KISS *by* KISS

NEW YORK TIMES BESTSELLING AUTHOR

KAYLEE RYAN

Cover Design: Lori Jackson Design
Cover Photography: Wander Aguiar

Cover Model: Tyler Collins
Editing: Hot Tree Editing
Proofreading: Deaton Author Services
Paperback Formatting: Integrity Formatting

CHAPTER ONE

I'S OUR REGULAR Monday morning meeting—the first since Royce and Sawyer have been back from their honeymoon. They waited until after the holidays to go, not wanting to miss time here with the family. That means we've spent the last hour shooting the shit, instead of actually working. That's the perks of owning the company. My brothers and I may have wasted this meeting to catch up, but that doesn't mean we're not dedicated to Riggins Enterprises. Our father built this company with our mom at his side. It's our legacy and one we take seriously.

"Knock, knock." Layla, who is our assistant, and my brother Owen's fiancée and baby momma, enters the room. "Sorry these are late. The bakery had some transportation issues."

I watch in fascination as my brother Owen jumps from his chair, the conversation he was having with our youngest brother, Marshall, long since forgotten now Layla is near. He takes the box from her, sets in on the end of the long conference table, and pulls her into his arms. One arm goes around her waist and the other rests on her belly, over their unborn son. Out of the five of us, Owen is the last one I would have guessed to be a father first. However, he met Layla and fell hard and fast.

He and my oldest brother, Royce, claim it's the "magic." That tells me they've spent too much time talking to our father. Stanley Riggins loves his wife, our mother, Lena, and swears it's "magic" that got them together. I think the old man just likes to tell tall tales, and now that my two older brothers are tied down, they're falling in line with his theories.

"Whatcha got there, Lay?" I ask my future sister-in-law.

"Oh, a new bakery just opened up down the block. You have to try these." She steps away from my brother to open the box.

"Well, we've lost Grant," Conrad, one of my younger brothers, comments.

He's the fourth brother. Royce is the oldest, then there's Owen and then me. I'm the middleman. Literally. The two youngest usually call me to pick them up when they've had too much to drink, and the two older brothers lean on me, more so than the younger two. I don't mind it. I love my family, and being the middleman keeps me involved in all of their lives.

"Hush—" I point at Conrad "—and step away from the pastries."

He throws his head back in laughter. "Lay, tell him to share," he says as any little brother would. It doesn't matter that we're all grown men.

"Now, boys, there is plenty for everyone," she assures us.

"But I get first pick, right?" I say, standing and walking to where she and Owen still stand at the end of the table. I bat my eyelashes, hoping to sway her to my way of thinking.

"They're all the same." She grins. "No way was I going to cause World War III over breakfast."

"Good call, Layla," Royce chimes in. "I'm going to take one to Sawyer," he says, standing with stars in his eyes as he mentions his new wife.

"I stopped there first." She smiles at him.

I place my hand over my chest. "Layla Riggins, you wound me." Her cheeks pink at the use of our last name instead of hers. She might as well get used to it. Hell, I'm surprised Owen hasn't raced her down the aisle yet. He's head over heels in love with her.

"Love that." I hear Owen whisper as I reach into the box and pull out a muffin. I bring it to my nose and pull in the scent. "Ah, banana nut, good choice." I nod, peel back the wrapper, and take a huge bite.

"I wanted one of everything." Layla laughs. "Pregnancy cravings, I guess. So, I told the woman behind the counter to surprise me, but that it all needed to be the same."

"Damn, sis, these are good," Marshall says, shoving the last half of his muffin in his mouth all at once, and fuck it, I do the same. We're classy like that, us Riggins brothers.

"Where is this place? I'm going to have to stop in and see what else they have."

"One block over." She points behind her, which tells me that I need to make a left when I leave the building. I make a mental note.

That muffin was too good not to stop into the bakery and see what else they have to offer. I work out five days a week, usually before coming into the office. I have a gym at my house, but usually I meet my two younger brothers at the gym. It's a good time razzing each other, and it's always better to have someone to work out with. Especially when you need a spotter. Royce and Owen used to sporadically join us, but now they both have beautiful ladies warming their beds, their presence has been nonexistent. Not that I blame them. They both hit the "significant other" lottery.

"Sawyer and I were talking about that the other day. We knew you'd be all over it as soon as you found out how close they were."

I point at her. "You've been holding out on me."

"All right, we need to get back to work," Royce says, doing the exact opposite as he reaches into the box and grabs himself a muffin. He takes a bite and moans his appreciation. "Maybe if I promise Sawyer fresh muffins every day, we can get one of those." He points to Layla's belly.

It's no secret that we all want kids. We want it all—the wife, the kids, the dog. Hell, I'll even take the white picket fence. None of us have an aversion to settling down. We've grown up watching the love that our parents share, and it's hard not to want that. It's just not the right time for us, and we've yet to meet the right woman to make it the right time. Well, at least me and my two younger brothers.

"I love the thought of our kids growing up together." Layla smiles up at Royce.

"You need me to explain to you how it's done?" Owen quirks a brow, barely containing his laughter.

"Trust me. We've got the how down pat. It's that daily pill that's getting in our way."

"Hey," Sawyer says, appearing in the doorway. "Royce, your nine o'clock is here." She's looking at him like he hung the moon.

"Thanks, babe." He walks to her, leans down, and kisses her lips.

I don't have a crystal ball or anything, but I can almost guarantee that those two will be the next to announce that the Riggins clan is growing. I couldn't be happier. I can't wait to spoil my nieces and nephews. I have some stiff competition for the title of favorite uncle, and that's a job title I'm going to take seriously.

"You planning on spending the night?"

I look up to find my baby brother, Marshall, standing in the doorway of my office. "Looks like I'm not the only one burning the midnight oil," I say. Glancing at the time on my computer, I see it's just after seven. I've been buried in paperwork all afternoon.

"I had a marketing plan to finalize for the San Francisco opening."

I smile. Marshall is the chief marketing officer, and he's damn good at it. "It's still hard to grasp the concept that we've taken this company across the United States."

"Dad paved the way," he says.

He's right. My father started this company with one truck and a dream. When my brother Royce took over, his dreams were even bigger. As each of us graduated from college and joined the business, we brought additional talent to the table, and I'm damn proud of what we've accomplished.

"That he did," I tell him. "You want to grab some dinner?"

He grins like the mischievous little brother he is. "Mom made chicken parmesan."

"Looks like I'm following you to Mom and Dad's." I laugh.

"You'd be crazy not to."

He's right. I would be crazy not to. Shutting down my computer, I leave the piles of work behind, grab my keys and my phone, and follow him to the elevator. "Is Conrad going to be there?" I ask Marshall as we step out of the building.

"Doubt it. He said something about taking a computer home to work on it."

I nod. Conrad is the chief information officer at Riggins Enterprises and our tech guru. You couldn't tell it by looking at him, not that I'm stereotyping, but Con just doesn't look like that's what he would be into. Kid's a genius.

"It doesn't matter how many times we tell him to delegate. He still won't do it." I shake my head.

"He loves that shit. I'm glad too. He fixed my laptop a few months ago. I hadn't backed it up in a while. Lesson learned."

"I'm sure he read you the riot act for that."

"Fucking older brothers," he mumbles, but there's a smile tilting his lips, and there's no heat in his tone.

"You love us, and you know it."

"Yeah, yeah." He smirks.

"Just think, if it were not for us, you wouldn't have gotten away with as much as you did growing up. By the time you came around, Mom and Dad were already desensitized to pretty much everything. We paved the way for you, little brother," I say, resting my hand on his shoulder.

"There's that," he agrees. "I honestly don't know how Mom and Dad are still sane after raising the five of us."

"We weren't that bad."

"One or more of us were always into something. They're saints."

"And to think she still makes enough dinner every night in case we want to drop in."

"We won the parent lottery."

"True that. See ya in a bit," I say as we part ways to go to our cars.

Pulling out of the lot, I need to go right to go to Mom and Dad's, but instead, I turn left. I need to scope out this new bakery that I plan to check out—maybe in the morning. Those muffins were too damn good not to sample the rest. Reaching the end of the block, my eyes scan and sure enough, there's a huge sign over the door. "Warm Delights," I read out loud. That's the perfect name for a bakery, and the muffins were indeed warm, telling me they were fresh, and they were definitely a delight. I like the way this place operates, and I can already tell I'm going to be a frequent customer.

CHAPTER *Aurora* TWO

"**N**o one should be this happy at 3:00 a.m.," my sister, Aspen, grumbles as I slide a cup of coffee in her direction.

"I can't help it," I tell her. "This has been my dream for so long, and it's finally happening. Thank you for doing this with me. I couldn't do this without you."

"Whatever." She rolls her eyes as she smiles behind her cup. "You and I both know that you don't need me."

"You're wrong. You stand behind me. You pushed me forward when I let my fear hold me back."

"That's what sisters do." She shrugs.

"Well, I love you, and I appreciate you." I drain the rest of my coffee and rinse my cup, placing it in the sink. "I'm heading downstairs to get started on today's special."

"What is it today?"

"Magic bars." I grin.

"You love me," my sister says, sliding off her stool. "I'm going to change, and I'll be right down." She disappears down the hall to her room.

Our small two-bedroom apartment is above my bakery, Warm Delights, and it's convenient not to have to drive to work. I looked for months when this location came on the market. It was going to be tough to swing rent on the bakery and an apartment, to the point where I was stressing out, but then this place came on the market, and it was as if it was meant to be.

Entering the kitchen, I flip on the lights, connect my phone to the Bluetooth speaker, and get to work. Aspen tells me I'm crazy for being too alert at this ungodly hour, but to me, I'm living my dream. There are people who told me I would never make it. That I was being silly, my recipes weren't good enough, that I was a fool. I pushed past the hurtful words, and with my sister as my biggest cheerleader, I'm standing in my bakery's kitchen, doing what I love, what I've always dreamed of. So, yeah, I'm going to do it with a big-ass smile on my face.

"Put me to work, boss," Aspen says, joining me a few minutes later.

"Grab the chocolate chips." I point behind her, and we get to work. We laugh and talk about anything and everything. Aspen is not only my sister, but she's my best friend. She's two years younger than my twenty-six. This move has brought us even closer together. When I brought up the idea of moving from Memphis to Nashville, Aspen didn't hesitate to agree to come with me. We talked about it at length, and she assured me she was all in.

She was working as an administrative assistant at a local newspaper at the time and was ready for a change. We both were. I called the realtor the next day, and here we are a year later, seeing all of our hard work pay off. We've only been open a month, but the support we've received has been incredible.

Closing my eyes, I send up a silent prayer to my grandma. Guilt hits me hard. I used my small inheritance money to lease the building and renovate it. I had to take out a loan with the bank for the equipment that I would need. I hate that I had to lose her to see my dream come true.

"Stop," Aspen scolds me. "I know what you're thinking. She would be happy for you. For both of us. She'd be happy that we took the chance."

"I miss her. I miss Mom and Dad. I hate that I'm happy here, and it took losing her..." My words trail off as I swallow the emotion clogging my throat.

"First of all, you have nothing to feel guilty about. You know Mom and Dad are thrilled to see you following your dreams. Second, you would have figured it out without the inheritance. You're a young business owner with the drive it takes to make things happen. She would be thrilled to know she helped you follow your dreams, something she would have offered had she still been living, and you and your stubborn ass would have more than likely fought her on it." She gives me a pointed look, and I can't help but chuckle.

"You look and sound so much like Mom right now."

"Thank you." She gives me a huge grin. "Now get your ass back to work. These magic bars aren't going to make themselves. I'm going to start on some fresh cupcakes."

Just like that, she helps calm my guilt, and I allow myself to be distracted with what I love—making delicious treats. I get lost in my work and before I know it, it's time to unlock the doors. My phone vibrates in my pocket. I smile when I see a message from Mom in the group message that Aspen and I have with her and my dad.

Mom: Have a great day, my beautiful daughters,

Dad: Now you're just trying to make me look bad.

My parents are the best people on the planet. Sure, I might be biased, but it's the truth. They've supported us in everything we've wanted to do. Although they didn't want us to move away, they knew I needed it. I think knowing that Aspen and I were going to be together helped.

Aspen: Love you!

Me: Love you!

With a smile on my face, I unlock the door and let the small crowd that's been waiting outside in. Today is going to be a great day indeed.

We've been slammed all morning, and I can't seem to stop smiling. Aspen is in the small lobby wiping down the tables that are finally empty from this morning's rush. "I'm going to run back and grab another pan of magic bars," I tell her.

"I can't believe how busy we've been." Her smile matches mine.

"Right?" I chuckle, disappearing into the kitchen to grab another pan of bars. "This is the last of them," I say, meeting her back behind the counter. She slides open the display case so that I can replace the full pan with the empty one.

"Do you want me to make more?"

"Nah, it's just before eight. We have a full pan and plenty of other options." Since we close at noon every day, it leaves the afternoon for catering jobs, which reminds me I need to hire a delivery driver. It's too much for Aspen and me to keep up with. It takes both of us to run the bakery, and we've had a few deliveries requested for the morning hours.

"Can you hold down the fort for a few minutes?" she asks. "I need to run to the restroom."

"Go, while you can." I laugh.

"That's a good problem to have, sister." She gives me a quick hug before disappearing into the kitchen to use the small staff restroom.

The chime over the door rings out and I lift my head to greet my next customer. I open my mouth to say hello, but no words come out as I watch the most gorgeous man I've ever laid eyes on saunter into the bakery.

"Morning." He grins.

I shake out of my fog and offer him a smile, feeling my face heat. "Good morning. Welcome to Warm Delights. What can I get you?"

"It all looks delicious," he says, but he's not looking at the display case. No, he's looking at me.

Me!

He has dark hair, cut short on the sides and a little longer on top. His eyes are a deep blue, and they're mesmerizing. He's wearing dress pants and a dress shirt with the sleeves rolled up to his elbows, tattoos on display. It's an unseasonably warm day for January, and it appears he's taking full advantage of it. My mouth waters as I lick my lips. "To-Today's special is magic bars." I point to the display case.

"Magic bars," he repeats, his eyes still locked with mine. "Tell me more," he says, leaning in a little closer.

"Well, they have a buttery graham cracker crust, topped with layers of chocolate chips, butterscotch chips, coconut, chopped nuts, and finished with a blanket of sweetened condensed milk," I rattle off the ingredients on autopilot.

"I'll take all you have left." He smiles.

"Um… that's an entire tray." I glance down at the tray I just slid into the display case.

"That's fine. I have four brothers who will be sure to steal these and two sisters-in-law, one of which is eating for two. I'll take them all." His eyes are still locked on mine, never once straying.

"Don't you want to try one first? You don't even know if you like them."

"Did you make them?"

"Yes," I say. My cheeks grow hot, and I'm not sure if it's embarrassment or this man's attention solely focused on me. It takes extreme effort to pull my gaze from his as I get to work packaging the entire pan of magic bars. I fight the slight tremble in my hands from his attention and pray to whoever is listening that he doesn't see it. When I finally have his order packaged, I have to steel my resolve and face him again.

"Can I get you anything else?" I ask.

He nods, a slow smile tilting his lips. "As a matter of fact, there is one more thing I can't leave here without," he tells me.

"Sure, what can I get you?"

"Your number."

I pause, replaying his words over in my mind, knowing that I must have heard him wrong. "Of course." I reach for a card on the counter by the register. "Our hours are listed on the back as well as our website."

"That's great, thank you. However, that's not the number I was referring to. I want your number. As in your personal number."

"You can reach me here." I smile, trying to hide my unease. I have no idea what he wants with my number. Men who look like him don't want chubby girls like me.

"You close at noon. What happens if I want to get dinner and would like the pleasure of your company?"

I turn to look over my shoulder to make sure I'm not getting punked. It's at that moment, my sister, the thinner, prettier Steele sister, comes from the kitchen, stepping up beside me. Good. He'll focus his attention on her.

"Hi." Aspen smiles.

"Hi." The handsome stranger pulls his eyes from me to glance at her. My shoulders relax. I'm used to Aspen getting all of the attention. "Can you help me with something?" he asks her.

"Sure," she says brightly, but I can hear the confusion in her voice at the same time. I take a step back to let her finish up, but his words stop me.

"You see, I'm trying to get this beauty to give me her number, and it would help if I knew her name."

Aspen, the traitor, giggles. "Aurora," she tells him. "I'm Aspen, her sister."

"Nice to meet you, Aurora," the sexy stranger says. It takes every ounce of effort I can conjure up not to swoon at the sound of my name rolling off his lips.

I stand here, my mouth hanging open, staring at him. It's not until I feel my sister's elbow dig into my side that I startle, and my hand shoots out in front of me. "Nice to meet you too…" I let my reply linger, waiting to see if he'll offer me his name.

"Grant. Grant Riggins."

"Oh, Riggins Enterprises," I say, nodding. "I met Layla."

"Layla is my brother's fiancée, and she's expecting the first Riggins grandchild. She's going to love these." He points to the box of magic bars. "Pregnancy has strengthened her sweet tooth. Something that she and I have in common." He winks.

"Do they know what they're having?" I ask him. I begin to relax a little. I remember Layla. She was nice and friendly, and laughed when she ordered a box of all the same thing. She said if I knew her brothers-in-law, I would understand. Now I get it.

"A little boy."

I nod and open the display case. Reaching in, I grab one of the baby boy sugar cookies that Aspen decorated this morning. "Here. Give her this." I put it in a small bag and hand it to him. "On the house."

"Thanks, beautiful. Now, about that number?"

"I'm sorry, I—" I start to decline when Aspen grabs a business card and scribbles my name and number on it, handing it to him.

"Here you go." She grins like a kid on Christmas morning.

"Thanks." He makes a show of taking a picture of it with his phone, then pulling out his wallet and placing it inside. "Just in case I lose it. It's too important." His eyes sparkle as he smiles.

"How much do I owe you?" he asks.

Aspen again elbows me, and I jump into action, ringing up his order and swiping his credit card. "Thank you," I tell him, handing him the receipt.

"The pleasure is all mine. I'll be seeing you, Aurora," he says. Is it just me or does his voice sound deeper? Sexier? Aspen clears her throat. "You too, Aspen. You ladies have a nice day."

"Enjoy the magic," Aspen calls after him.

He stops and turns to face us. It looks like he mouths "the magic" before nodding. "It's always about the magic." He grins, turns on his heel, and exits the same way he arrived, holding my attention.

"Holy freaking hotness." Aspen fans her face with her hand. "That man is fine, and that look on his face… It's as if he wanted to eat you alive."

"Come on. He's just flirting. I'll never hear from him." As I say the words, my phone vibrates in my pocket. Grabbing it, I see a text from an unknown number.

> **Unknown:** This is Grant. Save my number. Have a great day, beautiful.

"It's him, isn't it? I can tell by the blush on your cheeks. Told you so," my little sister gloats.

"Stop. It's not going to happen."

"You need a good man in your life. After what that dick Elijah did to you."

Before I can reply, the door chimes and in walks a group of older ladies. I give Aspen a look that tells her to drop it before greeting our customers. Grant might be the sexiest man I've ever laid eyes on, but that's where this ends. I'm not looking for a man in my life. The last one just about destroyed me.

CHAPTER THREE

Grant

I'VE CHECKED MY phone a million times today. Okay, maybe a million is a stretch, but it sure feels like it. Hell, even my battery that's flashing 25 percent is tired of me checking. I sent Aurora a text before I even pulled away from the bakery this morning, and nothing. I can see that she read the message, but it's been nothing but silence.

"What did that phone do to you?" Sawyer asks from the doorway of my office.

"Nothing." I toss it onto my desk. "What's up, sis?"

She steps into my office and takes a seat across from me. "Not buying the 'nothing,' Grant Riggins. What's going on?" There is nothing but love and concern in her voice.

"Just waiting on a reply."

"Oh, yeah?" Her interest is piqued.

"It's been hours," I say, frustrated as I run my fingers through my hair.

"Lady friend troubles." She nods, sitting back into the chair, obviously settling in for this conversation.

"Does she count as a lady friend if I just met her?"

"Yes."

She doesn't say anything else, and I'm thankful, but I know what she's doing. Sawyer is waiting me out. She's so damn easy to talk to. It's one of the reasons why she hit it off with my family and me immediately. Royce was a little slow to admit she made him feel something after years of self-isolation and throwing himself into his work. Sawyer, she waited patiently, and he eventually came around.

I've learned a lot watching my two oldest brothers fall in love, and when I find her—my own woman—I'm not holding back. I understand why Royce kept pushing Sawyer away, but he was an idiot and wasted so much time with her. Owen, on the other hand, he knew what he wanted, and he wasn't giving up until Layla was his.

"Oh, I meant to tell you those bars or whatever they are, were delicious. Thank you."

"Magic bars."

"What?" Sawyer tilts her head to the side, studying me.

"Aurora called them magic bars."

"Aurora?"

"The woman at the bakery."

"Ah." She grins. "Now we're getting somewhere."

"What do you mean, *ah?*"

"Let me guess? You gave her your number, and you've been waiting on her to call?"

It's eerie how close she is. "Not exactly."

"Enlighten me." Her grin grows wider.

"Why are you monopolizing all my wife's time?" Royce asks, waltzing into my office.

"She came to me." I smirk. He ignores me and goes straight to her. He's used to my two younger brothers and me doing what we can to rile him up when it comes to his wife.

He doesn't stop until he reaches Sawyer. His hand slides behind her neck as he bends to press his lips to hers. "Love you," he says, not bothering to lower his voice. My big brother is unapologetically in love with his wife. I can't stop the smile that pulls at my lips, seeing him this happy. He went through hell to get here, but he's finally found his other half. "What's going on?" he asks, standing behind Sawyer with his hands on her shoulders.

"Nothing." Sawyer is quick to reply, offering me a wink. "I just came to thank Grant for the magic bars."

"Is that what those things were? I had two of them."

"Yeah, I had to stop by and check it out after the muffins yesterday." Sawyer gives me a look that tells me she knows I was checking out more than just the bakery. My phone vibrates on my desk, and I lurch to grab it and fumble to look at the screen. Finally, after hours of waiting, I see the name I've been waiting for.

Aurora.

Aurora: You too.

That's it. You too, but I'll take it. She replied, which tells me she's interested. Glancing at the clock, I see it's after three. I've been waiting all day for a tiny morsel from her, and I finally have it.

"What's with the shit-eating grin? Who is that?" Royce inquires.

"Aurora."

"Aurora? What did I miss?"

Lifting my head from my phone, I smile at my brother and his wife. "She was working at the bakery this morning."

"Ah." Royce nods as if those eight words explain it all. In a way, I guess they do. "Thank fuck I'm not in the dating scene anymore."

"You weren't in it when you found me," Sawyer reminds him. Royce leans over her and presses his lips to hers to keep her quiet. I must admit his method works.

"I need to get back to work. Why don't you two love birds take that"—I wave my hand at them—"somewhere else."

"My pleasure," Royce says, his voice growing deeper.

"Go." I laugh. Sawyer waves before allowing Royce to lead her out of my office. I don't even know why she was in here in the first place. I guess if it's important, she'll let me know. I wait a total of maybe fifteen seconds before unlocking my phone screen and firing off another message.

Me: How has your day been?

I wait, my eyes glued to the screen to see if she's going to reply. It took her hours for the first response, so when I see the little bubbles pop up telling me that she's typing, I'm pleasantly surprised.

Aurora: Good. Yours?

Me: Great, actually. I met someone I'd like to get to know better.

I see the bubbles pop up and then disappear. This happens three more times before they disappear altogether. I know that the bakery is closed. They're open from six in the morning until noon. I've already familiarized myself with their website. I wasn't able to gain any personal knowledge. There is nothing listed about the staff. The only thing I learned was there are so many more items I want to try, and the hours of which I can stop in to do just that. I can only hope that Aurora is there the next time I stop in.

For the second day in a row, I find myself entering the doors of Warm Delights. The name fits this place perfectly as the smells of sugary sweetness warm my senses. I take my time making my way to the counter, seeing that Aurora and her sister, Aspen, are both standing behind the counter. I hold back, waiting for them to finish with the customers they are with, before stepping up to the counter.

"Morning, ladies." I make brief eye contact with Aspen, but

then my eyes lock on Aurora, and I can't look away. Today, her brown hair is braided, and her gorgeous hazel eyes show her surprise, but the smile never leaves her face.

"Good morning, Grant," she replies.

The way my name rolls off of her tongue, it causes me to have to shift my stance. "Aurora," I reply huskily.

"What brings you back today?" Aspen asks.

"Two things actually. One, I'm addicted to sweets, and two, I was checking on our girl here." I nod toward Aurora.

"W-What?" she stutters.

"You didn't text me back yesterday. I wanted to make sure you were okay." It's not a complete lie. I had a feeling she was fine but avoiding me. I'm not going to let her do that. Not until I have a chance to explore why my heart races as soon as I lay eyes on her or why she's consumed my thoughts over the last twenty-four hours.

"I-I'm fine. I was busy." Her eyes glance over at her sister before darting back to me.

"You didn't tell me he texted you," Aspen says to her sister, who is suddenly very fascinated with wiping down the counter.

"How about I buy you a coffee?" I offer.

"You want to buy me coffee in my bakery?" she asks.

I can't stop the smile from that little slice of information pie she just gave me. "Didn't know you were the owner," I confess.

"Go, have a cup of coffee. I've got this," Aspen assures her.

The bell over the door chimes, and I know Aurora is going to use that as an excuse to turn me down. She opens her mouth. I'm sure to do just that, but I speak before she does. "You close at noon, how about lunch?" I offer before she can.

"I have a lot of work to do to prepare for tomorrow."

"You have to eat."

"Thank you for the offer, but I just have too much to do."

"I can handle things here. As the man said, you have to eat."

"Aspen," Aurora hisses. She then looks around me. "Welcome

to Warm Delights. How may I help you?" she asks, stepping to the side to greet her new customers.

"What's her favorite?" I ask Aspen. My eyes are tracking Aurora's every move. I can't seem to stop looking at her.

"What's her favorite or what does she eat?" Aspen asks.

"Isn't that the same thing?"

"No." She shakes her head. "She doesn't allow herself to eat her favorites."

"Why the hell not?" I ask, finally turning my gaze to Aspen.

"That's a story she's going to have to tell. Her weakness is pizza and pasta. But she usually eats a salad or a wrap for lunch."

"Thanks." I nod, my mind already going through the local options and my schedule. I didn't even think about what I had going on today when I asked her to lunch. Pulling my phone out of my pocket, I scan my calendar, and there is nothing keeping me from leaving the office. I fire off a text to both Layla and Sawyer, letting them know not to schedule me for anything for the rest of the day.

I stand back, waiting for Aurora to finish waiting on her customers, before walking to where she stands at the end of the counter. "I'll see you around noon for lunch."

"I told you I've got too much to do to leave," she counters.

I give her my smile, the one that my brothers and I are known for. The same one that my momma says melts her heart. "That's why I'm bringing lunch to you. See you in a few hours, sweetness." With those parting words, I turn on my heel and exit the bakery. It's not until I'm in the elevator headed to the top floor of the Riggins Enterprises building do I realize I left empty-handed. That's fine. I got a lunch date, which is even sweeter.

CHAPTER
Aurora
FOUR

I WATCH HIM leave until I can no longer see him. I can feel Aspen's eyes boring into me, but thankfully I'm saved by the bell. Literally. The next four hours pass by in a blur. The bakery is busier than ever, with a constant flow of customers—many who inquire about our catering services. I'm all too happy to give them a rundown.

Normally, I'd be willing the conversation to end so that I can get busy prepping for the next day, but not this time. Not only does it keep me from my sister's prying questions, but it keeps my mind busy. Focused. I need to think about anything but Grant. The sexy man who walked into my life just over twenty-four hours ago.

"Finally," Aspen says dramatically as the final customer walks out the door. "I didn't think I was ever going to get you alone. What was that this morning?" She stands with her hands on her hips. I can see the defiance in her hazel eyes, ones much like my own. We both have our mother's eyes—something Dad always said was a blessing. I'm not getting out of this.

"That was word getting out about the bakery. Word of mouth is the best form of marketing." It's not a lie. Most of today's customers were a result of someone telling them about us. However, I know that's not what she's asking. I'm deflecting, and we both know it.

"That's great, and you know I'm thrilled for you, thrilled for us, but let's get back to the matter at hand. Grant." She gives me a pointed look.

"What about him?"

"He's into you."

"He doesn't know me."

"No, but he's about to." She nods over my shoulder, and I close my eyes. From the look on her face, I already know what I'm going to see when I turn around.

"Aurora." His deep sexy voice greets my ears.

After pulling in a slow, deep breath, I exhale before turning around. Grant has his dress shirt unbuttoned at the top, his tie no longer present, and his sleeves are rolled up to his forearms, giving me a chance to rake my eyes over his tattoos. He's all bad boy mixed with the air of a responsible professional. He's lethal, and I can't let myself fall.

Not again.

"Grant." I finally find my words.

"You ready for lunch?" He holds up a bag from the deli down the street and my mouth waters. I open my mouth to tell him I have too much to do, but he beats me to it. "You have to eat. Both of you have to eat." He flashes Aspen a grin. "I have lunch for the three of us."

My stance relaxes, knowing he bought lunch for Aspen too. I'm sure he's just trying to get closer to her through me. That's what they all do. "Okay," I concede.

"Actually, I have some calls I have to make," Aspen chimes in.

"At least take your lunch with you." Grant sets the bag on the counter and pulls out what appears to be a wrap and a bag of kettle chips.

"Thank you. Our fave." She smiles big, grabs her lunch, and disappears into the kitchen.

Traitor!

"Shall we?" Grant asks.

"Um, I need to lock the door." I step out around the counter, and his hand on my arm stops me.

"I've got it, go sit. You've been on your feet all day." With a gentle squeeze and a look that makes my knees weak, he releases me and makes his way to the front of the bakery to lock the door and flip the sign to Closed.

My arm is warm from his touch, which I don't understand. That's never happened before. I don't move a muscle as I watch him. He has an air of confidence that only a man like him can have. A man who knows who he is and what he wants, and right now, his attention is focused on me, but I don't know why. He places the takeout bag at a small corner table before walking toward me.

"Come here, baby," he says, holding his hand out for me.

Baby. A swarm of butterflies take flight in my belly. I've never had a man use a term of endearment with me, and this one, he seems to have plenty in his arsenal. On autopilot, I place my hand in his, and sparks ignite, coursing through my veins. From the look on his face, the way his mouth drops open and quickly closes, he feels it too. I allow him to lead me to the small table and pull my chair out for me.

It's on the tip of my tongue to tell him that I'm busy and don't have time for this, but I know it's going to fall on deaf ears. "Thank you," I say instead.

He gifts me with a boyish grin. His blue eyes have a light in them that tells me he's enjoying his time... with me. I want to ask him why. I want to tell him that he's putting his efforts into the wrong sister, but I don't. Instead, I stay quiet and wait for him to place our food in front of us.

"How was your day?" he asks, pulling open the wrapper around his meatball sub and taking a huge bite.

"Busy."

"That's good, right?" he asks, wiping his mouth.

"Yes. Most of the customers today were here from word of mouth. That's a good thing," I say. The excitement that my dream is finally coming true, and it's profitable, is palpable in my reply.

"How long have you been open?"

"Less than a month."

He nods. "Layla told me about this place. She brought in some banana muffins to the office, which were delicious by the way." I grin at his words. "This place is going to blow up. I predict it's just going to get busier. Trust me. I'm a sweets expert."

"We have more than sweets. We have fresh breads and croissants. Although not every day. Right now, it's just Aspen and me. However, at the rate that we're going, we'll be able to hire some staff soon."

"That's good."

"Is it?"

"Yep. I'm going to need you to myself for our date, so you hiring help is beneficial to both of us."

"You're awfully full of yourself." My pulse pounds in my ears. Trusting men is hard for me, and well, Grant is intimidating with his good looks and confidence. The thought of spending more time with him causes butterflies to dance in my belly.

He shrugs. "I want to get to know you."

"Why?" The words slip out before I can think better of it.

"Because I like what I see. Because in order to make these delicious treats—" He motions around the lobby. "You have to be just as sweet on the inside. They're made with love. I can taste it, and I want that in my life."

I look down at my lap, hiding from him. I'm not used to a man saying such nice things. In fact, it's the exact opposite of what I'm used to. All I've ever heard from men, other than my father, is that my job is the reason I'm fat. That I need to stop with the baking, so I can lose weight. That's just a glimpse of the hatred spewed my way.

"Hey." Grant reaches across the small table and places his index finger under my chin. He applies just the smallest amount of pressure until my eyes meet his. "Where did you go just now?"

"I'm right here."

"Physically. Where were you mentally?"

"That's not something you want to hear. Trust me." I close my eyes and sigh. What is it about this man that has me speaking words out loud that only my sister has had the privilege to hear?

"You're wrong. I want to hear it all."

"Another time," I say, picking up my wrap and taking a bite. I chew slowly before wiping my mouth with a napkin. "Thank you for lunch. This is one of my favorites."

He nods. "I might have had some help with that."

"Aspen."

"Don't blame her. She couldn't resist the Riggins charm."

I can't help it. I laugh. "You said you have four brothers, right? Your parents must be exhausted." I give him a wide smile, letting him know that I'm kidding. Even with my trust issues, I find myself warming up to him. He just seems like a genuine guy. I don't see any hate or cruelty hiding behind his eyes.

"Yep. I'm the middleman. I have two older and two younger. As for my parents, they're incredible."

"Are the others like you?"

"What do you mean, like me?"

"You know, pushy and don't know how to take no for an answer." My tone is light and teasing, but the reality is that I want to hear his answer. I want to see if there is any insight to the man sitting next to me.

"Well, if you ask my sister-in-law and future sister-in-law, they would tell you yes. Royce and Owen, my two older brothers, they're pretty stubborn when it comes to their women."

"Stubborn, how?"

"Not in a bad way." He's quick to reassure me. "Just opening doors, and Layla, that's Owen's fiancée, she's pregnant," I remind her. "He frets over her. Not that it's a bad thing, but they bicker about it. He wants to do everything for her, and she insists that she can still manage on her own."

"That's sweet."

"Maybe, but I bet Layla feels differently. I get it, though. I would be the same way if my wife or fiancée were expecting. That's precious cargo, *carrying* precious cargo."

My heart stutters, and my insides feel like mush, the butterflies taking flight for the second time in a matter of minutes. I know the definition of swoon, but this is the first time in my life I've ever felt as though the action was happening to me. I feel lightheaded from his confession, but my heart is full. It's reassuring to know that there are still good men out there. I don't know Grant Riggins well, but my gut tells me he is one of the good ones. He doesn't appear to be putting on a show. He's just speaking from his soul. That's a rarity in my experience.

"Did you always want to own your own bakery?" he asks.

"I was maybe eight years old. Aspen and I spent the weekend with our grandmother. We made cupcakes from scratch, and I loved it. Mixing the ingredients to create something incredible. I was addicted after that. The magic bars, they were her recipe. I just added a little twist, but it's mostly the same."

"They were delicious. I was right in buying the entire tray. Everyone devoured them."

"Thank you." I take a sip of the bottle of water he placed in front of me with our food. "What about you? What do you do at Riggins?" I rush to ask to hide my excitement that everyone loved my creation. I know Grant is not my ex, but old habits die hard I guess.

"It's a family business. We're a logistics company. My job is to oversee the day-to-day operations."

"All five of you work there?"

"Yeah. My dad started the company, and when he retired, Royce took over as CEO. The rest of us have our own niche, so to speak, that we bring to the table as well."

"How is it? Working side by side with your brothers?"

He shrugs. "We all get along. There are two years in between each of us. We're stair-stepped in age. That's what Mom calls it."

"I'm sure your parents are proud of you. Of all of you."

"They are. They're saints to raise five rowdy boys, but they've done one hell of a job if I do say so myself." He winks. "What about you? You and Aspen seem close."

Butterflies. I don't understand my reaction to this man. "We are."

"I'm sure your parents are proud of you."

"They are. It's my grandma who I wish could have seen this place." I look up, and the look in his eyes is unexpected. Sadness. "We lost her two years ago. Nothing tragic happened. It was just her time. Mom and Dad are still living in Memphis. It's just Aspen and me against Nashville." I feel a tug in my heart, just like every time I think or talk about Grandma Edna, and our parents. I miss them terribly. I know Mom and Dad are just three hours away, but I still miss them like crazy.

"I'm sorry for your loss."

I nod. The sincerity in his voice has me swallowing back my emotions. "Thank you. Thank you for lunch." I place the remaining half of my wrap in the packaging.

"When can I see you again?"

"Grant—" I start, but he shakes his head.

"I'm not taking no for an answer. You name the day and time, and I'll make it happen."

"I work crazy hours."

"Name it," he says, his blue eyes boring into mine.

"I go to bed early, and I'm up at ungodly hours to start the day."

"I want to see you again."

"We're closed on Sunday!" Aspen yells from somewhere in the kitchen.

"You need a sister?" I ask him.

"I have two."

"I thought you had four brothers?"

"My sisters-in-law are my sisters."

There he goes again, melting me with his words. "So, Sunday? My mom has Sunday dinner, but I can miss it."

"No." I'm quick to shut that idea down. "I don't want you to miss out on family time."

"Then come with me."

"W-What?" I sputter. "I can't come with you."

"Sure you can. The more the merrier."

"No."

"Please?" He juts out his bottom lip, and I admit it's hard to hold firm on my answer.

"I'm sorry," I say, standing.

He does the same and steps in close to me. I can feel the heat of his body and his eyes. The blue is mesmerizing this close. "Sunday, you're mine. Send me your address. I'll pick you up in the morning."

"I—No."

"Aspen!" he calls out.

"Yes?" She's grinning when she sticks her head outside of the kitchen door.

"I need your address."

My sister rattles off her number. "Text me, and I'll reply with all the info you need."

"I like her," he says, and my stomach sinks. I can't tell you how many times I've been told by the men in my life, well, one man in particular that I should be more like my sister.

"Hey." He cradles my face in the palm of his hands. "It's you I want. It's you I want to spend time with."

My skin tingles from his touch. I guess I didn't hide my reaction as well as I thought. "You can't skip dinner, and I can't go with you."

"We can see how the day goes. Is that fair?"

"Say yes!" Aspen hollers out, making me smile, and Grant laughs.

"Say yes, Aurora." He leans in close, and his musky scent invades the little space between us.

"Yes." My eyes widen at my agreement, and he throws his head back and laughs.

"I'll see you Sunday, beautiful." He leans in and places a kiss on my cheek.

I stand frozen with my hand on my cheek as he walks away. "Bye, Aspen!" he yells over his shoulder before striding out the door.

"Holy shit, that man is hot, and he wants you."

"I—" I start to reply, but I've got nothing. Aspen's arms wrap around me, and I'm grateful to be able to lean on her. My knees are weak.

Grant Riggins is dangerous for my heart.

CHAPTER
Grant
FIVE

'VE SPENT THE last few days obsessing over my date with Aurora. That's not me. That's not who I am. I don't stress over dates. Hell, I rarely go on dates. It's been... longer than I can remember. It's Saturday night, and instead of taking Conrad and Marshall up on their offer to hit the club, I'm sitting at home, watching mindless television. I'm not satisfied with the date I planned for tomorrow, and that's wigging me out a little. I want her to come to Sunday dinner with my family. I've never brought someone, and I know what it means if I do, what my brothers and my parents will think. I know what their assumptions about what she means to me will be. I can't seem to find it in me to care. I don't know what it is about her, but I can't seem to get Aurora out of my head.

I stopped by Warm Delights every single day this week. I didn't go this morning. Instead, I made myself go to the gym and meet my two younger brothers. I hated every minute of it. All I could think about was me missing the opportunity to hear her voice, and to see those beautiful hazel eyes trying to hide she's secretly glad I've thrust myself into her life. Her eyes are so expressive. It makes me wonder what else I can see in them, how they would look as I hover over her gorgeous body, raking my hands over her curves as our bodies connect as one.

Reaching for my phone, I start to send her a text, but I know that won't calm the desire to hear her voice, but calling her will. We've done nothing but text back and forth, but I need to hear her voice. Not giving myself the chance to change my mind, I click on her contact and place the phone next to my ear.

"Grant?" she greets me. Her voice is hesitant.

"I missed you." The words pass my lips before I realize that they're the truth. How is that possible? I barely even know her, but I missed getting to see her today.

"You… missed me?"

"Like a fucking limb." My voice is calm and serious, but her laughter tells me she thinks otherwise.

"You always laugh at a man when he's baring his soul to you?" I counter, with a hint of my own laughter in my tone.

"Oh, is that what you're doing?" she volleys back.

My smile is huge, and I'm kicking myself in the ass for not calling her sooner. Fuck texting. I want her voice in my ear. "I'm on my knees," I tell her. She laughs again, and I feel the sound deep in my chest. "How was your day?" I ask, settling back into the couch. It's as if hearing her voice is all that I needed to relax.

"Good. We were busy again today."

The smile in her voice is prominent. "That's great, babe. Are you ready for our day together tomorrow?"

"All day?" she questions.

"Yep," I say, popping the *p*. "You're mine all day."

She's quiet for several beats of my heart and so am I. I give her the time she needs to work through whatever it is that's plaguing her mind. "What are we doing?" she finally asks. Her inquiry is soft.

"I have some plans," I tell her. "Is there anything specific you want to do? I know it's your only day off. Is there anything that you need to get done tomorrow?" Whatever it is, we're going to do it together. I want the entire day with her.

"I—" She starts and then immediately stops. I can picture her thinning her lips, as her hazel eyes wage a war of indecision. It's a look I've seen on her every day this week when I mention tomorrow.

"Don't censor yourself with me. I want to know what you think, what you're feeling." I wait for her to speak, and when she does, her words are softly spoken.

"I want real. Don't pretend to be someone you're not. I've had enough fake in my life. I don't want or need more. If you can't be you… if you can't be real, then I don't want you in my life."

Damn. "Who hurt you?" My defenses are up. That's not a speech from a woman who's been cherished and told daily how amazing she is. Hell, I barely know her, and I already know that she's incredible.

"We all have a past, Grant. Mine is just that, mine. I agreed to do this, and I'm not going to go back on my word. But I need you to just be you. I don't need smoke and mirrors. I don't want you to try to impress me. I want you to be you. Grant Riggins. Whatever that is. If it turns out we're not into the same things, or compatible, then so be it. However, we will never really know unless we are both unapologetically who we are."

No bullshit, that's refreshing when it comes to women, and me and even my brothers. She's new in town, so she doesn't know who we are. She doesn't realize my net worth, and she still agreed to spend the day with me tomorrow. Suddenly everything I had planned is tossed out of my mind, and a new plan takes place. I'll give her me… something I've never done, but with Aurora, I want to.

"I'll be there at nine to pick you up. Dress casual and wear comfortable shoes."

"Casual? Jeans and a sweater?"

"Perfect. Maybe bring a change of clothes and different shoes for later."

"I'm not spending the night with you." Her words don't sound convincing.

"That's not why I mentioned it. We don't know where the day is going to take us, and if you decide to have dinner with my family, I want you to feel comfortable." I don't exactly know what we're going to be doing, but my original idea is not going to cut it. She wants the real me, that's what she's going to get.

"Grant, maybe this isn't the best idea."

"What? Of course, it is. I'll be there at nine," I say again.

"Why are you doing this?"

"Doing what?"

"Taking me out."

"Because you're the most beautiful woman I've ever laid my eyes on, and I want to get to know you better. I want to spend time with you." Her sharp intake of breath tells me that she's surprised by my answer. "I'll be there at nine. Sweet dreams, baby," I whisper before ending the call. I'm not giving her a chance to try and back out. She gave me her word, and I know she'll be ready when I get there in the morning. Glancing at the time on my phone, I see it's just before nine. I have twelve hours before I get to see her. That's more than enough time to change the course of our day.

She wants the real me, that's what she's going to get.

I'm early, half an hour early, but I can't seem to help it. I'm eager to see her and get this day started. I changed our plans last night, and I hope that the change is a good one. I had originally planned on taking her to breakfast, then a museum downtown, but something tells me Aurora isn't really a museum kind of girl. I'm not a museum kind of guy. I was trying to impress her, and that was my mistake. Luckily for me, our phone call last night pushed some clarity into my mind, and I was able to get online and change our plans.

Climbing out of my SUV, I make my way to the back entrance of the bakery. There's a buzzer just like Aspen assured me there would be. I press it and wait.

"Hello?"

"It's Grant," I tell the staticky voice. I can't tell which sister it is, but the lock releases, and I'm quick to pull open the door. The frigid January air is starting to make my teeth chatter.

"Come on up!" a voice calls from the top of a set of stairs.

Not wasting any time, I take them two at a time. "Morning," I greet Aspen.

"Good morning. She's almost ready." She steps back, allowing me to enter their apartment.

"Nice setup," I say, my eyes scanning the small living room and kitchen area.

"Thanks. We got lucky that this apartment was fully renovated when Aurora found the building. We only had to focus on the bakery, and the commute to work is nice." She grins.

"Definitely a perk," I agree. Movement from the corner of my eye catches my attention, and I turn to see Aurora. Her long brown hair is down for once and is falling over her shoulders in loose curls. She's wearing a pair of jeans that mold to her curves, a long sweater covering her ass, which is a damn shame. She's wearing a pair of black fuzzy boots with a flat heel. She's a fucking vision.

"Is this okay?" she asks cautiously. I can hear the concern in her voice.

I open my mouth to speak, but the words are locked and won't come. Instead, I move one foot in front of the other until I'm standing in front of her. Bending, I press my lips to her cheek and breathe her in. She's not working today, but she still smells sugary sweet. "You're perfect," I whisper in her ear, finding my voice.

"Maybe I should change." She takes a step back, but not far enough. Reaching out, I snake my arm around her waist, pulling her close.

"No. You're dressed perfectly for where we're going."

"Where are we going?" She tilts her head to look up at me, and her hazel eyes are both guarded and showing hints of excitement.

"Our first stop is breakfast. I hope you're hungry."

"She was too nervous to eat," Aspen answers helpfully.

"It's just me," I say, pressing my lips to her temple. She sucks in a breath, surprised by the gesture. "Aspen, I'll take good care of her."

"Be good, kids. Have her home before midnight, or don't..." Aspen laughs, letting her voice trail off.

"We'll keep you posted. Did you pack a bag?" I ask Aurora.

"I told you I'm not spending the night with you."

"Okay, baby. But you might want to change," I start to explain. "That's fine. We can come back here for you to change if you want to." She bites down on her bottom lip, showing me her uncertainty. "Trust me." My tone is gentle as I will her to give me her trust.

"You kids better get moving." Aspen claps her hands.

"I'll take care of her," I tell Aspen with a wink.

"Oh, you better." She gives me a sassy grin, and I know she's not talking about me bringing her sister home safely. My cock twitches behind the zipper of my jeans at the thought of "taking care" of Aurora like that.

Aurora steps out of my hold and slides her arms into her coat. I watch as she grabs her purse and a small bag that I know has a change of clothes packed neatly inside. I hide my grin by biting down on my cheek. Now is not the time to gloat.

Walking toward her, I offer her my hand, and she hesitates. Her eyes dart to her sister, then back to me, and then to my hand that's still suspended in the air waiting for her. I watch her as she straightens her spine and exhales slowly before placing her hand in mine. It's a small victory, but one I'm going to take all the same. It's going to be a lot of baby steps with Aurora, and I'm good with that. I don't know who hurt her, but I hope one day she'll tell me. In the meantime, I'll be sure to prove to her that she doesn't have anything to worry about when it comes to me.

I can't explain it, but I'm drawn to her unlike any woman ever before. To me, that's reason enough to stick around and see where this goes. With her hand in mine, I lead us out to my SUV. Taking the bag from her hands, I place it in the back seat before opening her door for her. Once she's in, I jog around and climb behind the wheel.

"Please tell me that whatever we're doing it's inside," she says as soon as my door is shut.

"Yes. I want to get to know you, not give you frostbite," I tease.

"Good." She rubs her hands together. "I was about to jump out if you'd given me any other answer."

"The objective is to keep you with me today as long as I can, not push you away." I keep my eyes focused on the road, but I can feel her stare. "What?" I ask, glancing over once I'm at the Stop sign.

"Why me?"

"Have you looked in the mirror lately?"

"Precisely why I am asking the question."

Something stirs inside me at her words. I can't really describe it—anger, sadness, and even determination to make her see herself how I do. Checking my mirrors, I signal to pull over and park on the side of the street. Putting the SUV in Park, I take off my seat belt and turn to face her. "I know we don't know each other really well, but let me tell you something about me. What you see is what you get. I'm not going to blow smoke up your ass to try and manipulate you. You're gorgeous. I don't know who has convinced you otherwise, but I'd like to introduce him to my fist. So, we have a rule."

"A rule?" she asks.

"Yes, a rule. When you're with me, none of that 'why me' bullshit. You're here sitting next to me because I want you to be. I want to get to know you, and today is how we start that process. Nothing more and nothing less. Got it?"

"Do I get to make rules too?" she sasses back.

"Name it." I love that she's being bold. That she's inserting herself into whatever this is between us. I don't like the thought of her being passive about me, about us, or hell, about anything.

"I-I'll get back to you," she says, crossing her arms over her chest.

I silently curse the coat that's hiding her breasts from me. "When you think of one, you let me know." With that, I pull back onto the street and head toward a small diner on the edge of town. Norma's is a staple, and only locals really know about it. They also have the best home-cooked food in town. It's a place my family and I used to frequent a lot growing up, and I want to share that with her.

"I didn't even know this place existed," she says as I pull into the parking lot.

"That's the best part. Stay there. I'll get your door."

"I'm capable," she tells me.

"Rule number two, I get to treat you the way you deserve to be treated. I'll get your door," I say again, pulling my keys from the ignition and rushing to her door.

CHAPTER *Aurora* SIX

"**T**HAT WAS DELICIOUS, thank you," I tell Grant, pushing my plate of half-eaten pancakes away from me.

"You barely ate any of it. Are you not hungry?" There's genuine concern in his voice, which is not something I'm used to. Not from a man, that is.

How do I tell him that it's my insecurities and the past evil in my mind that keeps me from letting loose and enjoying our breakfast together? "I'm full." I smile big, hoping he believes me. It's not a lie. I'm satisfied, but I could have eaten the entire thing easily.

"Well, I guess it's a good thing we're going to have a good lunch as well."

"Lunch? We're still sitting in front of breakfast, and you're already thinking about lunch?" I ask. I'm not judging him, just surprised.

"That's because lunch is the second part of our date." His grin lights up his handsome face.

"What are we doing in-between breakfast and lunch?" I ask cautiously.

"We have a little time to kill. I was thinking I could drive you by my place, so you know how to get there."

"And I need to know this because?"

"Because you and I are going to be spending a lot of time together, and you're going to need to know how to get to me when I'm not with you or at the office."

"You act like that's the only two places you're going to be." I laugh.

"Well, I do go to the gym with my younger brothers. The older two don't join us very often now that they're married or almost married. The only other place I frequent is my parents,' and you'll see their place later today."

"I don't think that's a good idea."

"Of course, it is." His confidence in this decision is resolute.

"We'll see," I say, not committing. I have no idea why he's so adamant that I go to this dinner with his family. But it's not something that appeals to me. I'm not in the mood to be judged.

"Ready?" he asks when the waitress brings back his change. He tosses a twenty on the table, and my eyes bulge out of my head. "I can afford it, and they work hard." He shrugs as if leaving a twenty-dollar tip for a bill that wasn't even thirty dollars is normal. Maybe it is for him. I have no idea what his financial status is.

"Yes," I answer as he offers me his hand to help me slide out of the booth, and I take it. I like the way it feels. The way the warmth of his skin seeps into mine. It's been a long time since I've felt the touch of a man, and even if it is just holding my hand, I'll take it.

Once outside, his SUV is already running. He opens the door for me and rushes around to his side of the truck. "Gotta love remote start," he says, rubbing his hands together.

"I was getting ready to ask you about that."

"It's one of the best features ever invented."

"It is nice," I say, settling into the heated leather seat.

"*This* is nice," he says, reaching over and lacing his fingers through mine.

He rests our joined hands on the center console, and I can't help but stare at them. I can't see his tattoos, not under his jacket or the long-sleeve Henley he's wearing today, but I know they're there. I've never given much thought to tattoos, but on Grant, they're sexy, and I want to see more of them and wonder if he has them anywhere else, someplace I can't see.

"This is me," Grant says, pulling into the driveway of a condo not far from downtown.

"It's nice."

"You haven't even seen the inside." He chuckles.

"I live over a bakery. It's a tiny two-bedroom, so this is nice. Trust me."

"Your place is cute. Convenient too."

"Yeah," I agree. I wait for him to tell me how I'm living in a shoebox compared to this place, or how crazy I am to have invested every penny into a business that I don't know will succeed. However, early numbers are showing are good. Warm Delights is doing well. I just hope we can maintain our momentum.

"You want to go in?" he asks, surprising me again.

I turn to look at him, trying to gauge how he wants me to answer. "Do you want to go in?" I answer with a question of my own.

He grins and shakes his head. "Yes and no. I'd love to show you my place, but we have reservations."

"What time is our reservation?" I ask, glancing at the clock on the dash. It's almost half-past ten.

"Eleven."

"Yeah, we better get going." I turn back in my seat.

"It'll happen," Grant says, putting his SUV in Reverse and backing out of his driveway.

"What will?" I ask, confused.

"I'll get you in there." He points through the front window of his SUV. "I'll get you in my space."

"You're awfully full of yourself."

"I'm a determined man."

"I don't really know how to take you at times."

My confession has him tossing his head back in laughter. "That makes two of us. I can't tell if you're into me, or if you're here just to be polite."

"If you remember, it was Aspen who accepted your invitation," I remind him.

"She did." He nods. "But you're still here, sitting next to me in my truck, spending the day with me."

"You're right. Take me home."

"What?" He presses on the brake, stopping us in the middle of the road and whips his head to the side to look at me.

"Gotcha."

"Oh, Aurora." He tsks. "What am I going to do with you?"

"Tell me where we're going?" I offer.

"Nope. Not after that little stunt. You'll find out when we get there."

"Are we there yet?" I ask. I don't know what's gotten into me. If I would have talked that way to Elijah, he would have lectured me for hours, told me how immature I was being.

"You're going to be a handful, huh?" He laughs lightly.

I don't respond, and he doesn't expect me to. Instead, we travel to the other side of town in complete comfortable silence. I don't feel the pressure to fill the silence, and for once, my mind isn't worried about how I look, if what I chose to wear is good enough, if *I'm* good enough. I don't know how he managed to pull it off, but Grant Riggins has got me out of my own head.

"Cooking class? We're taking a cooking class?" I turn to look at him. I know my mouth is hanging open in shock, but this is not what I expected. Not at all.

"Yep." He grins, and I can tell he's proud of himself. "I know you love to bake, so I thought maybe you would enjoy this too. I, for one, can cook. Mom made sure we all could, but I'm no gourmet chef. We're making homemade ravioli today."

"Really?" I ask again.

"Good surprise?" he asks.

"The best! I've always wanted to do this." I bounce in my seat a little from my excitement.

"Did you go to school to learn how to bake?" he inquires.

"No. My mom and my grandma taught me. Mom went to school for it, but I never did. I just picked it up. That's part of why I was so nervous about opening my own shop. I don't have an education."

"Passion."

"What?"

"You have the passion. Sometimes, especially in your case, that's worth more than an education. I've tasted your treats, many of them, and let me tell you, there is nothing they could have taught you that you don't already know. They're delicious, Aurora."

"Thank you." My cheeks heat from his praise. "I can cook the basics, but baking... that's my thing. So this—" I point through the front window. "—this is great. I'm so excited." I look over at him, and he's grinning, and I realize I'm acting like a fool. I immediately still. "I'm sorry."

"Sorry?"

I nod, but I can't make myself look at him. I'm sure the ridicule will start anytime now.

"Hey." He reaches over and gently lifts my chin so my eyes are connected with his. "What just happened?"

"Nothing. I'm sorry for acting a fool." I shake my head. I know better. I let my guard down.

"Aurora." His voice is stern. "You have nothing to be sorry for. Do you know how relieved I am to know that you are excited about this? That we get to spend the day together doing something we're both going to enjoy? That you're sitting in this truck with me? Do you?"

"No," I whisper.

"Fuck it," he breathes, and then his lips are pressing against mine.

I'm frozen, not sure what to do. This is our first date, and he's kissing me. The palm of his hand cradles my cheek, and his tongue traces my lips, and that's all it takes for me to relax and open for him. He takes the opportunity to caress his tongue against mine, just a quick taste before he's pulling away and resting his forehead against mine. We're both breathing heavily, and my mind is racing. I'm not sure what just happened, but I'll be the first to admit that it was too brief. I want his lips on mine again. And again. And again.

"I've been dying to do that since the moment I first laid eyes on you." He pulls back, and both of his hands rest on my face. "I don't know what the sorry was about, but I want your excitement. I want your happiness. Fuck me, but I want your sadness too. I can't explain it, and I don't want to. All I know is that you're all that I think about. I know that seeing you light up when we pulled into the parking lot has my heart expanding in my chest. Don't ever apologize to me for being happy or sad or mad. Fuck, I don't care what you're feeling. I want you to give it to me. All of it." His lips press to my forehead, just a quick peck before he's dropping his hands and pulling away. "Now, let's go make some lunch." He gives me a cheeky grin before removing the keys from the ignition and racing around the SUV to open my door.

I have a brief few moments to process his words.

He's not mad.

He's not Elijah. I know that, but after years of verbal abuse and certain expectations, it's hard to break old habits. When my door opens, the cold January air hits me. "Thank you, Grant. For today, for what you said. Just... thank you." I feel like I should say more, but the emotions clogging my throat, the past memories, and my current situation are almost too much to handle.

"Come on, baby." He reaches for my hand, helping me out of the SUV, and with his hand on the small of my back, he leads us inside.

CHAPTER
Grant
SEVEN

"**W**ELL?" I ASK once we're in my SUV and sitting in the parking lot of the cooking class.

"That was so much fun," Aurora says. Her hazel eyes are sparkling, and none of the fear she showed me earlier is present.

Fear.

That's what it was, and I'm still raging mad at the man who put that fear in her eyes. This beautiful woman has been torn down, and she doesn't realize how fucking incredible she is. I want to be the man to change that. I want to be the man who makes her see herself the way that I see her. A badass baker, a sexy, desirable woman, and I want that spark in her eyes always. The way her eyes lit up... damn, she's fucking gorgeous.

"Now what?" she asks.

"Well, this is the part of the day I'm not sure you're going to be on board for. I thought I could take you to my parents' and show you the land. I want to take you down to the lake to where my brothers and I spent a lot of our time growing up. Hell, we still do. It's our own private stomping grounds of sorts. Then, I thought we could have dinner with my family." My heart is hammering in my chest, and my palms are suddenly sweaty. I've never brought a woman to family dinner before, but this one, she's under my skin, and I know my sisters-in-law will love her. I know my momma will love her.

"I'm not sure. We just met, Grant."

"I know that, but I already know that I love spending time with you, and I know you and Aspen are new in town. Let's have her meet us there. She's more than welcome. We have plenty of room, and Mom makes enough to feed an army. We can even stop and pick her up and take her with us to tour the farm. Although selfishly, I'm not ready to share you just yet."

She chews on her bottom lip, and I can see the indecision, the war she's waging internally. "I want you there, but this is your decision. If you're not ready to meet my family, you don't have to." I say the words and mean them, but I really want her to say yes.

"Aspen can come?" she asks softly.

I fight the urge to fist bump the air. "Yeah, baby. She can come. Do you want to pick her up now? Or have her meet us there?" I can see she's not sure how to answer. "Hey." I reach over and trace her cheek with my index finger. I find that I'll take any excuse to touch her. "There is no right or wrong answer here. You tell me what you want, and we'll make it happen. It's that easy."

"If she meets us there, you won't have to drive me home."

"Oh, I'm going to drive you home." I lean in over the console, our lips a breath from one another. "I'm going to drive you home and walk you to your door. Then I'm going to kiss these soft lips." I trace the pad of my thumb over her bottom lip. "One taste wasn't enough."

"I-I'll call her."

I nod, pulling away from her, giving her some space to call her sister. I don't know what's going on here. I've never felt this kind of attraction to a woman before. I just want to be with her. That's never happened to me before, but I know enough from watching my brothers, I'm not going to fight it. Royce fought Sawyer, and he was miserable until he let himself admit what she meant to him. Owen, he dove in headfirst, and I've never seen him happier. Hell, now that Royce has dragged his head out of his ass and made Sawyer a Riggins, he's the same. I'm going with this. Something tells me she's worth it.

"Hey, Aspen, it's me." Aurora's sweet voice fills the silence. "Yeah," she says, glancing over at me. "It's been fun. Listen, Grant wants us to have dinner with his family." She listens to whatever it is Aspen is saying. I can hear her talking, but I can't make out what she's saying. "I want you to come with me," she tells her sister.

My heart soars. That means she wants to be there. I want her to be there. I want to see her with my family, and with Sawyer and Layla. I can't explain it, but the need is there, and my gut tells me having her there is the right thing to do.

"I'll text you the address," she says, her voice breaking me out of my thoughts. "Thanks, Aspen," she says softly before ending the call and turning to look at me. "She's going to meet us there. I just need to give her a time and the address."

Unable to help myself, I lean over the console and press a kiss to the corner of her mouth. "Thank you," I say quietly. I rattle off the time and address, and she sends the message to Aspen.

"Are you sure this is okay?" she asks.

"Positive, but if it will make you feel better, I'll call my mom." I don't wait for her to answer before hitting Mom's name on my phone, and the call rings through the Bluetooth speakers.

"My middle son." Mom chuckles.

"Your favorite son," I counter. My smile is wide.

"Only when your brothers aren't around. What do I owe the pleasure? Don't tell me you're going to try and get out of dinner," she says.

"Nope. Actually, I was calling to make sure it was okay if I bring someone." I glance over at Aurora. "Two someones."

"Of course, you don't have to ask, you know that. There is always more than enough to go around, and until I get all you boys married off, there is still room at the table." She chuckles once again.

"Even then, there will be room," I remind her.

"Yes, but once my grandson gets here, hopefully, you boys will give him some cousins, and we'll need to start a kiddie table," she says wistfully.

"Isn't that something you should be talking to Royce about?"

"Oh, I have," she says with a smile in her voice. "The more the merrier, Grant, you know that."

"Thanks, Mom."

"So, who is she?" she asks.

I can imagine her smirking. No way can I beat my mother at her own game. "Her name is Aurora. She runs Warm Delights, the new bakery in town. Her and her sister, Aspen."

"Oh, Sawyer and Layla were telling me about her place. I've been meaning to stop by."

"We're actually going to be there before that. At least Aurora and I are. I'm going to show her the lake and the property. Aspen is meeting us at the house at six."

"Perfect. I'll put together some hot chocolate for you to take with you. Love you."

"Love you too," I say, reaching for the dash to end the call on the screen.

"Your mom sounds sweet," Aurora comments.

"She is, but she's also fierce. She had to be living with six Riggins men."

"I can't even imagine," she says with a laugh. "Thank you for inviting me and inviting Aspen."

"You're welcome, but it was purely selfish. I'm not ready to end my time with you."

"Tell me more about this lake," she says, and I know she's finally accepted that this day is ours. Hers and mine. I tell her about the lake that Dad built, and how my brothers and I spent every minute we were allowed to there when growing up. "We still do," I tell her. "We have boats and Jet Skis. It's a good time. We have a huge fire pit and a gazebo. That's where Royce and Sawyer were married. That's where he proposed."

"That's amazing. To have that history... to have so much family. Aspen and I lost our grandma two years ago, and now it's just us and our parents. Both of our parents were only children. Grandma Edna was the last of our grandparents to pass."

There is a tightness in my chest for her, and her family. "What made you move to Nashville?"

"The building. I've always wanted my own bakery. My grandma always said she would come and work for me, and even though she isn't here, I still wanted to do it. I hope that she's watching over me, and she's smiling."

"You know she is," I assure her. "What about Aspen? Did she always want to bake as well?"

"No." She laughs. "Aspen went to college and got her associate's degree, but she hated every minute of it. She was working as an administrative assistant for a local newspaper when I brought up the idea of the bakery. She was on board to go wherever we ended up and stand by my side while I took the biggest risk of my life."

"And your parents?"

"They supported me and were glad to hear that Aspen was coming with me. In a way I think they were relieved I was getting out of Memphis. Starting over was scary, but I needed it. I'm just lucky to have a little sister who is my best friend to come on this crazy ride with me."

"Sounds like that risk is paying off," I tell her.

"Yeah, we've been successful, but it's still too early to determine if we can go the distance."

"Well, I've tasted the goods." I wink at her, and she blushes. "I have no doubt that you have what it takes. Besides, the move brought you to me." I glance over and give her a big cheesy grin.

"Stop." She swats lightly at my arm, laughter bubbling up in her chest.

"Admit it, that's the best part of the move," I say, keeping my eyes on the road. I hated the sadness in her voice. I'll take her laughter any day.

"Wow," she breathes when we turn down the lane to my parents' place. "This is where you grew up?"

"Yep."

"I guess with five boys you needed space to roam."

"Yeah, it was Mom and Dad's way of also keeping us out of the public eye. Dad built the business from the start, and as it grew along with his bank account, it was hard to go out without stares, and random people stopping us asking him for a job, even a loan. Complete strangers would stop him asking for money. I don't remember that part as much. But I've heard the stories. That's when they bought this place and built the lake. It's our own little oasis."

"It's beautiful," she exhales, staring out the window. "I bet it's gorgeous when the snow falls."

"The forecast is calling for snow next week. If it happens, I'll bring you back. You can see for yourself."

"What makes you think I want to come back?" she asks.

I pull up to the house and put the SUV in Park. Removing my seat belt, I face her. "Think with this," I say, placing my hand on her chest, over her heart. "Not with this." I lift my hand and tap my index finger against her temple. "Or maybe think this these," I say once again, running the pad of my thumb across her lips. "Definitely think with these."

"I'd like that. I mean, I'd like to come back. With you."

"There's my girl." I lean in and kiss the tip of her nose. "Come on. Mom's got hot chocolate ready for our adventure."

"It's freezing out. Will we be warm enough?" She looks down at herself; I'm sure gauging the warmth of her outfit for an outdoor escapade.

"We'll take the Ranger. It's enclosed and has a heater." I wink at her, before climbing out of the SUV. This time she doesn't wait for me to open her door, but that's okay. We can take some small steps. After all, she is here with me. I didn't think I would be able to convince her to come. The rest will fall into place.

Meeting her at the front of the truck, I place my hand on the small of her back and guide her up the front porch. "Mom!" I call out as we enter.

"In the kitchen!" she calls back.

"Ready?" I ask Aurora.

"Is anyone ever really ready to meet the parents?" She peers up at me, and I can see the indecision in her eyes.

"Yes. Mine are awesome. Trust me, babe." We move toward the kitchen to find Mom tightening the lid on a thermos that I know is full of her homemade hot chocolate. "Mom, this is Aurora Steele. Aurora, this my mother, Lena Riggins."

"It's nice to meet you. You have a lovely home." Aurora holds her hand out to my mother.

"We're huggers," Mom says, walking around the kitchen island and drawing her into a hug. "And thank you. We're glad to have you," she says, pulling away. "I've got you all set up. Dad fueled up the Ranger, and there are a couple of blankets, laundered blankets, on the seat," Mom says with a shake of her head.

"Hey, that's your eldest two," I say, holding my hands up in defense.

Mom glances at Aurora and rolls her eyes. "You're just like them." She throws me a mock glare that isn't the slightest bit scary.

"On that note, we're out. Thanks." I lean in and kiss Mom on the cheek. "Tell Dad thanks as well. We'll be back before dinner. If she beats us here, her sister's name is Aspen."

"Go on. I can handle it. Oh, and, Aurora," Mom says, waiting for Aurora to look at her. "Make him work for it." She winks and turns toward the sink, dismissing us.

Aurora's mouth drops open, and I throw my head back in

laughter. "Come on, let me show you where I grew up." Hand in hand, we head back outside and toward the barn. We just got here, and I can already tell this is going to be my favorite part of the day. Other than the kisses. Those are at the very top of the list.

CHAPTER
Aurora
EIGHT

GRANT EXPERTLY MANEUVERS over the trails. I'm sitting with a blanket on my lap, and my eyes glued to the scenery. It's breathtaking. I know that Tennessee is beautiful, but seeing it like this, away from the city lights, is something else altogether.

"What are you thinking about over there?" Grant asks.

"How Aspen would love to see this," I tell him honestly.

"We'll have to bring her out with us next time."

"She would love that. *I* would love that," I say, turning to look at him. I don't comment on his assumption that there will be a next time. I know him well enough already to know that if he wants it, he's going to do whatever it takes to make it happen.

"This is the lake." He pulls up to the edge of a huge body of water. "My dad had this made when we were kids."

"Wow." I take in the beauty of the lake.

"It's a blast in the summer. We have boats and Jet Skis, and we go tubing. It's a good time."

"What about the winter? Do you ever get to ice skate?" I ask.

"We do, but not here. Dad dug a smaller ice-skating rink. We don't use it much anymore. We used to play hockey on it when we were kids."

"Why separate?"

"It's thinner, only about a foot deep. It's guaranteed to freeze faster and be solid. Not only that but if the ice cracks, it's not going to swallow anyone whole. Mom was worried we would risk it on the lake, and it would end in tragedy. Dad agreed and dug us a rink."

"I can't even imagine having this as a playground growing up."

"It was a good time. My brothers and I spent hours out here. My parents too when they could. Dad was busy with the business, but he always kept Sundays and most Saturdays for family time. He made it to all of our games and looking back, I'm not sure how he managed it all."

"He wanted to."

"Yeah." He nods. "He did. He made sure that all five of us, and our mother, knew what we meant to him. Mom is the love of his life, and he's been known to go overboard when it comes to her."

"Ah," I say, nodding.

"Ah? What do you mean, ah?" he asks.

"That must be where you get it." I smile at him.

"I'll take that as a compliment." He winks at me.

"It's not a bad thing. It's just... different for me. I've never met a man so determined to spend time with me." I let the truth float between us. I don't tell him that I've never had a man look at me as he does. I've never had a man make the butterflies in my belly take flight from a simple glance or touch.

"I don't know if that makes me happy or sad, a little of both I think." He leans over, his mouth a breath from mine. "It makes me sad that you've not been treated like you deserve, but it also makes me happy that I'm the man who gets to give you that. I get to show you how special you are. I get to kiss these soft lips." He angles closer and kisses the corner of my mouth.

"This all seems fast," I confess. I'm breathless from his nearness.

"It's fast, but there is no timeline. We do us, and as long as we are true to not only ourselves but each other, we're free to do what we want. Take me, for example. I can't stop thinking about you. You're all I've thought about since the day I stepped into Warm Delights. That's never happened to me before. I've never met a woman who consumes my thoughts. Not just when I'm with you, but all day, and all night long. That's enough for me to know that you're special, and I want to see if there is something between us. I know I'm coming on strong, but I don't play games. I don't see the point. I'm always going to be open and honest with you, and although some things might be too soon, if I feel it, I'm going to tell you. Good or bad. That's the only way I know how to operate."

"I've never met anyone like you."

"Good." He places his hand on my thigh. "I'm hoping that will give me an advantage." He chuckles. "I'm not telling you I'm in love with you, Aurora. What I am telling you is that you intrigue me, you're beautiful, and you're the only woman I see. I want to explore that and find out why. If you'll let me."

I don't even think about it. I nod my agreement. The last thing I need is to fall into a relationship, but there is something about Grant that pulls me in. He's not the only one feeling this... connection that we seem to have. I want to explore it too. It scares the hell out of me, but it's the truth. The butterflies in my belly won't let me push him away. It's a new feeling, one that I would love to feel every day of my forever, but even I'm not naïve enough to think that's where this is going.

"Come on. I'll show you the rink."

We ride around the lake, with his hand on my thigh. It's surreal that I'm here. That this is how things are going between us. I swore I was done with men. After Elijah, I never thought I would be able to trust another man. I'm not sure that I can trust the one sitting next to me. What I do know is that my gut is telling me I can. I don't know that I ever had that "gut" feeling with Elijah. In fact, I know I didn't. Maybe in the beginning there were some butterflies. All new romances have those, but not like this. Placing my hand over my stomach, as if it will stop my jitters, has him glancing over.

"You okay?"

"Yeah. Yes, I'm fine." I smile to let him know that I am indeed, okay. I'm going to be okay, and there is nothing wrong with us getting to know each other better. I just need to keep reminding myself of that.

"Wow," I say as Grant stops next to the rink. "When you said rink, I didn't expect this." I turn to look at him. "Does anyone in your family do anything halfway?" I ask.

"Nope." His deep chuckle fills the cab. "There were seven of us, five being rowdy boys. We all needed our space."

"This is huge."

He nods. "Do you skate?"

"Yeah, I mean, I can. It's been a while since I have. Aspen and I used to go skating all the time with our parents. It's been years." I think back to the last time I went skating. It was Aspen's sixteenth birthday. After that, we were both too involved with being teenagers to spend that time with our parents. If I only knew then what I know now. Teenage me would have spent as much time with them as I could. Adulting sucks, and in my case my choices have taken me and my sister three hours from our parents. I swallow hard. I miss them so much.

"You miss them," Grant says, at the same time I feel his thumb swiping across my cheek.

"I'm sorry," I say, not realizing I was crying.

"You have nothing to be sorry for. I can't imagine not living close enough to just drop in on Mom and Dad. You should invite them up. You know my mom would be down to host them. They could stay with me or even with my parents."

I give him a watery smile and turn my gaze back to the rink. "I'll keep that in mind. I don't know if we're there yet."

"Of course we are," he says, giving me a charming smile.

"Think about it. Really think about it. I'd love to meet the man and woman responsible for giving me you."

"You're unlike any man I've ever met." I know I've said it before, but it's worth repeating.

"Good." He hands me a cup of hot chocolate before leaning over and kissing my cheek. Comfortable silence surrounds us as we enjoy our drink. "We better start heading back. Aspen will be there soon, and I don't want her to have to go in alone," he says.

"Are you always this considerate?" I ask.

"I'm a gentleman." He grins.

"I'm not worried about Aspen. She doesn't know a stranger."

"Good. We're not strangers." He reaches over and laces his fingers through mine. "Not anymore."

I nod because I have no words. My emotions are running high, and I don't trust myself to not say something I'll regret later. The ride back to the house is quiet, with his hand holding mine tightly. It's as if he knows I need the connection. I don't know how he does it, but Grant seems to know what I need when I need it. Like today. I needed today. I didn't realize how much I missed the company of a man. One who doesn't belittle me, one who my gut tells me I can trust. I never thought I would trust again, but with Grant, it's as easy as breathing. I don't know how or why, but it just is.

With his hand on the small of my back, Grant leads me into the house. I can hear my sister's laugh as soon as we open the door. That's Aspen for you. She's never met a stranger and can hold a conversation with anyone. I used to be like her. I used to be full of life, but then I met Elijah. At first things were good, but then he changed, and suddenly there wasn't much to laugh and smile about.

"Hey, you two," Lena says as we enter the kitchen. "How was your ride?" she asks, her eyes sparkling.

"Good. Thank you," I say politely.

"I should be thanking you. You kept that one out of my hair. I swear those boys of mine pick at everything I'm cooking. It makes it impossible to get anything done." She turns to look at Grant, as do I. His hand is still on the small of my back, but in the other, he has a roll that he's just taken a huge bite of.

"What?" he says with his mouth full.

"See what I mean?" Lena smiles at her son. "Can I get you something to drink?" she asks me.

"No, thank you. We just had hot chocolate. It was delicious."

"Yo, Ma, where are you?" a male voice calls out.

"In the kitchen!" Lena calls back.

I turn to Grant to ask which brother, but before I can, he appears in the doorway of the kitchen. "Well, what do we have here?" he asks. His smile lights up his face as he darts his eyes from me to Aspen.

"Conrad, this is Aurora, and her sister, Aspen."

He steps next to me and takes my hand in his, bringing it to his lips. "Hello, beautiful," he coos.

"Back off, Con," Grant all but growls. The sound has Conrad's grin growing wider.

"Is that how it is, big brother?" he asks. There is mischief in his voice, and the smile tells me he likes to rile his brother up.

"That's how it is," Grant says, stepping a little closer to me. The warmth of his skin seeps into me, and my shoulders relax. I don't understand how I can be so comfortable with him in such a short amount of time.

"And this one?" Conrad points to Aspen.

"This one can speak for herself, and I'd back off if I were you, *Con*," Aspen says sweetly, repeating Grant's earlier words.

Conrad throws his head back in laughter. In a couple of long strides, he's around the huge kitchen island and grabbing my sister's hand, pulling it to his lips just as he did with me. "It's a pleasure to meet you, beautiful," he says, laying on the Riggins charm.

"Aspen." My sister corrects him with a laugh. She is not the least bit affected by his antics.

"What's going on?" another guy says.

"Marshall, this is Aurora, and her sister, Aspen," Grant introduces us.

"Ladies," Marshall croons. "Brother, you didn't tell me you were bringing me new friends," he says, sliding up next to me.

"Marsh," Grant warns.

"'Bout fucking time." A voice comes from behind us.

I turn to look over my shoulder, and a tall guy with a thick beard and blue eyes, so much like Grant's, is smiling. He has Layla pulled to his side—one arm around her waist and the other resting on her swollen belly.

"What did I miss?" another man, who is clearly a Riggins, asks. He looks down at the woman standing by his side. "Babe, what did I miss this time?" he says to her. The entire room erupts in laughter.

"Are you boys bothering your momma again? I'm starving," adds an older man, who the five other men in the room closely resemble.

"The old man is my father, Stanley," Grant starts, pointing out the newcomers. "That one's Owen, and his fiancée, Layla, and my nephew." Grant indicates toward Layla's swollen belly. "This is Royce, and his wife, Sawyer. Everyone, this is Aurora, and her sister, Aspen." Grant points behind us.

"Told you," Owen and Royce say after all the introductions, hugs, and handshakes have taken place.

"Yeah," Grant says, rubbing the back of his neck.

"This is going to be fun." Royce rubs his hands together.

"What are they talking about?" I whisper to Grant.

"Nothing." He shakes his head, clearly amused. Everyone begins to filter from the room at Lena's instructions to make our way to the dining room.

"Grant," I say, placing my hand on his arm. He immediately

stops, and I have his full attention. I swallow back the fear of being ridiculed. "Tell me, please." My voice is pleading. "I-I don't want secrets. I can't do secrets. I don't know what this is, but I've been with a man who kept me in the dark. He kept me at arm's length, and used me." I swallow hard, stopping there. I've already said more than I ever intended to.

"Hey." He cradles my face in the palm of his hands. "No secrets. They've been razzing me, telling me that when I fall, it's going to be hard. I gave them both hell when they met my sisters-in-law, and this is payback for that. Nothing more, nothing less."

I nod. I can't speak over the emotions clogging my throat. Swallowing hard, I manage to push "Okay," past my lips.

"You're the first woman I've ever brought to dinner. My brothers and I, we don't bring just anyone. She has to be special. We have to see more than just a few dates or a roll in the hay with her. They know that."

"Just me?" I ask him.

"Yeah, baby. Just you." He pulls me into a hug, holding me close to his chest. "No secrets," he whispers. "Come on, let's get in there before the vultures eat it all." He eases back. "You good?" I nod. He studies me, searching for the truth. He must find what he's looking for because he returns my nod and leads us into the dining room.

No one pays us any attention as he holds the chair out next to his and tells me to sit. I make eye contact with Aspen, who is sitting between Marshall and Conrad. I give her a subtle nod, and she smiles softly. It's her way of telling me she's here, and I have no doubt she's going to grill me once we're home.

Funny, I'm not dreading it. I need to talk to someone about today, about Grant, and about all of these damn butterflies.

"Spill it," Aspen says as soon as we're home.

"It was... a good day."

"That smile tells me it was more than a good day. Come on now, you can do better than that." Her phone rings, and a look that can be described as pure mischief crosses her face. "Hi, Mom."

"No," I whisper to her.

"Oh, we're fine. We just got back from dinner. At Aurora's new man's parents' place."

"Aspen!" I hiss.

She throws her head back in laughter. "Technically, he's not her new man, but he wants to be." She laughs at something our mom says. "Hold on." She pulls the phone from her ear and taps the screen. "You're on speaker," she tells Mom.

"Aurora, tell me more," Mom says, her voice giving away her excitement. After my ex, I swore off men and dating. Mom was disappointed. She said I was letting him win, but I didn't care. I was jaded, and I still am, but everything about Grant screams that he's different.

"He's a nice guy."

"How did you meet?"

"He came into the bakery."

"Nice. Does he have a handsome brother for your sister?"

"He does actually. He has four brothers but two of them are taken."

"There you go, Aspen. You have two to choose from," Mom teases her.

"Hey, I thought this was about Aurora." Aspen pouts.

"I want both of my girls happy."

"We are," we say at the same time.

"Fine. I won't press, but I'd like to see a picture of this young man."

"I've got you," Aspen tells her.

"Great, now tell me what else has been going on? Don't leave out a single thing."

Aspen and I spend the next half hour or so talking to our mother. Dad joins the call too, and it makes me miss them even more. I miss them, but I really am happy with where I'm at in my life right now. I think Aspen is too. We both love Nashville. It was good for both of us to get out of Memphis. We were both just kind of going through the motions. Here, it feels like we're living.

Really living.

CHAPTER NINE

Grant

MOST WOULD SAY that me coming into her bakery every morning is obsessive. I like to think of it as resourceful. It's not just the fact that I get to lay eyes on the beautiful Aurora. Her creations are mouthwatering, out-of-this-world delicious.

"Fancy seeing you here." Aspen smiles. "What can I get for you?"

"Is Aurora here?" I ask her.

"Yep."

"Can I see her?"

"She's in the back." I move to walk around the counter. "Hey, what are you doing?"

"Going to see her."

"Employees only."

"I'll be sure to leave you a big tip," I say. The bell on the door chimes, telling me she has another customer, and I know she's not going to try and stop me. Pushing through the swinging door, I find Aurora filling cupcake pans. "Morning," I say, and she startles, dropping the scoop she's using.

"Shit. You can't sneak up on me like that." She picks up the scoop and tosses it in the sink, before reaching into a drawer and pulling out another one. "What are you doing back here?"

"I wanted to see you. How has your day been?" I ask her, leaning against the wall and crossing my feet at the ankles.

"It's not even—" She glances at the wall. "—eight in the morning. How bad could it be?"

"I don't know. You started your day hours ago, so I thought it was worth asking." I shrug.

"Do you forget anything?" she asks.

"Not when it comes to you." A ghost of a smile tilts her lips before she can stop herself. "What flavor?" I ask, pointing to the cupcakes.

"Red velvet."

"They smell like heaven."

She laughs. "Thank you."

"So, how about dinner tonight?"

"I don't know. I have to be in bed early. My day starts at three most days."

"You name the time, and I'll make it happen."

"I usually eat at four."

"Done."

"Don't you have to work?"

"I do, but I can also work from home later this evening. Besides, it's a perk of owning the company."

"Don't tell me you're one of those spoiled 'I can leave whenever the hell I want' guys?"

"No. I work hard. Riggins Enterprises is my family's legacy. I'm proud of that. However, if my girl needs an early dinner, I can make that happen."

"You're not going to let me say no, are you?"

"Nope."

Another smile, this time, she doesn't try to hide it. "Pick me up at four."

"I'll be here." I stand to my full height and make my way to where she's standing. "Have a good day, Aurora," I say, pressing a kiss to her cheek. "I'm going to go have Aspen ring up a box of these. I think Layla will love them."

"You really are one of the good ones, huh?" she says. I'm not sure if it's a question, but I answer her anyway.

"Yes. Later, babe." I turn and walk back out to the front and wait in line for my own box of cupcakes.

"You have to try these," I tell Royce. I'm standing at the front reception desk where I've just set a box of red velvet cupcakes on the corner. Layla didn't waste any time indulging, and neither did I.

Royce looks at the name on the box before diving in for his own cupcake. "This is the third time this week that you've brought in treats," he says before taking a huge bite of his own cupcake.

"So?" I shrug. It's no secret in my family that I have a sweet tooth.

"It's Wednesday," Royce points out.

"Well," I say, winking at Layla, making her laugh, "my nephew needs them to make it through the day."

"Your nephew does not need them, and neither does his mother," Layla chimes in.

"But yet you're eating one."

"I'm pregnant and eating for two. You can't just put all this sugary goodness in front of me and expect me to be able to resist. I have no willpower, Grant Riggins, and you damn well know it," she says, giving me what I imagine will be her attempt at the mom look.

"Are you giving my wife a hard time?" Owen asks, joining us. He kisses Layla's cheek before grabbing his own cupcake.

"Fiancée." Royce is quick to correct him. Owen might be giving our parents the first grandchild, but Royce is going to hang on to the fact he gave them the first daughter-in-law, twice, but we won't talk about the first one. She's better left in the past.

"We really need to fix that," Owen tells Layla.

She shrugs. "So, let's fix it."

Royce, Owen, and I all stop chewing and stare at her. Owen has been asking her for months when they can set a date. Hell, he was asking the minute he proposed.

"What are you saying, Layla?"

"I'm saying this little guy will be here in a few months, and it might be nice for his mom and dad to have the same last name."

"Tell me when and where and I'll take care of it."

"As long as Ronnie and Linda are there, I don't really care."

"We'll go to them."

"Um, I want your family there as well."

Owen looks at us, and I nod, but it's Royce who speaks up. "You tell us when and we'll make it happen, brother."

"How about we get married on the beach?" Owen asks her.

"I do love the beach." She smiles up at him. There is so much love and devotion shining through in that one look. It hits me deep in my gut. I want a woman to look at me like that. No, not just any woman. I want Aurora to look at me like that.

"Call Mom," I tell Owen. "She'll be all over this."

"Lay?" he asks.

"I would love nothing more than for her to take care of it all. I just want to worry about this little guy." She rubs her belly. "The rest is just semantics. I know your mother will make it a day we will both remember. I'll help with anything she needs, but honestly, I don't even know where to start."

Owen drops to his knees and wraps his arms around her waist. Royce and I share a glance before stepping away and going to our own offices, giving them a moment alone. Pulling my phone out of my pocket, I set it on my desk while I fire up my laptop. The urge to send Aurora a message is strong, and I'm not sure that I should in this moment, for fear of what I'll say, but I do it anyway. Grabbing my phone, I type out a message. She wants real. I'm going to give her real.

Me: How is it possible that I miss you already?

I hit Send before I can think better of it. It's cheesy as fuck, and if my brothers were to read this message, they would crucify me. However, it's also a valid question. I want to know how I can miss her already. I barely know this woman, but she's under my skin. She has me thinking about things I've never thought of before. Dreaming of a future that I once thought was so far beyond me in years, that it would be a while before they ever came to mind. Not now. Not after meeting Aurora.

Aurora: Is this a trick question?

I can't hide my chuckle.

Me: Not a trick. I just... can't wait for our date tonight.

Aurora: Some date I am. I have to be home by eight to go to bed.

Me: I'll take any amount of time you're willing to give me.

Aurora: There they go again.

Me: What? Who are they?

Aurora: The butterflies. You're always making them flutter around.

Me: I give you butterflies?

I'm smiling like a fool. I can't help it. It's been difficult to get anything out of her. This is progress.

Aurora: Every day.

Every. Day.

Me: I'll be there at three-thirty.

Aurora: I thought we agreed to four?

Me: I can't wait that long.

Aurora: I'll be waiting.

I have to force myself to shove my phone in my desk drawer to keep from texting her again. I need to get some work done, especially since I'm leaving early. I have a date that I refuse to be late for.

"You win the lottery or something?" Conrad says from my door.

"Nope. Just having a good day."

"Does it have anything to do with these?" He holds up his half-eaten red velvet cupcake.

"Not so much the cupcake as the creator," I admit.

"No, shit. You're joining them on the other side?" he asks.

"By them, I assume you mean Royce and Owen? And on the other side, I assume you mean a relationship?"

"That," he says, shoving the rest of the cupcake in his mouth.

"I hope so."

He swallows and wipes at his mouth with a napkin. "Didn't expect you to admit it."

"Why? I have nothing to hide. She's incredible."

"You barely know her."

"That's why we're dating to get to know one another. And what I do know, she's incredible."

He begins to sing "Another One Bites the Dust," making me laugh. I grab a highlighter from my desk and toss it at him, hitting him in the chest.

"We're all going to fall, Con. It's just a matter of when and for who."

"Yeah," he agrees. "But not for a while. I've got more wild oats to sow."

"These are so good," Marshall says, stopping to stand next to Conrad. "I think I might ask her to marry me. Can you imagine living with someone who can create these?" he asks. There is a light in his eyes that tells me he's picking a fight, and he's going to get one.

"Fuck off. She's taken."

"And then there were two," Marshall says dramatically.

"Go." I laugh, waving them out of my doorway. "I have work to do."

"Hot date tonight?" Marshall asks.

"Yes, and you jokers need to leave me alone so I can get shit done and get to her."

"Oh, it's worse than I thought, Con," Marshall quips.

"Fuck off." I toss another highlighter. Their laughter follows them down the hall. They can give me all the shit they want. It's not going to change a thing.

Not with her.

Never with her.

CHAPTER
Aurora
TEN

"**T**ELL ME, DEAR sister, what date is this?" Aspen asks from her spot on the side of the tub.

"I don't know." *Lies.* I know exactly how many dates this makes for us, but I'm not going to admit it.

"Liar," she calls me out.

"Fine," I sigh dramatically. "Eight." I pretend to not notice her smile of victory.

"Eight." She nods. "How long, like two weeks?"

"Three."

"I like him."

My shoulders relax. "Yeah, I like him too." I really like him—more than I should. I was supposed to be focusing on me and my business, but Grant Riggins is hard to resist.

"Are you happy?"

"We're just dating." That's what I keep telling myself, but I know my heart doesn't understand. With every message, every phone call, and every date, I fall harder for him.

My sister throws her head back in laughter. "If you call the way Grant looks at you 'just dating,' then the rest of us are screwed. Quite literally screwed. That man is more than just dating you, Aurora."

"I thought maybe that was in my imagination."

"Nope." She grins. "Whatcha gonna do about it?"

"Nothing. We're taking things slow, getting to know one another."

"Maybe tonight will be the night." She wiggles her eyebrow.

"The night for what?"

"You know? Brown chicken, brown cow," she singsongs.

"Stop. That's not going to happen." It's not that I haven't thought about it. I mean, Grant is sexy and charming, and it's been way too long for me. I don't have the experience that a man like Grant would want or need. It's best not to go there. He's going to realize I'm not the one for him, and all this will end. No use in adding in sex to make things more complicated. I'm already having a hard time keeping my heart in line with the "don't fall for him" concept.

"Date night, the man is a saint. Has he tried anything?"

"Other than kissing or hand-holding? No."

"Aw, sis, don't sound so disappointed. I know he wants you. He's just giving you time. He's one of the good ones."

"I don't know what this is," I finally admit. "Look at me. I'm not the kind of woman a guy like Grant goes for. He's so nice. I'm having a hard time figuring out his angle."

"Aurora, that's because he doesn't have an ulterior motive. He's into you. And if I hear you say that shit again, you and I are going to have words. I hate Elijah and what he did to you. You're beautiful and sexy. You have curves, curves that drive men wild, even men like Grant. Elijah was a dick who wanted to manipulate you. Don't let him ruin this for you. He's already stolen so many years of your life and left you—"

I stop her. "Don't. I can't go there right now. Hell, I don't ever want to go there again." Thinking about my ex before my date with Grant is not a good idea.

"I'm sorry." Aspen is quick to apologize. "Where is he taking you tonight?"

"I'm not sure. He just said dress casual." I look down at my black skinny jeans, black tank top, and burgundy open-front sweater. "Is this good enough?"

"You look hot. He's going to go crazy."

Before I can second-guess my outfit, the buzzer sounds. "Will you let him in?" I ask my sister. I just need a few more minutes. With each time I see him, my feelings grow. I always have a good time with him. He never makes me feel pressured or less than him. It's a feeling I'm quickly becoming addicted to. Squaring my shoulders, I take one last glance in the mirror and go to meet my date.

"Wow," he says as soon as I step into the small living room. "You look great."

"Thanks," I say shyly, looking down at my feet that are now covered in my knee-high boots.

"Ready?" he asks.

"Yes."

"Aspen, do you want to join us?"

"No. You crazy kids go ahead." She gives us a knowing smile, like she has this big secret that she knows we're about to discover. That's Aspen for you. Always optimistic and looking at the bright side of life. I wish I could be more like my little sister.

"Want me to bring you something back?" I ask.

"Nah, I'm good. Besides, one of us needs to eat your leftover chicken parmesan from last night's date." She smirks.

"Fair enough." Grant chuckles. "Let us know if you change your mind." We wave to Aspen and then we're off. With his hand on the small of my back, he leads me to his SUV.

Date number eight is officially underway.

"I'm impressed," I tell him, finishing off the rest of my wine. "That was delicious."

"I'll admit I was nervous. I wasn't sure I remembered everything from our class."

"Is this what you call a two for one? Using what you learned on our cooking date to preparing the same meal on your own as another."

"It got you here, didn't it?" He smirks.

"Yeah," I agree. "It got me here." I stand and start clearing our plates.

"Sit. I'll get that. You're a guest."

"I am, but you cooked. This is the least I can do."

"Aurora, go sit," he says, taking our empty plates from my hands. "Why don't you refill your wine, and go pick out a movie?"

"You're going to let me pick?" I ask, raising an eyebrow.

"We could stare at a screen full of fuzz as long as you're sitting next to me." He kisses my cheek and turns to start filling the dishwasher.

Doing as he suggested, I pour myself a little more wine and head to the living room. He already has the movies pulled up, so I scroll through looking for something that would interest both of us. I'm still scrolling five minutes later when he comes and takes a seat next to me with a bottle of water in his hands.

"Any luck?"

"No." I hand him the remote. "You pick." My anxiety about choosing wrong is taking over. I know it's all in my head and that I'm overthinking this. I also know he's not Elijah, but that's just it. Elijah wasn't always an asshole. No, he got me in his clutches before he became the devil here on earth. At least to me.

"Oh, no. That's your job. I already told you I don't care what we watch." He places the remote on my thigh.

My breathing accelerates, and I hate myself for it. This is

foolish. I'm a grown woman who has choices. I should be able to make these kinds of decisions with a man and not freak the hell out.

"Hey." Grant turns to look at me, his hands resting on my cheeks. "Breathe for me, beautiful," he says softly.

Keeping my eyes on his, I focus on slow, even breaths. Once I have gained control of my breathing, I turn my head to hide my embarrassment, but Grant won't let me hide. Not that I expected him to.

"Come here." He moves to settle against the couch and pulls me into his arms. My head rests against his chest, and the steady beat of his heart calms me. "You want to tell me what that was about?"

"Not really. I was hoping that we could forget that it happened."

"No way. I need to know what I did to cause that reaction in you, so I'm sure to never do it again."

"It wasn't you."

"No? Then tell me what's going on. I'm right here, and I'm not going anywhere." He's quick to assure me.

I don't know how, but he always seems to know what I need or what I need to hear. "My ex was... not a nice guy."

His body stiffens. "Did he hurt you?"

"Not physically."

"Explain that for me, babe."

"I'm sure you'd rather watch a movie than listen to my past relationship woes." I'd do just about anything to get out of talking about this.

"You see, that's where you're wrong. I need to know what triggered that reaction, Aurora. I want to be a man you can depend on. If you can't open up to me, I can't be that for you."

"Reverse psychology?" I chuckle.

"Not exactly, but if it works." I can feel him shrug.

"Cliff's Notes, he was a good guy in the beginning. He made

me fall for him and then tore me down every chance he got. We've been broken up for almost two years. After my grandma's death, he was… let's just say he wasn't there for me, and I finally saw my situation for what it was. I was in an abusive relationship. Mentally. I got out."

"You're glossing over a lot there, sweetness."

"I just don't want to talk about him. Not right now. We've had a nice night, and I'd like to forget that I'm ruining it with the drama of my past. It's way too early in this dating thing we have going on to bring you down with all of that."

"This is more than just a dating thing, but you'll realize that with time. Tell me what brought on tonight's episode, and I'll let it be for now."

I sit up and look him in the eye. "It was me making the decision. It's not something he ever approved of, and I had to hear it. I'm a work in progress."

"We all have our issues, Aurora." He leans in and kisses the tip of my nose. "I promise you I won't stop until everything he did to you is nothing but a distant memory in your past. I won't stop until you understand how amazing and beautiful you are. And know this. If you pick something, I'm good with it as long as I get to spend time with you. If it's something I absolutely hate, we'll discuss it. You won't tell me, but I assume there were never any discussions with this asshat. We are a team, Aurora. That's what I want us to be, tonight and twenty years from now. However long you allow me to be a part of your life. We are a team."

I give him a watery smile with a slight head nod. That's all I'm capable of with the emotions rolling through me—the fear, the relief, and the hope that what he says is right.

"I'm going to close my eyes and hit the button on the remote. Whatever pops up is what we're watching."

"What if we both hate it?" I laugh. How he always manages to calm me is beyond my comprehension, but I'm grateful for it.

"I'm not going to be watching it anyway."

"No?"

"Nope. Not if I'm holding you." With that, he places his arm around my shoulders and pulls me back into his chest. I don't fight it. I settle in close, letting the warmth of his arms soothe me, as some action movie begins to play. Neither of us moves until the movie ends. I don't remember any of it. I couldn't focus on his hands running through my hair and tracing up and down my arm.

It's not until the movie finishes that his lips finally connect with mine. He kisses me like he always does. Like I'm the air he breathes. He never takes things further, and I can't help but wonder if that's intentional, or if he doesn't want to see the rest. My heart cracks a little at the thought. I know he's not like that. But he's also all I think about. Grant is the man who's slowly bringing me back to life. I can't help but wonder how I will deal with the carnage when he decides I'm not the one he wants.

CHAPTER
Grant
ELEVEN

WALKING INTO WARM Delights, I take in the smell of sugary goodness. My stomach growls, and I'm not even hungry. I had breakfast after I hit the gym this morning with Marsh and Con. My eyes scan the room, and it's packed, which has my smile growing. My girl is killing it. She's making a name for herself, and I'm thrilled for her. My eyes scan until they land on her. What I see has my smile dropping. There is a man at the counter, and he's leaning over, leaning toward Aurora. She doesn't look impressed.

My feet carry me to them. "Hey, babe." I stand tall next to the asshole talking to my girl. Aurora visibly relaxes.

"Who are you?" the guy asks. This guy is lanky and rough around the edges.

"I'm her boyfriend." It's not a lie, but not the truth either. Aurora and I have been dating for a month this week. I've been taking things slow, not wanting to scare her. I assume I'm the only man in her life. She's the only woman in mine. It's time we have that conversation just so that we're both on the same page.

His beady eyes move toward Aurora. "And she's mine." I hear from beside me. I know without looking it's Marshall's voice.

"Fucking figures," the guy mumbles, grabbing his bag and stalking out of the bakery.

Marsh and I watch him go. "What are you doing here?" I ask my brother.

"I saw your SUV outside. I thought I'd stop and grab something too."

"I'm not eating. I'm just here for Aurora."

"Suit yourself." He turns his attention to the girls where they're still standing behind the counter. "Hey, Aspen, what's today's special?" he asks, his eyes dropping to scan the display case.

"Apple fritters."

"Perfect. I'll take a dozen. Might as well get some for everyone," he says, pulling his wallet out of his pocket.

"You good?" I keep my eyes trained on Aurora.

She nods. "He was harmless."

"You looked scared to death." I give her a pointed look, daring her to argue with me. She's only given me bits and pieces about her douche ex, but I'd say the fear in her eyes isn't from the guy who just stalked out of her bakery. My guess it has everything to do with the ex who she refuses to talk about.

"I wasn't scared. I've dealt with guys like him in the past." Something flashes in her eyes, and my suspicions are confirmed.

"Well, now, you don't have to. I'm just down the block. If someone fucks with you, they fuck with me. You call me." I turn to look at Aspen, who is boxing up Marshall's order. "Aspen." She stops to look up at me. "You ladies need me, you call the office. If I'm not available, one of my brothers will be."

"We got you," Marshall says. "Besides, that gives us an excuse to grab a sweet treat." He winks at Aspen.

"We're big girls, Grant," Aurora replies defensively.

I release a heavy breath. "I know you are, but you don't have to do it on your own. Not anymore."

She closes her eyes, and I'm ready for her to fight me, but she surprises me when she nods, those hazel eyes slowly opening and staring into my soul. "I'll be at your place at five," I say, leaning over the counter for a kiss. Today is Valentine's Day, and I have plans for us. For her.

"I'm working," she says, trying to refuse my kiss.

"And I need to go to work, but not until I feel your lips against mine. We can do this the easy way or the hard way," I tell her with a smile.

She rolls her eyes but leans into my kiss. Her lips press to mine, and it takes more restraint than I knew I had to not deepen the kiss. Hell, I want to say fuck work altogether.

"Have a good day, baby." I kiss her one more time.

"I should get another dozen on the house for having to see that," Marshall jokes.

"Oh, hush," Aspen tells him. "It's sweet."

I laugh, and the smile on Aurora's face tells me she's not the least bit upset with me for my insistence to kiss her. "Call me if you need me."

"Yes, dear," Aurora replies, her sugary voice sweet.

"Have a good day, *dear*," Aspen tells Marshall, mocking us.

"Thanks, snookums," he croons, and the four of us explode in laughter.

I hold the door for Marshall as we exit onto the sidewalk. "You're fucked, brother," he says with a laugh.

"Yep." There is no point in denying it. I've fallen hard and fast for her. It's amazing the way your heart can latch on to someone in just a few short weeks. Now, I can't imagine my life without her. I refuse to dig deeper into what that means. I'm not ready to admit it. I know that once I do, I won't be able to hold back with her. So, instead, I pretend that the beat of my heart doesn't pound her name in my chest.

I've been sitting at the back of the bakery for the last thirty minutes. I left the office a few hours ago to get everything ready for our date tonight. It's the first Valentine's Day, where I've had plans with a woman who I care about. It's a big deal. My brothers, the younger two, gave me shit. The older two were too busy thinking about their own plans to worry about mine. That's fine. I can take the heat. Any amount of time spent with Aurora is worth it.

When the clock turns over to read four-fifty, I can't take it anymore. Pulling the keys from the ignition, I make my way to the back door. I buzz, and Aspen's voice greets me immediately.

"Is that you, boyfriend?" she asks.

I chuckle. "Caught that, did you?"

"Yep," she replies as the buzzer sounds and the lock releases.

I take the stairs two at a time, anxious to get to Aurora. I'm excited about our date and to show her what I have planned for us. I rap my knuckles against the door, and it's immediately opened. Aspen stands there with a smirk on her face.

"Is she pissed?"

"No." She shakes her head. "However, word of advice. When you refer to a woman as your girlfriend, you might want to discuss that with her first."

"Oh, don't you worry. We'll be discussing it." That's all I've thought about all day. I've given her time. Hell, it feels as though I've given her a lifetime. I need to know she's mine. That some asshole isn't going to swoop into her shop like the one today and take her away from me. I just found her.

"Have a seat." Aspen points at the couch as she takes the chair, pulling her legs under her. "So, what are your plans for the night?" she asks.

"You'll have to ask your sister when she gets home."

"Oh, she's coming home?" she asks coyly.

"The choice is hers." I don't tell her that I've imagined her sister in my bed beside me every single night since the day I met her.

"Good. She's not always had that luxury."

Before I can ask her what she means, Aurora appears, looking so much like the beauty that she is. The only thing I told her about our date was that she needed to dress warm and comfortable. She's in leggings, fuzzy boots, and a thick oversized sweater. Her long brown hair is curled and falling down her back. I want to bury my hands in those long locks and kiss the breath from her lungs.

"Why are you looking at me like that?" Aurora asks.

"Like what?" I ask, slowly making my way toward her.

"Like you want to eat her alive." Aspen laughs.

Once I reach Aurora, I snake an arm around her waist and pull her into my side, burying my face in her neck, breathing her in. It's a move I've seen my dad, Royce, and Owen do several times, and I never understood. I always chalked it up to them being saps, but that's not it. Not at all. There is nothing in the world that smells better than Aurora, and her in my arms, that's something to be cherished. I get it now.

"You look beautiful," I tell her, pulling back.

"Thank you. Is this okay? You said, comfortable and warm."

"It's perfect. You're perfect," I say, pressing my lips to the corner of her mouth.

"I'm not perfect."

"No," I agree, and her face falls. "You're not perfect because none of us are. We're human, we all have our flaws, but," I add, "you are perfect for me. That's all that matters."

"Damn, Rory, he's good," Aspen says, fanning her face with her hands.

"Rory?" I ask, raising my eyebrows. This is the first time I've heard the nickname.

"It's what Grandma used to call me. She started the nickname, and my parents and Aspen ran with it." Her watery eyes find her sister. "It's been a long time since I've heard it." She swallows hard.

"I like it. It suits you."

She nods, smiling up at me through the emotions welling in her eyes. "We should go," she says, pulling away and wiping at the corner of her eyes.

"Yes, you should go. You don't want to keep your *boyfriend* waiting," Aspen says, her voice giddy, knowing that she's giving her sister a hard time. "She turns into a pumpkin at midnight," she adds.

"I have to work tomorrow," Aurora says. I'm not sure who she's reminding, her sister or me?

"She's in good hands," I tell Aspen.

"Oh, I'm sure she is." She grins.

"Come on." Aurora slides her arms into her jacket. "She can do this all night."

"What are you going to do all night?" Aspen fires back.

"See what I mean?" Aurora tries to look annoyed, but I know better.

"You two kids have fun," she calls after us as we leave the apartment and make our way back down the steps to my SUV.

"So, where are we headed?" Aurora asks as I pull out onto the road.

"It's a surprise."

"Don't I get a hint?"

"Nope."

"I'm not good with surprises."

"No? Is there a reason?" I know as soon as I ask the question and glance over seeing that she's biting down on her bottom lip that I've hit the nail on the head. "You know you can talk to me about him."

"Who?" She's trying to play like she doesn't know, but we both know her efforts are fruitless.

"The man who tore you down."

"What makes you think that?"

"Because you have no idea how fucking beautiful you are. You worry about what to order when we go out, and you hate surprises. If he treated you right, like a man is supposed to treat a woman he cares about, none of those things would cause you anxiety. That poor lip of yours can't take much more. And besides, I plan on stealing lots of kisses tonight. I don't want to hurt you." I pull up to the Stop sign and reach over and take her hand in mine. "I'm ready to listen whenever you're ready to talk."

"What if I'm never ready?"

"It's going to take more than that to scare me away. However, I want to be the one you lean on when you need to. I want to be there for you."

"Why?"

"Because you're my girlfriend."

"Ah, I did hear something about that earlier today," she says, smiling, the tension leaving her body. "Funny, I don't remember discussing that title."

"No? Well, I guess we'll have to do that tonight."

She shakes her head and turns to look out the window. We're almost to our destination, so I let her have this moment. I'll give her this time to think about what I've said, and maybe tonight will be the night that she opens up to me. Regardless, I'll be here ready and waiting. In the meantime, I'll keep working to show her how special she is to me, and that I take the boyfriend title very seriously. I want to show her what it's like to have the affection of a man who cherishes her. Because I do. In just a short span of time, she's become everything.

CHAPTER *Aurora* TWELVE

"**W**E'RE GOING TO your parents'?" I ask as soon as we turn onto their road.

"Yes, but not to hang out with them. I have more game than that," he says, glancing over smiling.

"Of that, I have no doubt."

"Okay." He pulls up to the barn. "This is where we change vehicles, and I'm going to need you to wear this." He hands me a blindfold.

"You want me to wear this blindfold and let you drive me out into the wilderness in the middle of February?" I ask. I'm only half teasing. I know putting this much trust into someone I've known for a matter of weeks is probably not a great idea, but with Grant, I always feel safe.

"Yes." He turns to look at me, his face more serious than I've ever seen him. "You're safe with me, Aurora. Always. I won't stop until I erase everything he did to you. I'd never hurt you. Never."

"He didn't hit me or touch me at all for that matter." The small confession slips before I can think better of it.

He nods. "You have my word, but if it makes you feel better, text Aspen and tell her where we're going to be. Better yet..." He pulls his phone out of his pocket and taps on the screen, holding it out in front of him.

"Son?" His dad answers.

"Hey, Dad. I have Aurora with me." He turns the phone so that his father can see me sitting in the passenger seat.

"Why in the hell are you calling me if you've got your girl sitting next to you on Valentine's Day? I thought I taught you boys better than that," Stanley says. I can hear the disbelief in his voice.

"I just wanted you to know that we're here, and we're taking the ranger."

"This is information I already know, Grant. Are you feeling all right?"

Grant laughs. "Yeah, I'm good. I just wanted her to feel safe. You know, a man taking her into the wilderness."

"Haven't you already done that?"

"Yeah, but everyone knew."

"We all know," Stanley counters with a deep chuckle.

"Well, I wanted her to have the reassurance that I'm not a serial killer."

"He's good, Aurora. Maybe a little crazy chatting with me when he's got you within reach, but we can only teach our children the skills they need in life. What they do with them is altogether different." I can't help it. I throw my head back against the seat, laughter spilling from my chest. "Now, hang up the damn phone and go canoodle with your girl."

"Sure thing, Dad." Grant laughs, ending the call. "Now, call Aspen and let her know where you are."

"No. I don't need to do that."

"Maybe not, but it will give you peace of mind."

"He's right. I've already ridden the land with you."

"That doesn't change the fact that you feel different this time. Call her, babe."

I know I'm not supposed to, but I can't help but compare him to my ex. There is just something about Grant and his constant confidence and reassurance that's endearing. He didn't have to call his parents, but he wanted me to be comfortable. He's doing this for me, and that makes the butterflies take flight. Retrieving my phone from my purse, I pull up her name and call her, just like he did his dad. "What are you doing calling me? You're supposed to be on a date with your boyfriend," Aspen answers.

"I just wanted to let you know where we are."

"Aurora." I can hear the emotions in my sister's voice, and it has me swallowing back my own.

"We're at his parents' place. We're going out on the property."

"To the lake," Grant speaks up.

"Okay. Thanks," Aspen says. Grant can't see her face on the screen, but I know he can tell by the sound of her voice that my sister gets it. She gets me. I wish I could get past this. Past the worry. Maybe one day.

"Grant?" Aspen says. I turn the phone so that she can see him. "Take care of my sister."

"With my life," he says. The conviction in his voice would bring me to my knees if I were not sitting in his truck.

"Now, hang up and go enjoy your date. Love you, Rory."

Tears fill my eyes. "Love you too." I end the call and slide my phone back into my purse. "I'm sorry. I don't know why I even started this. I know I can trust you."

"You didn't start it. I did. I didn't want you to have a shed of doubt. If you don't like how the night is going, tell me, and I'll take you home."

"Just like that?"

"Just like that. We've been to dinner a few times a week since we met. I know that I'm determined, and I can be a lot to take on, but, babe, I would never pressure you into anything you don't want."

"No. It's not that I think that you will. I-I don't really know what's going on with me," I confess. "I like spending time with you." The confession slips past my lips without thought.

His smile is wide. "Well, I know what's going on. You and I are going to get this Valentine's Day date started. Stay there." He grabs his keys and climbs out of the SUV. When my door opens, he surprises me, sliding his hand behind my neck and leaning in so that our lips are barely a breath apart.

"Happy Valentine's Day, Rory," he whispers, ghosting his lips across mine.

"You called me Rory," I say when he pulls back. He nods. "Why?"

"I got the impression only those close to you do. Those that you hold in here"—he places his other hand over my heart—"call you that." His blue eyes bore into mine. "I care about you. Hell, I'm fucking crazy about you."

"I like it. I mean, I like you calling me Rory. It's something I haven't heard in a while, and I miss it."

He nods. "Come on, baby. Dinner is going to get cold."

"Are we eating outside?"

"Kind of. Come on." I turn in the seat, and before I can start to move, his hands grip my hips, and he lifts me from the seat, setting me on my feet. He leads me to the Ranger, the same one we took out the first time I was here. Inside is the same quilt I covered up with, and an extra, plus a thermos. "Mom." He smiles over at me. "I might have left work early today to get set up and recruited my parents for help. Well, I recruited my dad. Mom found out and added her own touches."

"You're lucky to have them."

"I know. You are too, according to Mom. She swears I was going to mess this up without her expertise."

I can't help but laugh. "So, what part did she take care of?"

"The quilts are clean and fresh, the hot chocolate and dessert. I bought a chocolate cake, and she was insistent that I couldn't serve my miracle baker girlfriend store-bought cake. She was horrified and read me the riot act. I let her take over from there."

"She's awesome," I say with a smile. "So, what's for dessert?"

"I don't know. She wouldn't tell me. Just that it was going to be a surprise. She and Dad dropped everything off. I texted them before I came up to your apartment to get you."

"You put a lot of thought into this."

"Only the best for my girl." He winks, and those damn butterflies take flight. "Now, I'm going to need you to put this on." He produces the blindfold from his jacket pocket. I don't hesitate to take it from him and slide it over my eyes. That's why I don't see him coming until his lips press against my cheek. "It's just a short drive." He places his hand on my thigh, and instinctively, I place my hand over his and weave our fingers together.

I've not been much for surprises during the last few years, but something tells me that whatever he has planned is going to be good. Suddenly, I'm excited to experience it with him.

"We're here," Grant says. "Stay there. I'll help you out." He raises our joined hands and places a kiss to the back of mine.

I miss his touch instantly, but when I hear the door shut on the Ranger, I know that my time is almost up. All of the anticipation of the past few days and the ride here is going to be over. "I've got you," he whispers huskily, reaching for my hand and helping me step out of the Ranger. "Watch your step," he says. His hold on me is tight as he guides us to our destination. "Right here." He steps behind me and wraps his arms around my waist. "Happy Valentine's Day, Aurora," he says sweetly. "Take off your mask, baby."

My hands are shaking as I pull the mask from my eyes. I blink a few times and gasp at what I see. "Grant," I whisper. "This is… incredible." My eyes scan the vision before me.

We're standing in front of the ice-skating rink on his parents' land. There are lights strung up around the entire rink, and on the ice, rose petals are spread out on the ice, and they spell out *Happy V Day, Aurora*. Hot tears prick my eyes. This is the sweetest, most romantic thing anyone has ever done for me.

"Well, what do you think? I bought you some skates. Aspen helped me with your size." I blink hard a few times, trying to fight the tears threatening to spill. "Aurora?" he asks.

I can't tell him with my voice. I have no words to explain what this means to me, what he means to me. Turning in his arms, I cup his face in the palm of my hands. His blue eyes are taking me in. I can see the worry when he catches sight of my tears. These are happy tears. Standing on my tiptoes, I press my lips to his. I kiss him with everything I have in me. With all the breath in my lungs, and all of the love in my heart. I kiss him until he understands that my tears are not from pain, but from the hope he gives me. The light he brings into my life.

I can't get close enough. Can't kiss him deep enough. It's as if he can read my mind. He knows what I need, what I want without me having to pull my lips from his. Kiss by Kiss, I'm telling him that he's everything. He bends at his knees and places his hands on the back of my thighs, and I jump into his arms, wrapping my legs around his waist.

When we both need air, I'm forced to pull my lips from his. He rests his forehead against mine as we both pull in much-needed oxygen into our lungs. "Good surprise?" he asks.

"The best."

"I want you, Aurora. All of you. The pieces I know, and the ones that I have yet to discover. Will you be my girlfriend?" he asks.

"Did you really just ask me that?" I've never met a man like Grant. He's not afraid to express how he feels, and he doesn't have a single care as to who knows it.

"I did," he replies, pulling away to look at me. "I don't want there to be any confusion as to what's happening between us. I don't want any other man to get your attention, or your hugs, or your kisses. I want them all for me."

"And what about you?"

"All I see is you, Aurora. From the moment I walked through the doors of your bakery, you've been the only woman I see. I want us to be official. I don't want it to be a surprise when I introduce you as my girlfriend. I want you beside me at family dinners. Hell, I want it all," he says, kissing my forehead.

My arms tighten around his neck as I pull him into a hug. He wants me. Me. Aurora Steele, the chubby girl, the one who is always the second choice. He's choosing me.

"Babe, this is where you say, 'Yes, Grant.'"

"You're choosing me?" I ask, my voice barely a whisper.

"Rory, baby, I'll always choose you."

He can't possibly know that. Things change, life changes, but for now, I choose to believe him. I choose him too, and as his lips press to mine, I feel some of the pieces of my shattered heart being put back together.

Kiss by Kiss, I start to feel whole again.

CHAPTER THIRTEEN

Grant

"**A**RE YOU GOING to leave me in suspense?" I ask her. The smile on her face and the mist of tears in her eyes tells me what I need to know, but I also need to hear her say it. I need the words from her luscious lips.

"Yes." She nods.

My lips connect with hers, my arms pulling her a little closer, holding her a little tighter. I kiss her like we have all the time in the world, and we do. She's officially mine. No more wondering if she feels this connection we share—no more worrying that another man will garner her attention. We're together. For the first time in my adult life, I have a girlfriend, and not just any girlfriend. Aurora. The woman who is perfect for me in every way. Not to mention, she's a baking genius.

Fucking finally.

She's mine.

"Come on. I have something for you." With my hand laced

with hers, I guide her to the tent that I set up earlier. Inside there is a propane heater, table, two chairs, and two coolers that hold our dinner and dessert—hopefully keeping them at the correct temperatures. "Sit." I point to one of the chairs and grab the white box with a red bow around it. "Here." I hand her the box.

"These…" She points to the vase of roses in the center of the small table. "They're beautiful."

I lean in and press my lips to hers. "So are you. Now open the box." Standing to my full height, I watch as she carefully removes the box and then the lid.

"Grant," she breathes. Reaching into the box, she pulls out one of the brand-new white skates. "You didn't have to do this. When you said you brought some skates, I assumed they were a borrowed pair from your mom or one of your sisters-in-law." She stares down at the new skates like I've given her a million dollars.

"No one likes to wear used skates." What I don't say is there is nothing that I wouldn't do for her. Nothing I wouldn't give her. These skates are just a small token of that.

She looks up at me, her smile lighting up her eyes. "I should have known."

"What do you say? Feel like skating with me?"

"After all of the work you put into this? How could I say no?" She makes quick work of pulling out both skates and pulling off her boots. "What about you?"

"I have mine." I point to where they sit behind the coolers. "I didn't want you to see them and spoil the surprise."

"It's really warm in here," she comments, pulling on the first skate.

"Yeah, this tent, the material's thick, and it helps that I had Dad crank this up when I got to your place earlier." I wasn't sure that this old tent would still hold heat, but Dad assured me it would.

"I can't believe you did all of this."

"It's our first Valentine's Day together." I finish tying my skates. "You ready for this?"

"Yes. No. I don't know." She laughs. "It's been years since I've been on the ice."

"I've got you." I offer her my hand, and she doesn't hesitate to take it and allows me to help her to her feet. "Ready, baby?"

"As I'll ever be."

Reaching into my pocket, I hit Play on the playlist that I made for tonight, and the music begins to play from the small outdoor Bluetooth speaker I have set up just outside of the tent. Hand in hand, we make our way to the ice. I step on first and hold my hands out for her, helping to keep her steady.

"Is there anything that you didn't think of?" she asks, as we begin to slowly skate around the rink.

"Come on now. This is me we're talking about." I wink at her, and she laughs.

"You can turn around," she tells me. "I think I've got this."

"Just like riding a bike. However, I like this," I say as I continue to hold onto both of her hands, skating backward.

"You're awful good at that. Is this where you bring all the girls?" she teases.

"You know that's not true. I've never brought anyone here. Never. Just you. This place is special."

"I thought it was just dinner with your family?"

"Nope. This is my sanctuary of sorts, my brothers too."

"So, they never bring anyone out here either?"

"Well, Royce and Owen brought Sawyer and Layla, but they're married now, or almost married. Baby momma status and an engagement ring is close enough in my book."

"What about the younger two?"

"Nope," I say, popping the *p*. "You know what that means, right?" I slow, allowing us both time to stop before drawing her into my chest, wrapping my arms around her waist.

"What?" she asks, staring up at me.

"You're special." She looks away, but I'm not having any of that. "Eyes on me, baby." Her eyes pull back to mine. "There she is." I tuck a loose strand of hair behind her ear. "You can ask anyone in my family. They'll all tell you that you're special. They know me, and they know what it means to have you here. Hell, they know what it means that I want you tied down."

"Tied down, huh?" she asks, humor lacing her voice.

"Tied to me. Is that better?"

"As long as it's not tied to the bed," she says and immediately slaps her hand over her mouth. "Oh my gosh, I can't believe I just said that. Aspen is rubbing off on me. I'm sorry."

"Don't be. I'm not ruling out the tying to the bed scenario, but only when you're ready." I wink at her. Her cheeks are pink, and although it's cold outside, I'm positive that some of that is from her embarrassment.

"You can't say things like that," she scolds.

"You're my girl," I say, kissing her softly. "It's bound to happen."

"I-I'm not into that."

"Into what?" I play dumb. I'm enjoying this way more than I should.

"Tying and all that," she says, burying her face in my chest.

"All that?" I ask, goading her.

"Grant! You know what I mean." She laughs, the sound drowning out the slow hum of the music.

"You're too damn cute." I kiss her forehead and pull away. Keeping one of her hands clasped in mine, we skate around a little more. "You hungry?" I ask after a few laps.

"If you are."

I stop, and we both almost fall, but I'm able to correct us before it happens. "Aurora." My voice is stern. "Are you hungry?"

"A little."

"Don't hide from me, baby." I wish I could beat the hell out of the fucker who hurt her. He better run if I ever meet him. Jackass. "I'm starving, and we need to get you warmed up. Your nose looks like Rudolph." I let go of her hand and grin at her. "Wanna race?"

"I don't know." She begins to ponder the request, when out of the blue, she takes off, skating as hard and as fast as she can. I don't rush after her, not when I'm enjoying the view of her ass in those jeans.

When she's almost to the edge, I take off after her and almost eat it, making us both laugh. "A little rusty, Riggins?" she teases.

"Hush it, woman." I chuckle. "Come on." I pull back the side of the tent so that we can enter. It's not as cozy as a house, but it sure as hell takes the chill off. "Have a seat, and I'll grab our dinner."

"What are we having?"

"I had to bring Mom in on this one. She makes the best homemade vegetable soup. I thought something warm would be ideal. We have homemade biscuits too, and triple chocolate cake for dessert. Her specialty."

"Did you help?" she asks.

"That would be a negative. No way am I attempting to bake for my hot-ass baker girlfriend. I don't need that kind of negativity in my life."

She grins. "Come on. I think it would be sweet."

"You want me to bake for you?" I ask her.

"Maybe one day. Not now. It won't mean as much with me telling you to do it."

"Women." I shake my head, and we both laugh.

"So, how are things at the bakery?" I ask, after serving us both a cup of soup.

"Great." Her eyes light up. "Better than I could have expected. I was worried the newness would wear off, but the numbers are steady, and it's been a little over two months, so I'm happy. I hope it stays that way."

"You've tried your treats, right?"

"Treats?" She laughs.

"What else am I supposed to call them?"

"Warm Delights," she fires back with a smirk.

"My girl's got jokes." I know I'm smiling like a fool, but I couldn't care less. This woman sitting across from me makes me happy. I can't not smile knowing she's mine.

"There they go again." She places her hand on her belly. She must see my confusion. "The butterflies," she adds.

"I gotta admit. I like that I have an effect on you."

"I don't understand why some woman hasn't snatched you up yet."

"She did." I point to her.

She rolls her hazel eyes. "I mean before me."

"It's simple," I reply with a shrug.

"Care to enlighten me, old wise one?"

"I was waiting for you." Her eyes widen, and she squirms in her seat. "Now, eat up. We still have dessert, and if you want to go back out on the ice, we can do that. I also need some Rory time, so we need to pencil that in before I take you home as well."

Her laughter is the sweetest sound. "What's Rory time?" she asks, taking a bite out of her roll.

"Rory time is you in my arms. It's me kissing you, and if I'm lucky, holding you too."

"It's getting late, and I have to be up early. Rory time might be cut short."

"I'll take whatever time you'll give me."

"I'm your girlfriend now, so my time is all yours."

"Music to my ears, baby. Now eat up." I shove the rest of my roll in my mouth, making her giggle. Conversation lulls as we finish eating.

"Where do we start?" she asks once she has her skates off and her boots back on.

"I'm just going to pack up the generator I used for the lights and load up the food and the heater. I'll come by tomorrow after work and take down the tent."

"Can we do it now? That way, you don't have to do it tomorrow?"

"You're cutting into my Rory time." I give her a heated look.

"It will be easier to take down in the daylight anyway. I'll have one of my brothers come and help me. It won't take us any time at all."

"Are you sure?" She looks around. I can see that leaving all of this out here bothers her.

"Hey." I offer her my hand, and she takes it, letting me pull her into my chest. "Am I sure that I want more Rory time? Hell yes. Am I sure that leaving this out here tonight is okay? Yes, again. Nothing will happen to it. We're taking the generator, the heater, and the food. Everything else is minor."

"Okay." She peers up at me. "If you're sure."

"I'm more than sure. Now, I'm going to go start the Ranger and get the heat going before you get in."

"I'm not fragile, Grant."

"No. You're not, but you are precious cargo, and I take that shit seriously." I kiss her quickly before ducking out of the tent to start the Ranger.

CHAPTER
Aurora
FOURTEEN

"**W**HERE IS LOVER boy taking you tonight?" Aspen asks from her spot on the couch. We're both lounging after an early day at the bakery.

"We're having dinner at his place."

"Oh." She sits up a little straighter. "Alone time." She nods as if she's approving our plans.

"I'm exhausted, and we still have to go grocery shopping, and I have laundry to do. I don't feel like going out." It's the truth. I got up at three to start today's special lemon bars. We sold out by 9:00 a.m. I made another triple batch, and we sold out of them as well. I'm thrilled that Warm Delights is doing so well, but it's exhausting. I have zero energy for anything else in life—even dating.

"I can do the grocery shopping. You stay here and do your laundry and take a cat nap for your date." She stands from the couch and stretches.

"It's my turn," I remind her.

"And I said I would do it. Besides, I don't have anything better to do."

"You should go out tonight. You can come with me," I offer.

"Nope. Not going to be the third wheel."

"I can't believe that I have a social life, and you don't." I grin.

"You deserve it, Rory." Her eyes soften. "For years you let him belittle and control you. You weren't living. I can't tell you how happy I am to see you smiling and not letting your anxiety control you."

"Oh, it's there," I tell her. "Trust me. It's just Grant can tell when I'm freaking out or getting ready to, and he talks me out of it. I don't know how he knows or how he manages to calm me, but he does. Everything inside me, well except for the butterflies, calm when I'm with him."

"You're still getting butterflies?"

"Every. Single. Time."

"Wow," she breathes. "That's a big deal. It's been a couple of months now."

"I know. I keep waiting for the day that they go away. It hasn't happened yet."

Aspen tilts her head to the side, studying me. "Maybe they never will. That's what true love is about, right? Always feeling like it's new with the one you love?"

"I don't know. It's never happened to me before." Neither one of us mention that I was engaged to be married. I thought I loved him, but I was wrong. I was so wrong. The longer time passes from that day—the day it all ended—I see that. Even more so as Grant and I grow closer. I've never felt the way I do when I'm with Grant. My heart beats a little faster, and those damn butterflies run wild. It's not just when I'm with him; it's when I hear his voice, get a text message, or even think about him. I'm in trouble. So much trouble.

"I love this." Aspen claps her hands together.

"What are you talking about?"

"I love getting to see you fall for a good man. A man that deserves you."

My phone rings and a picture of Grant and me that he took on one of our many dates pops up, requesting a video call.

"It's him, isn't it? I can tell by the giddy smile on your face," Aspen says knowingly.

"Hey," I greet him.

"How was your day?" he asks.

"Busy. We sold out of lemon bars. Twice."

"Damn, I should have come to see you. I've been working all day. We have a new location opening in Pennsylvania, and I've been buried in paperwork."

"I saved you some," I tell him.

"You love me." He laughs.

It's just an off-handed comment, but it has my heart stalling in my chest, and the butterflies, they're insane. "I knew you were working, and I know you love them."

"I love everything you make, babe."

Aspen does a little dance around the living room and points at me, mouthing, "I told you so." I don't know what she thinks she told me. It wasn't a confession of love, but my heart, it's still beating just a little faster.

"So, there's a slight change of plans tonight if you're willing. Owen and Layla invited everyone to their place for dinner."

"Sure." I'm quick to agree.

"That's my girl," Grant says softly.

He doesn't have to elaborate for me or even Aspen to know what he's talking about. When we first started dating, I never would have agreed so quickly, not without stressing over what to wear or if I would fit in. Don't get me wrong, I still worry, but it's not controlling me. I've met his family several times over the past couple of months, and I know they are good people who have accepted me as a part of Grant's life.

"What time?"

"I'll be there to pick you up around five if that works?"

"Sure. I'll be ready."

"Oh, and Aspen is invited as well."

I glance at my sister, and she shakes her head. "I'll tell her. She's getting ready to go to the store."

"I thought that it was your week?"

He's always listening when I talk. "Aspen volunteered so I can get caught up on laundry and maybe take a short nap."

"Okay, babe. I'll let you go so you can get it all done. I'll be there at five."

"I'll be ready," I say as we end the call.

"You've got four hours, sister. You better get to napping."

"I'm going to start a load of laundry and then lie down. Are you sure you don't mind doing the store this week?"

"Positive."

"Are you going to come with us?"

"Nah, not this time."

"What are you not telling me?" I ask.

"Fine," she sighs. "I have a date myself."

"That's great. Who is he?" I hate that I've been so wrapped up in my own life, that I failed to miss that my sister is dating. I need to make sure that I'm making time for her. After all, she did uproot her life to follow me and help me make my dream a reality.

"Just some guy who came into the bakery last week. He asked for my number, and we've been texting. I finally agreed to dinner. And before you ask, I'm meeting him there so that I have my car."

"Good. Call me if you need me."

"Wait, what time? You're going to need a nap too."

"I'm not meeting him until seven. I have plenty of time to go to the store and come back and nap before I have to get ready."

"Well, I'll toss your clothes in with mine."

"Teamwork." She high-fives me. "The list still on the fridge?"

"Yes."

"Text me if you think of anything else," she says, sliding into her coat.

"Thank you, Aspen."

"What are sisters for. It's not like I'm not eating the food too." She waves and walks out the door.

Needing to get my tired ass in gear, I make my way to her bedroom and do a load of her clothes first before lying down in bed. All I can think about is Grant and how excited I am to see him. I saw him last night for dinner. He's like my drug, and I can't seem to get enough. After staring at the ceiling for thirty minutes, I realize sleep isn't going to happen. Instead, I pull myself out of bed and begin to clean the apartment. Might as well make myself useful.

"I'm so glad you came," Layla says, stepping forward and wrapping her arms around me in a hug.

"Thank you for having us. Your home is beautiful."

"Thank you. We just finished a few renovations." Something passes in her eyes, but it passes before I can decipher it.

"Can I help with anything?"

"Nope. We ordered pizza. You want something to drink?" she asks, moving into the living room.

"No, thank you." I follow her and take a seat when she points to the couch. "How are you feeling?"

"Great." Her smile is wide and genuine. "This little guy is active, keeping me up at night, but I wouldn't trade a minute of it."

"See, babe." I hear from behind me. I turn to see Royce and Sawyer enter the room. "It's fun." He points to Layla and her swollen belly.

"Go to your brothers." She laughs, pushing him away.

My eyes immediately go to Owen and Grant, who are chatting in the kitchen. Grant catches me looking and winks.

"Give us all the dirt," Sawyer says, sitting next to me.

"The dirt?"

"Yeah, how are things with you and Grant?"

"Good." I nod. I don't know them well, but from what I do know, they are genuine, and I feel comfortable with them.

"Speaking of dirt," Layla speaks up. "What about you? How's the baby-making?" She wags her eyebrows.

"Practice makes perfect." Sawyer smirks.

"Practice makes babies," Layla counters. "You know that's how this little man got here."

Sawyer nods. "I stopped taking the pill. Royce is determined for it to happen like yesterday." She laughs.

"I've heard it happens when you stop trying."

"Tell that to my husband," she replies. "We just officially started trying a couple of weeks ago. It's still early."

"It only takes once," Layla says.

"What only takes once?" Owen asks, sitting next to Layla on the loveseat.

"Making a baby."

He nods. "You jokers need some pointers?" he asks his brothers.

"I've got it handled, right, babe?" Royce asks Sawyer. He offers her his hand, hauling her from the couch, taking her seat, and pulling her back into his lap.

"What about you?" Owen smirks, directing his question to Grant as he takes the open seat next to me.

"We're not there yet, but when we are, I'm certain I can handle it all on my own." He smiles at me, and my heart melts. Straight up melts in my chest. He's talking about the future like he often does, but this... kids? With me?

"So, what's the occasion?" Royce asks.

"Figures, they started the party without us," Conrad says, entering the room, Marshall right behind him.

"Oh, Aurora. Did you bring me anything?" Marshall asks, batting his eyelashes at me.

"I did. They're on the kitchen counter." When I couldn't sleep, I cleaned and had the laundry caught up, so I made some fudge brownies to bring tonight.

"You ever get tired of this one. You know where to find me." He winks.

"Back off, little brother," Grant warns.

"I think you can take him," Conrad tells Marshall. "I mean, this is your stomach we're talking about. No mercy," he says, and we all laugh. Conrad sits in one of the two remaining chairs. Marshall takes the other, shoving a brownie into his mouth.

"Well, we've been talking about the wedding. Owen doesn't really want to travel with me being pregnant."

"You know it's safe, right?" Sawyer asks him.

"Yeah, sis, I do, but I'd rather not if we don't have to," Owen replies.

"So we were thinking of doing it here." Layla looks over at Owen. "This is our home, and new memories are what we need." The way she says it makes me think that something happened. It also makes me think that Owen needs it more than she does.

"You sure about that?" Marshall asks her. He's suddenly more serious than I've ever seen him.

"I am. This is what I want. This is our home, and that night doesn't define us. It's the memories we make here. Getting married here, and bringing our little man home. This is where I want to raise him."

"Layla," Owen starts, but she places her fingers to his lips to stop him.

"I want this. I've always loved this house. I want to make it our home. I won't let her take another damn thing from me. We've already renovated. It doesn't even look like the same place. The security is top-notch, and we have plenty of room for a small ceremony and reception."

"What did I miss?" I whisper to Grant.

"I'll fill you in later," he says, kissing my temple. I fight the urge to sigh. He's always doing sweet things like that, and I fall harder every time.

"What can we do?" Sawyer asks.

"I need a dress, and we'll need food and a cake."

"I can take care of the cake," I speak up, surprising myself.

"Really?" Layla asks.

"Sure. I can put together a tasting if you want." Grant gives my leg a gentle squeeze, showing me his support.

"No. I trust you. We both eat anything. Just… thank you, Aurora."

"Sure. I'll take care of it. Just let me know how many people."

"Small," she says immediately.

"All of you. Stanley and Lena, your sister, and Ronnie and Linda." She points to Conrad and Marshall. "If these two want to bring a date." She chuckles.

"Nah," the two youngest brothers say at the same time.

"When is this shindig taking place?" Marshall asks.

"This little guy is due to be here in four weeks." Layla looks over at Owen. "We were thinking two weeks." She turns her gaze to me. "Is that okay? Can you do two weeks?"

"Yes." I nod.

"What about you? Can you find a dress in that time?"

"I just want something simple. I'm sure I can find something. I was hoping Lena could do the food."

"She's going to be all over that," Royce says.

"I'll help," Sawyer adds.

"I can help too."

Layla's eyes well with tears. "I've never had a family, not a functional one. I love you all so much, and I'm thrilled to be able to call all of you my family." She wipes at her eyes. I find myself doing the same, and a quick glance at Sawyer shows she's in her feelings too.

"Damn it, sis," Conrad says, clearing his throat. That breaks the tension, causing us all to laugh.

"I'm sorry. It's the pregnancy hormones, but I meant every word. I don't know what I did to have each of you come into my life, but I will be forever grateful."

"Fucking love you," Owen says, not caring who hears before his lips crash with hers. The doorbell interrupts them, but Royce stands.

"I'll get it," he tells his brother, making his way to the front door, Marshall on his heels to help carry the food.

The rest of the night is filled with laughter and a whole lot of love. Plans are made, and even Lena and Stanley show up after Owen called them to fill them in. It has me missing my parents more than ever, but it also solidifies that the Riggins family is the real deal. I can only hope that Aspen and I both find this kind of love and acceptance in our futures. I glance across the room at Grant. I don't know what the future holds for us, but I can't help but let a little sprout of hope fill my heart that this too is my future.

CHAPTER
Grant
FIFTEEN

Looking across my brother's living room, I watch as Aurora covers another yawn. "We're out of here," I say, finishing off my bottle of water and tossing it in the trash.

"You don't have to run off," Owen says.

"Aurora has been up since three. She's dead on her feet," I tell him.

"You good to drive?" Royce asks.

"Yeah, just had water." I look at my two younger brothers. "You two need a ride?" I ask.

"Nah, Mom and Dad said they would drop us off," Conrad says, tipping back his beer.

My eyes scan to Marshall, and he nods, letting me know that's the plan. "All right, see you tomorrow," I say, walking toward my girl.

"Hey, babe. You about ready?" I ask Aurora. I'm leaning over the back of the couch. She tilts her head back to look at me and nods.

"Aw, don't leave," Layla begs.

"Sorry, my girl's been up since three. I need to get her home," I tell her.

"Call me next week, and I'll bring you by a couple of samples," Aurora tells her.

"You don't have to do that. I trust you."

"I want to," Aurora assures her.

We spend the next five minutes saying goodbye, as the woman in my life hugs it out with each of my sisters-in-law and then my parents. By the time I get her to the SUV, it's nice and warm. "Thank you for that," I say once we're on the road.

"For what?"

"The cake. That was nice of you."

"Of course. I'm happy to do it."

"I'll pay you. Just let me know what it costs, and I'll cover it."

"What? No, I want to do this for them."

"Rory, you're a new business. You can't afford to just give your cakes away."

"I can when it's my boyfriend's brother's wedding," she fires back.

"Is this our first fight?" I ask, not able to hold my grin.

"No." She crosses her arms over her chest in a pout. I pull up to the Stop sign at the end of Owen's road and glance over. That's when she realizes she's stood up to me. Her body goes stiff, and she bites down on her bottom lip. "I-I'm sorry."

"You have nothing to be sorry for." I pull my eyes from her and back to the road. "I'm proud of you. You told me how you felt." I reach over and place my hand on her knee. "I want you to always tell me how you feel. Even if you think that it's going to upset me, that's how this works, Rory. It's a relationship. It's going to take work and give and take from both of us."

"How did you get so smart?" she asks, finally releasing the grip her teeth had on her bottom lip.

"What can I say? When you've got it, you've got it," I say, tapping her knee and making her laugh. "I thought we could go to my place. I know you're tired. I just... I'm not ready to take you home yet."

"So… you want me to stay with you?"

"Yes." I don't hesitate with my answer. We've been dating for a couple of months, and I'm fine taking it slow, but having her in my bed, in my arms, that sounds really damn good right now. "I'll be on my best behavior," I tell her.

"Okay."

"Okay," I repeat. I keep my eyes on the road and fight like hell to keep the smile off my face. Gloating that I got my way is not a good idea. At least not until I get her in my place, in my bed where she belongs.

"Go ahead," she says a few minutes later.

"What?" I ask, glancing over at her.

"Let it out." She laughs.

"I don't know what you're talking about." My grin says otherwise.

"Come on, let's hear it."

"Finally," I say, releasing a heavy breath. "I've been waiting forever to have you in my arms all night."

"Forever," she repeats dramatically.

"Exactly," I say, turning into my driveway. "You better call Aspen and let her know you're not coming home."

She nods and pulls her phone out of her purse. I expect her to call, but as her fingers fly across the screen, I know she's texting her instead. I was hoping to hear that conversation, knowing that Aspen would more than likely have something hilarious to say about her sister finally staying with me. Those two could not be more opposite, yet they are so alike in many ways too. I know without a doubt they share a bond, much like the one my brothers and I share. I know they will always have each other's backs.

That's why I'm not worried about what they're texting. I know Aspen is team Grant, and they both know that I'm team Aurora— whatever that looks like. I'm all in for whatever she wants or needs.

"All set," she says, sliding her phone back into her purse.

Reaching up, I hit the button to close the garage door and climb out of the SUV. She meets me at the door to enter my condo. "Are you ready for bed?"

"Yes," she says, covering another yawn.

"Come on, sleepyhead." Holding her hand, I lead her to my bedroom. "I'll get you something to sleep in." Digging through my drawers, I find an old Riggins Enterprises T-shirt and hand it to her. "Bathroom." I point to the door on the right-hand wall. "There are toothbrushes I get from the dentist in the bottom drawer. Make yourself at home." She nods and disappears into the bathroom.

As soon as the door closes, I begin to pace. She's in my bathroom, stripping down. I'm a gentleman, but I'm a man—a man who is insanely attracted to his girlfriend. I've been giving her time. I know that she's been hurt in the past, and I don't know what he did to her. She said he didn't hit her, but still, she's skittish, and she's getting naked.

In. My. Bathroom.

The door opens, and she appears looking like the fucking goddess that she is, in nothing but my T-shirt. "Thanks." She looks down at the shirt that comes to just above her knees.

"I'm going to change. Make yourself at home. If you're hungry or thirsty, you know where the kitchen is. You can put your clothes wherever. Wait." I stalk to my dresser and pull out a stack of shorts and toss them in the chair in the corner. "Use this drawer. I'll clean out more so you can leave stuff here or whatever," I say, rambling like a nervous teenager.

"Thank you, Grant."

I nod in response, grabbing some sleep pants and disappearing into the bathroom.

I brush my teeth and change into a pair of pajama pants. I usually sleep in nothing but boxer briefs, but I'm not sure how comfortable she'll be if I do that. So, pajama pants it is. I can look past it knowing that I get to sleep next to her.

Turning off the light, I open the bathroom door to find my sexy girlfriend standing next to my bed, staring down at it.

"Everything okay?" I ask, stopping to stand next to her. I place my hand on the small of her back, just above her ass. I itch to slide my hand under her shirt. To feel her skin under my fingertips.

"Do you have a side?" She points to the bed.

"Whatever side you're on." A smile tilts her lips. "Climb in, baby. I'll get the light." I force myself to walk away from her to the other side of the room to hit the light switch. My legs carry me back to the bed, navigating my bedroom in complete darkness. I go to the side of the bed where she was just standing and feel around tapping her legs, her thigh, working my way over her chest and her face, ending on her head.

"Grant." She laughs.

"What? It's dark in here."

"Get in bed, crazy." She chuckles.

The tension eases from the room as I carefully climb over her body. I don't bother moving to the other side of the bed. Instead, I settle in close, wrapping my arms around her. We're both quiet for several minutes. I don't know what she's thinking, but for me, I'm in awe of how good this feels. To have her lying next to me. This is a giant step forward for us, one I've been craving, and deep down, I know that she has been too.

I need more of her. I just need to feel her skin. Taking the risk, I slide my hand under my shirt that she's wearing and rest my palm on her belly. She immediately freezes in my arms. "Rory?" I whisper. "What's going on?"

"Nothing." Her reply is short, and her tone is laced with worry.

"Talk to me," I say, gently drawing circles with my thumb against her soft skin.

She sighs loudly, and when she opens her mouth to speak, I never could have guessed where this conversation was headed. "I'm waiting for you to freak out."

"What? Why would I freak out?"

"No man, especially not a man that looks like you, wants the chubby girl."

Anger, red hot anger like nothing I've ever felt before crashes through me. I'm not mad at her, but whoever made her feel this way. "Aurora." My voice is strong and firm as I try to rein in my anger. I don't want to scare her, and the last thing she needs is to feel worse about herself. I roll out of bed and turn on the lamp that sits on the bedside table, on what I guess is now my side.

I walk around to her side and drop to my knees. "Look at me, baby." I wait patiently as she forces herself to open her eyes and look at me. I can see the shimmer of tears. "I don't know who hurt you, but I want to kill him. You are not chubby." I toss back the covers and, with my eyes on hers, pull up my T-shirt. My hand goes to her belly once more. "You're perfect."

"I'm not. I bake all day, and it's hard to not taste them, and it's quality control. I cut back as much as I can, but I'll never be model skinny. I never have been. That's just not who I am."

"Babe, I don't want you to be anyone but you. Model skinny is overrated. I love your curves." To prove it to her, I let my hand roam, tracing said curves while my eyes remain locked on hers. I want to watch the path my hand is traveling. I want to memorize every inch of her, but there's time for that. Right now, I need her to know she's here because I fucking crave her. All of her.

Her eyes are closed, and her bottom lip quivers. That doesn't stop me. No, it fuels me to show her how I see her, how every red-blooded man in the damn city sees her. I've walked into the bakery on more than one occasion to find some asshole chatting up my girl. I won't stop until she sees herself as I do.

"Do you trust me?" I ask her. Her eyes blink open slowly, and her reply is a subtle nod. "You hold the power, Aurora. If you want me to stop, I will." Another nod. That's all I need to explore her. To lavish her body with the reverence she deserves. "Sit up for me," I whisper. She hesitates for a few seconds before sitting up, her hazel eyes watching me intently. "Lift your arms for me."

More hesitation.

"You can say no, but I want to see you. All of you."

She pulls in a deep breath and slowly raises her arms over her head. I jump into action, sliding my T-shirt up her body and over her head, dropping it to the floor. She's still wearing her bra and panties, and although I want her naked, I know I need to take this slow. "Lie back," I instruct. This time there is no hesitation as she lies back on the pillows.

"Fuck, baby, I don't know where to start." My eyes roam over her. My mouth waters at the vision before me. Gingerly, I climb back on the bed and settle next to her. Propping my head up with my elbow, I keep one hand on her as I explore her curves.

"Your skin is so soft," I say reverently — my hand traces across her ribs and back to her hip. "You doing okay?" I ask. It's important that she feels like she has a choice in this. I don't know what kind of backstory she's hiding from me, so I have to take all options into consideration.

"I'm okay."

That's my green light. I shuffle, moving down the bed. Tentatively, I lean over and place a kiss on her belly, causing her to suck in a breath. I peer up at her, and she gives me a small nod. My lips go back to her skin, and I kiss her, everywhere her skin is exposed. My cock is hard as steel, but I ignore him. This is about her. She needs to know her value. My lips trail up her body. When I reach her breasts, I move to settle between her thighs. I need to be closer to her. My lips find her hard nipples easily through the material of her bra, and I suck gently, causing her back to arch off of the bed.

"You with me?" I ask, my breath hot against her neck. I don't wait for a reply as I lick and nip at her neck, making my way to her mouth. "You're fucking gorgeous," I whisper before my lips connect with hers. She opens for me immediately as I push past her lips. Her hands grip my hair as she gives as much as I take. I grind my cock that's still covered with pajama pants and my boxer briefs against her pussy.

"Oh," she moans, lifting her hips.

I smile against her lips as I continue to explore her mouth. She meets me stroke for stroke, taking what she wants, what she needs. I kiss her until we're both breathless and overcome with need and desire for one another.

"There isn't a single inch of you that I don't crave. When I say I want you, Aurora Steele, I mean all of you. Does this feel like the cock of a man who thinks you're not sexy?" I ask.

"I—" She immediately clamps her mouth shut.

"No, don't do that. Don't sensor yourself. Not with me. Hell, not with anyone. Tell me what you want, baby. No matter what it is, I'll give it to you." I move next to her, resting on my side. She mimics me so we're facing one another. "Tell me," I whisper, resting my palm against her cheek.

"I want—" She stops and swallows hard.

"It's just me, Rory. The man who is falling so damn hard for you. You can trust me. You can tell me anything. There isn't anything in this world you could ask for that could make me climb out of this bed." Unless, of course, she asks me to do exactly that. From the way she kissed me back, I don't think that's what she's going to ask for. At least I hope not.

"I want to lie with you."

"Done." I move a little closer and pull her into my chest.

"N-Naked. I want to be skin to skin. I-I've never done that." Her confession is so quiet I would have missed it had I not been solely focused on her.

What kind of fuck was she dating? "Done." I roll away from her, and in one swoop, I have my pajama pants and boxer briefs pulled over my thighs, kicking them off the rest of the way.

"Your turn." I grin at her.

"Can we turn off the light?"

I shake my head. "No way. I'm finally getting you naked, all the way naked. I'm not going to miss this." A blush coats her cheeks. Part of me feels like an ass for saying no, but I don't want her to hide from me. Ever. I need her to know that I'm seeing all of her, and nothing changes. Well, maybe my need for her grows. In fact, I know it will. But I'm not running for the hills like she thinks I will. No, I'm right here, exactly where I want to be. Where I'm meant to be. I feel it in my soul.

CHAPTER

Aurora

SIXTEEN

I CAN'T BELIEVE this is happening. I feel as if I'm living in someone else's life. Someone else's body. The way Grant's looking at me, the blue of his eyes is so deep, so profound, and he's not faking. You can't fake... that. He's sitting back on his knees on the bed. His hard length in his hand as he strokes himself from root to tip. His eyes are connected with mine, and he's doing... that.

"You need my help?" he asks huskily.

"No." I shake my head. I can do this. I need to do this. Not only do I need to undress myself in front of him, I want to. I've never in all my life had a man look at me the way he is right now. I've never had a man take the time to learn my curves. Then again, I have limited experience. Elijah was my first serious boyfriend, and—No, I'm not bringing him into this. This is between Grant and me.

"It's just me, baby. This is what you do to me." He nods down at his cock that he's fisting.

You can do this, Aurora.

Hooking my fingers into the side of my panties, I shimmy them down my hips. Grant reaches over and tugs them the rest of the way down my legs. His eyes lock on my pussy, and he groans.

Keep going.

Sitting up, I close my eyes and pretend that he's not watching my every move. Reaching behind my back, I release the clasp on my bra. My hands shake as I hold the cups in place. I know that this fear is irrational. I know that. I know that my ex tore me down, that he mentally abused me. I also know that I let him. I was his doormat, and I refuse to be that ever again.

You are not a doormat.

This time is different.

Grant is different.

"Let me see you, Rory." His husky plea surrounds us.

Slowly, I open my eyes. My breath hitches at the sight before me. Grant is still on his knees, his hard cock standing proud, almost as if it's saluting me. His hands are locked behind his head, and his eyes are boring into mine. He gives me a small nod of encouragement. I finish removing my bra, dropping it over the side of the bed.

"Lie back," he says, moving next to me. "Roll over," he instructs, and I do as he asks. The bed dips, and the room is bathed in darkness. I feel him settle in behind me as he tugs the covers up over us. "I'm going to hold you. Is that okay?"

"Yes."

He pulls me close, my back to his chest, and doesn't stop until our bodies are perfectly aligned. His hand travels a slow journey as he runs them over every inch of my skin that he can reach. When he's satisfied, he rests his hand on my belly and presses his lips to my bare shoulder.

"Is this okay?" he questions.

He's always making sure I'm good. He's never pushy, and that makes me want him even more. He's giving me choices. Not so much as choices, but he's helping me speak them without fear.

"It's okay."

The room is dark, and the only sound is our breathing. My body is wide awake, craving the feel of his skin against mine. It's a feeling that I've only read about. Something I've always wondered about. It's intimate. I feel like he's giving me this huge gift, so I should give him something in return. We've been dating for a couple of months, and it's time I tell him my ugly truths. I have this irrational fear that Grant hearing what another man thought will change his mind, but I know in my heart that's not right. That's not who Grant Riggins is. Squeezing my eyes closed, I prepare myself for this conversation.

At least it's dark.

"His name was Elijah." I stop to see if Grant's going to comment, but all I feel are his lips pressing against my shoulder yet again. "He was my first and only serious relationship. He was my first in a lot of ways. I gave him my virginity and my heart. He took my soul and my spirit, and then he destroyed them both." I pause, needing a break. I hate talking about this, but Grant deserves it all. I want us to move forward. I want this happy life he paints for us. I can't have that until he knows my past. It's mine, but it made me who I am. I need him to better understand my hesitations and insecurities.

"He wasn't like that at first. He was nice and charming. He was never much on showing affection, but I just chalked that up to just being him, you know? Everyone has their own quirks, and I assumed that was his when it should have been a red flag." I shudder a breath. This is harder than I thought it would be.

"I'm right here, baby. I'm not going anywhere," Grant finally speaks. I don't know how he always knows what I need to hear.

"We dated for about a year, and I ignored all the signs. I thought he loved me, and I loved him, and it was just a quirk. He never introduced me to his friends and family, telling me he didn't have any worth mentioning. He never wanted to hold my hand or hold me. Not like this. We were barely naked when we slept together." Grant's arms tighten around me. "And after, he would get dressed or simply roll over and go to sleep. I'd try to snuggle with him, and he always said it was too hot or that he didn't like to be touched like that."

"Fucking prick," Grant mumbles but otherwise says nothing.

"When my lease was up on my apartment, he asked me to move in with him. I was twenty-three, and the idea of us living together made me giddy."

Here comes the hard part. I pull from the strength his arms wrapped around me brings. "I hadn't lived there a week when he started to make comments. Things like you're eating again? Or those pants look really tight. Have you gained weight? Things snowballed from there. We would go to dinner, and he would order for me. A steak or something for him, and salad no dressing for me. He would make comments to the waiters that I was dieting, that I needed to lose thirty pounds."

"What the fuck? Where in the hell would you lose thirty pounds from? That would make you too damn skinny," Grant seethes.

I ignore him and keep pushing on. "He would then test me. He would order and let me order on my own. The first time he did, I ordered a steak just like he did. He ridiculed me the entire dinner. He didn't bother lowering his voice, and everyone in the restaurant heard him. When we got home, he apologized. He seemed sincere. He said he was just worried and wanted me around for years to come, but my weight was worrying him." I go on to tell him how he would say my job made me fat and that I needed to buy looser clothes to hide my fat rolls.

"I was so blinded by my love for him that I believed him."

"You're perfect."

"I'm a little bigger now than I was then."

I feel pressure on my shoulder as he rolls me over to face him. The room is still bathed in darkness, but his hand is resting on my cheek. I can envision his deep blue eyes boring into mine. "You're perfect. You don't have fat rolls. You have curves." His hand drops from my face and roams over my side and hip. "Sexy as fuck curves. Tell me that you know that."

"I'm getting there."

"Get there," he says. "Fuck, Rory, I hope I never meet this asshole."

I nod, even though he can't see me. "My parents tried to tell me, but I was lost in him. I thought he loved me. He told me often. He was doing all of this because he loved me and needed me to be the best, so he would have me for years to come. My parents—" I swallow hard. "—they told me it wasn't right, they didn't like him, but they knew that I loved him. It wasn't until Grandma passed away and he wasn't there for me that I started to see it. He didn't so much as give me a hug. Instead he told me she never liked him, so why should he be sad? He showed up at the after-memorial service at my parents' house. I was sitting on the couch with Aspen and eating a piece of cake, my grandma's best friend made. It was always my grandma's favorite. Anyway, he barged in and berated me in front of everyone. It was humiliating, but I still stayed with him. When he asked me to marry him, I agreed easily. I thought he loved me. I was wrong."

"What happened?"

"Aspen tried to talk me out of it. She told me I deserved better, but I thought he was it for me. That he loved me, and all of his ridicule was being done out of love. Turns out it was all just a game to him. The day of our wedding, it was small, but my friends, and what distant family I had left were there. Aspen was my maid of honor." I stop to catch my breath. I hate talking about this. I wish I could just leave it in the past.

"I'm right here," Grant says, holding me a little tighter.

"He left me. I can still remember the look on Aspen's face when his mom came to the door to tell me that the wedding was off. Aspen was ashen, and Elijah's mom had no remorse. It was as if she agreed with her son's decision to leave me on our wedding day. I never made it down the aisle." Another deep breath. "I packed up and moved out that very same night. Aspen and I moved into our grandma's place while waiting for it to sell. She was having issues with her roommate, and since Grandma's was still on the market. It gave us some time to regroup, and then I found this building here the same week my parents got a contract on the house, and well, here we are."

We're both quiet as I will my heart rate to slow. Grant's hands roam over my body, warming me, bringing me back from the memories to the present. His touch soothes the pain and turns me on all at the same time.

"I need to turn on the light. I need to see you. Can I do that, Rory?" he asks. There's something in his voice that I don't recognize.

"Yes," I whisper. I'm scared as hell, but if he's going to end it, I'd rather it be now before I fall any further in love with him because I'm finally willing to admit it to myself.

I'm in love with Grant Riggins.

The bed dips, and the click of the lamp follows, lighting the room with a soft glow. Grant slides back over to me and lies down, facing me. The palm of his hand comes back to rest against my cheek. "I want to erase him from your life. I want to soothe every hurtful thing he ever did or said to you." He breathes in deeply. "I want to hurt him for what he did to you. I want him to pay for how he treated you." He moves closer, his lips a whisper from mine. "Most of all, baby, I want to love you. I want to show you what you mean to me every single day. I want to hold you like this every night, and I want to ravish your body until you can look me in the eye and tell me that you're beautiful, and mean it." His breathing is labored, and his eyes, even in the dim light of the room, are a deep blue. They're mesmerizing.

His lips close in on mine. His tongue gently dashes across my bottom lip, and I open for him. There really isn't another option. Not when it comes to Grant. I fear that I'm getting too close, and this sweet, tender, loving guy is going to turn evil, but my heart knows better. Elijah never put forth the effort as Grant has, and he never said sweet things to me. It was always I love you, and that's why I'm hard on you, never that he wanted to love me or that I was beautiful.

Grant makes me feel beautiful.

He slows the kiss and pulls back just enough for his eyes to find mine. "I love you, Aurora Steele." My breath hitches. "Let me show you." I can't speak, so I nod.

He loves me. I want to shout it from the rooftops. I want to take an ad out in the paper with the hopes that he'll see it. That the demon from my past can see that he was wrong. I am worthy of love. I want to freeze this moment in time and never leave this bed. I never want this feeling, this heart-racing, butterflies-going-crazy, soul-soothing feeling to ever end.

Heartbreak be damned. I want Grant to show me. I want to know what it feels like. I want to experience it. Kiss by kiss, he's bringing me back to life. He makes me want to reach for more, and with each passing day, Elijah is nothing but a horrid memory, and the damage to my heart and my soul, well, Grant's taking care of that.

"I love this," he says, as he runs his large hand over my side. "This dip of your hips," he whispers. His hand is everywhere, tracing over my bare skin. His hard body is pressed to my soft one, and I don't have the time to feel self-conscious. He's driving me wild with want and desire.

"Tell me what's off limits, baby. What are my boundaries?"

Boundaries? I don't want any. Not between us. "No boundaries," I reply softly.

"No? So, I can do this?" he asks, sliding his hand between my legs. With a feather-soft touch, his index finger traces through my folds. "Fuck me," he mumbles.

I should be embarrassed about how wet I am for him, but I can't seem to find it in me to care. Not when his deep blue eyes are looking at me like a man finding a fresh spring in the middle of a drought.

"How about if I do this?" he asks, sliding one long digit inside me. Sucking in a breath, I grip his forearm. "Tell me what you want, Aurora. Tell me what you like."

I think about his question, and I realize I'm not really sure. "I don't know," I answer honestly.

"What do you mean?"

"Elijah, he never… he was more of a get his and rollover kind of guy." I hate talking about him again, but he's my only experience.

"Not that I like bringing that asshole into bed with us, but for the sake of clarity, I need to know. Did he never play with your pussy? Did he never taste you?" he asks, licking his lips.

I shake my head. "He barely touched me. Just enough to get off, and then… nothing."

"Have you ever had an orgasm?"

"Not with a man." His eyes widen, and then something that can only be described as determination fills his eyes, and suddenly the embarrassment of my confession is gone, replaced with need for him.

Sliding his arm under my neck, he pulls me close while lazily pumping his finger in and out of me. "We're going to change that. From this moment on, he's your past. I'm your future, baby, and I promise you, I'll cherish you always." His lips connect with mine as he adds another finger. I dig my nails into his back. It's a new feeling for me. It's not uncomfortable, but foreign, and it feels… good. Really good.

CHAPTER
Grant
SEVENTEEN

I WANT TO fucking devour her. My cock is hard as stone, begging for release, but he's just going to have to wait. Right now, my girl needs to know how sexy she is. She needs to know that I want nothing more than to ravish her body. I could keep her in this bed for days and never be satisfied. I'll never have my fill of her.

Never.

Topping my overwhelming need to consume her, she's telling me I have no boundaries. She's mine for the taking, and I suddenly feel like a kid in a candy store. I want it all, and I don't know where to start.

She's wet and ready for me, but I need to make sure. That's what I tell myself as I move to slide down her body. The truth of the matter is that I don't want to rush this. I *can't* rush this. I need to take my time and make sure she feels nothing less than cherished.

"W-What are you doing?" she asks, lifting up on her elbows to stare down at me.

"I need a taste," I reply, licking my lips as I settle between her thighs. My cock aches, wanting in on the action, but I won't hurry this moment. No, tonight is the night that dreams come true. I can't even say how many nights I've laid in this very bed imagining having her like this. She's here, I'm here, and I want it all.

"Grant." She whispers my name, drawing my attention from her glistening pussy. With tremendous effort, I pull my gaze to her eyes. "I—This is new." Is that fear in her voice?

"Do you want me to stop?" It would kill me, and if she says yes, there is a serious case of blue balls in my future, but if that's what she wants, that's what's going to happen.

"No." She shakes her head vigorously. "I don't know what to expect. I don't know what to do." There is a hint of panic in her voice.

"You grip my hair, the sheets, whatever you need to. And you lie back and enjoy it. Just feel, Rory. I'll take care of the rest." Sliding off the bed, I grab her ankles and pull her to the edge before dropping to my knees. One at a time, I place her legs over my shoulder. "Just feel," I tell her again before lowering my head.

I lose myself in her taste that explodes on my tongue. I grin when I feel her hands grip my hair and tug. Sliding two fingers back inside her, I suck on her clit gently, but it's enough to have her arching off the bed. That simple act is followed by a low, throaty moan, and that's all the encouragement I need to double my efforts.

It doesn't take long before she's writhing and calling out my name. I don't remove my hands or my mouth until her body sags into the mattress. Sated. My chest swells with an indescribable emotion, knowing I'm the man who gave her that. Peering up at her, I see a dopey smile on her face, and her entire body is flushed. I've never seen anything sexier in my entire life.

Wiping my mouth with the back of my hand, I stand on shaking legs, ignoring my cock that's screaming for attention, and lift her into my arms. With careful steps, I carry her into the bathroom. Something tells me that I can't push this. That I need to make tonight about her, and her alone. I can handle my cock, literally and figuratively.

"What are we doing?"

"You're taking a bath."

"But what about…" Her voice trails off, but the question is still there hanging between us.

"This might be cold," I say, placing her on the counter.

"My entire body is warm."

"To answer your question, tonight's about you. I need you to see that I desire you. That you're sexy, and this"—I reach down and fist my cock—"is all because of you."

"Doesn't that hurt?"

"It would, but I plan on taking care of it." Her eyes widen.

"W-What do you mean?"

"I mean, I'm going to run you a warm bath, and then I'm going to leave you to relax while me and my friend Rosey palm"—I hold up my hand with my fingers spread wide—"are going to go out there"—I point to my bedroom—"and take care of it."

"Why would you do that? Do you not want me?" There is pain laced in her voice.

"Hey." I place my index finger under her chin and lift her eyes to mine. "This shows you that I want you. I just fucking ate your pussy like a starving man. I want you, Aurora. Don't ever think differently."

"Then… I don't understand."

"I don't either. Not really. What I do know is that he used you. He fucked you and got off, never caring about you or your needs. He belittled you and beat you down so much so that you fucking struggle to order when we go out to eat. I know that I'm madly in love with a woman who doesn't know her self-worth. I know that I won't stop until you do. That means that me and Rosey are going to remain close." I wiggle my fingers, and a small smile tilts her lips.

"I want you," she whispers.

I nod. "I know that too. But we need to give this time to grow."

"We've been dating a while."

I nod again. "We have, and we're going to continue to date." I lean in and kiss her slow and deep, letting her taste herself on my lips. "Now," I say, pulling back, "let's get you in the tub."

She eyes the tub and then the walk-in shower. "How about a shower instead?"

"Whatever you want, beautiful." I press my lips to her forehead before stepping away to start the shower. I make sure the water is warm before turning toward her again, only to find her standing right behind me. "You're all set," I say, stepping back.

"Are you not joining me?"

Not if I'm going to keep my hands and my cock off of you. "Do you want me to?" She opens her mouth to speak but quickly clamps it shut and nods. "Tell me." I bend my knees so that we're eye level. I keep my eyes on hers, even though her naked body is still on full display for me to feast on. "There is nothing you can't tell me, Aurora."

"I've never—" She shrugs.

Standing back to my full height, I offer her my hand. "Then we'll shower." My cock aches as the words pass my lips, but this is what she needs. She needs to know that I respect her and that her body is something to be cherished, not repulsed. Stepping under the hot spray, I pull her into my arms. Her naked body pressed against mine with the warm water raining down on us is intimate and erotic.

"That has to hurt," she says again, looking up at me.

"I'll be fine," I assure her.

She looks down between our naked bodies and then back up at me. "Can I touch you?"

"Always. You never have to ask me. I'm yours, and only yours." I turn so that my back hits the wall of the shower, leaving my hands at my sides and closing my eyes. This is her show, and I'm going to let her run it. I'm only so strong, and denying her isn't something I'm capable of. I'm trying to be a gentleman to give her time, but if this is what she wants, I'm not going to stop her.

Her small hand wraps around my cock, and I take in a slow, steady breath. I force myself to think about something other than how soft her hands are and how they feel stroking me.

"I don't know what to do?"

When I force my eyes to open, the sight before me has me reaching for the wall to hold myself up. Aurora on her knees, her hands on my cock, that's a vision I will never for the rest of my life ever forget.

Never.

"Help me," she says, running her thumb over the tip.

I swallow hard. "You're doing just fine on your own, darlin.'"

"I don't want to hurt you."

"Right now, the only thing that could hurt me is if you stop."

"Grant."

"Aurora," I counter.

"I'm serious."

"So am I. There is nothing that you could do that I won't like. Go on your instinct. I promise you if your hands and mouth are on me, I'm going to enjoy it. I'm close to losing my damn mind as it is. I'm standing here thinking about fluffy puppies trying not to come."

"Really?" She smiles.

The little minx. "Yes, really."

"So, what if I did this?" she asks.

I'm still staring down at her, and when her tongue peeks out and licks me, I fight hard to keep my knees from buckling. "T-That works," I say, once again resting my head back against the wall of the shower and closing my eyes.

"Grant."

Fuck me. She's trying to kill me.

Opening my eyes, I peer down at her. "Yeah, baby?" I grit out. "Watch me."

What. The. Fuck.

My girl went from being shy and timid to a sex goddess in one night. Don't get me wrong. I'm not complaining. That's what I wanted for her, to have the confidence with me to take what she wants, but this… this is more than I expected, and everything I've ever wanted.

Doing as she asks, I keep my eyes locked on her as she takes me into her mouth. The water is raining down on us, her hair is wet and matted to her face, and her mouth's stretched wide with my cock. My hands tremble at my sides, and my knees, they're weak. I've never in my life felt like my knees were going to give out from the sight of a woman on her knees. Then again, this isn't just any woman. This is my woman. This is Aurora. The woman who swooped in with her sweet treats and fragile heart and stole mine.

"Babe." I tap her on her shoulder. She stops and looks up at me, letting my throbbing cock fall from her pretty pink lips. "I'm close," I tell her, fisting my cock. "I didn't know if you were ready for that, so…" I let my words hang as I continue to stroke myself. "I'm close," I tell her.

She nods but doesn't look at me. Her eyes are glued to my hand stroking myself. I watch as her tongue peeks out and swipes at her lips, and that's all it takes. I'm crying out her name and spilling onto her chest. I sag against the wall. That was the most intense orgasm I've ever had. Forcing myself to open my eyes, I look down to see her staring at her chest. Fuck. Panic rips through me. I knew this was too much too soon. I quickly fall to my knees, which gets her attention. A slow smile pulls at her lips.

"Aurora?"

"Thank you." Her smile grows.

Relief washes over me. "Come here, you." I pull her into me and hug the hell out of her. "You're incredible." I kiss her slowly. I hope it says: I love you, thank you, and when can we do it again.

"Let's get cleaned up." I stand, bringing her with me, and we quickly shower, which was the original plan.

Not ten minutes later, we're both back in bed, sans clothes, her head resting on my chest. My arms are holding her tight, and as sleep claims me, I send up a silent prayer that this is what our forever looks like.

CHAPTER
Aurora
EIGHTEEN

MY EYES FLY open when a pair of lips press against my shoulder, and "Good morning, beautiful," is whispered in a sexy, husky morning voice.

Grant.

Last night wasn't a dream. Heat floods my cheeks when I think about what we did, what I did. I've never been that bold before, not in my life, and not while naked. I'm glad he can't see my face so I can hide my embarrassment and unease. What happens today?

"Stop thinking. It's too early." Grant chuckles, pulling me closer, snuggling his face into my neck. "You hungry?" he asks, just as a phone starts to ring from somewhere in the house. "Ugh, who is calling me this early?"

"It's after eight."

'Right? Too damn early."

"This is sleeping late for me."

"Because you go to work in the middle of the night." The phone that has stopped ringing begins again. "Wait, is that my phone or yours?" he asks.

"I'm not sure."

"I'll go find them both. You stay here. I want to come back to this." He grins and climbs out of bed. A few minutes later, he's walking butt-ass naked back into his room and perching on the edge of the bed. "It was mine." He taps the screen and places the phone next to his ear. "What's up, brother?" he asks.

I can only assume it's one of his brothers. Trying not to listen and give him privacy, I unlock the screen of my phone and see a text from Aspen.

> **Aspen:** I want details, sister!

> **Aspen:** The suspense is killing me.

> **Me:** We just woke up.

Her reply is immediate.

> **Aspen:** You slept until after 8:00 a.m.?!

> **Me:** Yep.

I can't help but grin, knowing giving her little bits and pieces is indeed driving her crazy—however, the joke's on me when my phone rings. I fumble with my phone and quickly answer it. "Hello?" I greet in a rushed whisper, as Grant's deep chuckle meets my ears, and his hand slides under the blankets and rests on my bare thigh.

"You are not holding out on me," Aspen says into the phone. "That man is hot, and I need to live through you."

"I'm good," I tell her.

"He's there, isn't he?"

"Yep."

"Rory," she whines, and I can't help but laugh at her.

I tune her out when Grant smiles down at me. "I'll check with

Aurora and call you back." He ends the call and bends to press his lips against mine. "I'm going to go make us some coffee." Another quick kiss, and he's off the bed and striding toward the bedroom door.

"Like that?" I blurt.

He stops and looks over his shoulder. "It's just us here, baby." He follows it up with a flirtatious wink and walks out of the room for the second time this morning in nothing but his birthday suit.

"Aurora!" Aspen scolds. "What's happening? What did I miss?" she demands.

"Nothing. Grant's making coffee."

"Oh, I heard that. I also heard the kiss he gave you."

My cheeks once again betray me as they flood with heat. "I'll fill you in when I get home."

"And when will that be, my dear sister?"

"I-I don't know." She's silent, and I'm sure I've shocked her just as much as I've shocked myself. I'm not ready to leave him. Not yet. I'm afraid that if I do, this bubble of bliss that we've created will pop, and that will be the end of the fairy tale.

Before either of us can formulate a reply or try and decipher what it means, Grant's walking back into the room. "Aspen, I'll call you back. I'm going to see what the plan is for today."

"I'll wait," she sasses, and I can hear the laughter in her voice.

"Fine." I pull the phone from my face. I don't want to sound needy, but let's face it, I'm needy as hell when it comes to Grant.

"That was Owen. He wants us to come over and move some furniture to get ready for the wedding."

"So soon?"

He chuckles. "He's not taking any chances of Layla backing out. Tipping their house upside down is his way of making sure she's committed."

"She is."

"We all know that, but Owen is crazy in love with her, and well, he's my brother, and we're going to be there regardless. I told him I would meet them there in an hour. Do you want to come with me?"

"No, you and your brothers have it handled. I'll have Aspen come and get me."

"I can take you home."

"I know, but she won't mind." To prove my point, I lift my phone to my ear. "Aspen—"

She cuts me off. "I'll be there in forty-five," she says, ending the call.

"She'll be here in forty-five minutes," I tell him.

"I only need five to shower. So what shall we do with all of our extra time?" He leans in close, and just when I think he's going to press his lips to mine, his head drops to my neck, and he kisses me there.

"I need coffee," I say, deflecting. Now that it's the light of day, it's different. I'm different, and I need some time to process that.

"Fine," he grumbles good-naturedly. "Meet me in the kitchen in five."

"Grant." He stops and turns to look at me, giving me a full view of his hard length and the sexiness that is his body. I take my time, letting my eyes roam over his tattoos, and memorize his chiseled abs.

"Aurora," he says, his tone is filled with heat and warning.

"Sorry." I shake my head. I don't know what's gotten into me. "Can you maybe cover up?" I ask him.

"Is my sexiness distracting you?"

"Yes." I nod vigorously, making him toss his head back in laughter.

"Sure thing, baby." I watch as he walks to his dresser and pulls out a pair of well-worn gray sweatpants, and slips into them. "Better?" he asks.

I take in the V of his hips, the abs and tattoos that are still on display, and the bulge between his legs. "No." I shake my head.

"Get moving, baby." He smirks and walks out of the room.

As soon as the door closes, I'm patting my chin to make sure I'm not drooling before pulling myself out of bed and getting dressed. I reach for my clothes and decide to mess with him like he's messing with me. I grab the T-shirt he gave me to sleep in and slip it over my head. My hair is a hot mess, but there is nothing I can do about it. I have nothing here. I wasn't ready for this. Hell, I'm not sure I'm ready for him. Pushing my shoulders back, I pretend I'm my sister, always full of confidence, and stride out of his room and into the kitchen.

"Hey, do you—" Grant turns and stops talking. He takes the time to let his eyes roam over me before grinning. "Are we playing it like that?" he asks.

"You started it." I point to his sweatpants.

"Come here, Aurora." He crooks his finger, summoning me to come to him, and I do without hesitation.

I don't know who this person is, being so open and free, but I like her. I like her a lot. "Hey!" I screech when his hands land on my hips, and he lifts me to the kitchen counter.

His strong arms surround me as he rests his hands on the counter. "I like this," he says, kissing the corner of my mouth. "You here in my home, in my bed. I like it a lot, Rory."

"Yeah?" I slide my arms around his neck. "Me too," I confess softly.

"You should leave some stuff here. I hope this is a new normal for us."

I nod. "I'll see what I can do."

"Good." He kisses me again. "Now, as much as I love you in nothing but my shirt, Conrad is on his way to pick me up, so you need to get dressed." The words are barely out of his mouth before he lifts me into his arms and carries me back to his bed. Together, we get dressed before making our way back to the kitchen, where I finally get my coffee. Grant makes us some toast, and we both slather it with strawberry jelly. It's one of the best mornings I've ever had.

"Con should be here any minute," Grant says. I'm sitting on the counter, and he's standing between my legs.

"Yeah, Aspen too."

"You coming to Sunday dinner with me tonight? Aspen is welcome too."

"Yeah, we'll be there."

"I love you," he says, pressing his lips to mine. My heart soars with his words. I never thought I would trust those three little words from a man again, but Grant, he proved me wrong.

"Yo!" Conrad yells out as he enters the kitchen. "Damn. Another one bites the dust," he says, grinning. "Morning, Rory." He smirks.

"It's Aurora, asshole," Grant fires off. There is no way that he knows my family calls me that. The smirk tells me he thinks he's made it up on his own.

"I like Rory." His grin grows wider. "You don't mind if I call you that, do you, sis?" he asks me.

How do I say no to that? Besides, I like it. I feel like Aspen and I are a part of this big, crazy, loving family. I've missed this feeling of… family. I miss my parents. Mom keeps asking when they can come and visit, and I realize now that we need to make that happen. "Sure." I shrug.

"Traitor," Grant whispers against my lips.

"You coming with us?" Conrad asks, making himself a cup of coffee.

"No. Aspen is on her way to pick me up."

"I could have taken you home," Grant grumbles.

"Yes, but now you don't have to. You guys can leave from here," I tell him, just as there's a knock at the door. "That's probably Aspen."

"I'll get it. You two"—Conrad points at us—"get all of that out of your system so we can head out." He's laughing as he goes to answer the front door.

"It's really hard for me to pull away from you right now," Grant says, wrapping his arms around me.

"I'll see you in a few hours."

"Yeah," he says, leaning in for another kiss.

"Be warned." I hear Conrad tell my sister. "It's sugary sweet with lots of canoodling in there," he says, his tone falsely serious.

"Oh, good. I didn't miss it." I hear Aspen clap her hands as they step into the kitchen.

I roll my eyes at my sister as Grant pulls away and turns to face our siblings, his back resting against my front. "Show's over," he says, crossing his arms over his chest.

"Damn it." Aspen laughs. "I always miss the good stuff."

"Hang out with this group for long, and you'll get your fill. Marsh and I are the only two normal ones," Conrad tells her.

"Normal? You telling me you don't like a good make-out session, Conrad Riggins?" Aspen asks, placing her hands on her hips.

"I'm all for a good make-out session." He winks at her. "But this—" He points to Grant and me. "—it's nauseating."

"You're just jealous," Grant fires back.

He looks at me and winks. "I mean, if I had a woman who looked like Rory here, I guess I could understand it." He's grinning like a fool knowing that he's goading his brother.

"Fuck off, she's mine," Grant says, turning to the side and wrapping one arm around my waist.

"Aw," Aspen coos.

"Come on, lover boy. We've got furniture to move," Conrad says, draining his coffee and placing his empty cup in the sink.

"I'll be right out," Grant tells him. He doesn't wait for them to reply, or to leave for that matter, when he cups my face in his big hands and kisses me slow and deep.

It's just us. Everything else fades to black as he seduces me with his lips. "You want me to swing by and pick you guys up later?"

"No, we can drive."

He nods and lifts me from the counter. Hand in hand, he leads us to the door where we slip into our shoes and jackets. I grab my purse from the table by the door and step out onto the porch waiting for him to close and lock up. Conrad is standing next to the driver's side door of Aspen's car, and the windows are down. It's March in Tennessee, so it's still chilly. I'm about to ask her what's going on when I hear music flowing out of her car windows. It takes me a minute but as soon as I hear it, my face flames. Grant roars with laughter and pulls me into his chest as The Lonely Island's "I Just Had Sex" blares through the morning air. Do you know the one with Akon? Yeah, that song.

Aspen is laughing, and Conrad is bent over at the waist, doing the same. Grant's chest shakes with his laughter, and all I can do is hold onto him and let my laughter bubble-free as well.

"Come on, babe, you have to admit that was a good one. I'm surprised my brothers haven't pulled that same thing."

"That's classic!" Conrad says, gasping for air over his laughter.

"Hey." Grant tilts my chin up to look at him. "I love you."

Butterflies go crazy as I stare into his eyes, and I know without a shadow of a doubt he means it. This strong, amazing, gorgeous man loves me. He really loves me. "I love you too." I smile. Even with the ribbing of our siblings, I'm happy. Happier than I've ever been. My heart feels lighter, and I owe that all to this incredible man who's holding me close to his chest. For the first time in a very long time, life is looking up for me, and I can't wait to see what happens next.

CHAPTER
Grant
NINETEEN

I'M STILL LAUGHING when I climb into Conrad's truck. "Was that your idea?"

"Nope, but fuck, I wish I would have thought of it. That was epic." He grins, backing out of my driveway.

"She's something else." I shake my head thinking about Aspen and the look on Aurora's face.

"You and Aurora looked awful cozy."

"She's my girlfriend. Is there another way for us to look?" I ask.

"No." He chuckles. "She just seems to be more relaxed."

"Yeah, with each day she drops another layer of the shield she has erected. I swear if I ever meet the jackass, I'm going to kill him," I seethe.

"Wow, hold up now. What jackass and those are some strong words, brother."

"Her ex is the jackass, and you better hope one of you are around if he and I do ever cross paths."

"What did he do?" Con's voice is deadly calm, which is the opposite of my happy-go-lucky carefree little brother.

"He tore her down," I say, running my fingers through my hair.

"Can you elaborate?" he asks, pulling into Owen's driveway.

"I might as well wait until we get inside. I don't feel like repeating this story a million times."

"There are only four of us," he reminds me.

"Yeah, but add in Mom and Dad, and the girls, and I can see me having to retell it over and over again. Not to mention, I'm not telling you all everything. I'll give you enough to understand why I want to kill him. The rest is her story to tell."

"You think she'll ever tell it to anyone but you?"

"I don't know. I hope so. They're here all alone. Their parents are in Memphis but from what she tells me, there is no other family."

"No, shit?" he asks, grabbing his keys from the ignition. We climb out of the truck, and I follow him up the porch steps and wait as he knocks. "I guess I need to start doing this at your place now too." He smirks.

"Might be a good idea."

"Well, Marsh and I still have open doors," he says, opening the door when someone from inside yells out to come on in.

"Only a matter of time, Con," I tease, following him inside.

"What did we miss?" Royce asks as we step into the living room.

"Oh, you know, this guy—" Conrad points at me from where I stand next to him. "—he's all shacked up."

"No, shit? Aurora's moving in? That's great." Royce walks toward me with his hand out for me to shake.

"No, she's not moving in. She stayed at my place last night."

"Minor details," Conrad replies.

"Details are important, Con," Sawyer speaks up.

"Where is she?" Layla asks.

"She went home. Aspen picked her up. They're coming to dinner tonight at Mom and Dad's." I don't even bother hiding the smile that graces my face, knowing I get to see her again soon.

"Ugh, there." Marshall points at me. "The goofy lovesick grin is in full swing."

"Yep." I'm not going to hide what she means to me. Especially not after what that douchebag put her through.

"So, tell me," Conrad says.

"Tell you what? What did we miss?" Marshall asks.

"Nosey fuckers," I mumble.

"And proud of it." Sawyer winks.

"Aurora, she's had it rough. Her ex did a number on her. You know that, right?"

"Yeah," they all agree.

"Her ex is a total fuckstick. I won't tell you everything, but I can tell you that he tore her down. She thinks her weight is an issue, among other things." My hands ball into fists when I think about the way he must have treated her. Mentally and emotionally abusing her and taking never giving.

"Calm down there, hulk." Owen chortles.

"Stop." Layla, who is glued to his side, smacks him lightly on the chest. "What can we do to help her, Grant?"

"You got lucky with this one." I point at her, keeping my eyes on Owen. "You too," I tell Royce, pointing at Sawyer.

"We know," my two older brothers reply at once, making the girls smile, despite the roll of their eyes.

"Tore her down, how?" Layla tosses out another question.

"Her self-esteem is shit."

Layla nods slowly. "I'm all over it." She glances at Sawyer, who nods as well. They hold an entire conversation with just a look. I don't know what they're saying, but from the looks of it, I'm not the only one who's going to be showering my girl with love.

"The girls and I will take care of it." This comes from my

mother, right behind me. I turn to look at her. "Momma's on it, son." She winks, and we all laugh.

Reaching out, I pull her into a hug. "Love you, Mom," I say, kissing her cheek.

"You were always my favorite," she says, her voice loud, which has my four brothers protesting.

"Oh, hush, you're all my favorites, you two as well." She points to Layla and Sawyer. "Now, I believe we have wedding details to go over. Get busy." She claps her hands, and we all jump into action.

We spend the next couple of hours moving furniture around Owen and Layla's living room. The Riggins women couldn't seem to make up their minds, but we didn't mind. Anytime we get the opportunity to all be together is welcome. I just wish Aurora were here with us.

I rode with Conrad to Mom and Dad's with the hope that I could catch a ride home with Aurora and Aspen. If not, one of my brothers will take me home, but I'm hopeful that it's Aurora that I leave here with.

"Boy, you keep watching the driveway, you're going to stare a hole in it." Dad laughs.

"You need to work on your jokes, old man," I counter, moving away from the window. He's not wrong. If stares could cause holes to form, there'd be many forming in their driveway right now. Aurora texted me almost twenty minutes ago and said they were on their way.

"Things are going well with the two of you?" Dad asks.

"Better than I could have imagined."

He nods. "You know what that is, right?"

"Love?" I ask, knowing damn well what he's talking about.

"That too." He grins. The lines around his eyes are more prominent as he ages. "It's the magic, Grant."

"Come on, Dad. I know you preached that shit to Royce and Owen, but do you really believe in magic?"

"I do." He nods. His face is stone serious. "Your momma…" He shakes his head. "That woman is my heart." He taps his chest. "She helped me build an empire to leave to you boys, and then there's the five of you. She gave me that, and her love." He swallows hard.

It's not new to see my father get emotional when he's talking about Mom. I've never seen a love as strong as theirs, well not until Royce and Owen fell in love. They've quickly adopted Dad's magic logic.

"There's someone here for you," he says, as the sound of Marshall greeting Aurora reaches us in the living room. "Before you go, when you look at her, tell me you don't feel the magic." He looks around me. "Hey, sweetheart," he says.

I feel Aurora step next to me before I see her. I reach out and slide my arm around her waist and press my lips to the top of her head. My heart skips a beat from just having her in my arms. I look up at Dad, and he's smirking.

"Good to see you. Is that sister of yours with you?"

"You as well. Yes, Marshall took her into the kitchen."

Dad nods. "That's where I'm headed. I need to see if my Lena needs any help." With those parting words, he walks away and my lips descend on Aurora's. "I missed you."

"Yeah?"

"You can go ahead and bank on the fact that if I'm not with you, I'm missing you."

"You're a smooth talker, Grant Riggins."

"No, I'm speaking from the heart."

"I like your heart."

"Yeah?"

She nods.

"Well, you're in luck because I love yours." I lean in for another kiss.

"Cut that shit out," Marshall grumbles. "It's time to eat."

"You hungry?" I ask her as we turn to head toward the dining room.

"A little."

"Babe, this is my family and me. You can be you. Tell me, are you hungry?" I stop walking until she answers me.

"Yes." She nods. "I'm hungry."

"Good. Mom cooks for an army. You know that. Come on." With her hand held tight in mine, I lead her into the dining room. Everyone is already sitting at the table, with Aspen seated between Conrad and Marshall.

Conrad looks up and grins. "Remind me to tell you guys a story," he says, looking at each of our brothers. "It's a good one. I just sent you the link to the song," he says, cracking himself up.

"Hey!" Aspen smacks his arms when her phone pings, and she opens her message. "That's my material that you're using."

Conrad slides his arm over her shoulders, and together, they fall into a fit of laughter. "Epic, I'm telling you... it's epic."

"Do we even want to know?" Dad asks.

"No," Aurora and I say at the same time.

"Trust me," I tell my father. Aurora slinks into my side, and that's when it hits me. She's probably worried that I'm embarrassed, and I'm not. I just don't want her to be. However, we don't hold back in this family, and she needs to get used to that. She also needs to know that I'm not ashamed of her. "On second thought, it was pretty good," I admit.

Aurora tilts her head back to look up at me.

"They know I love you," I say, not bothering to soften my voice as I lower my head and kiss her.

"So, get this," Conrad starts.

"Wait!" Aspen laughs. "Let me get the song ready." She messes with her phone and then nods at Conrad.

He throws his arm back over Aspen's shoulder and pulls her close. "So this one came and picked Rory up this morning from Grant's place. I was there. We left the love birds to say goodbye and walked outside. Aspen got in her car, and we were chatting until those two"— he points across the table at where we are now sitting across from them—"decided to come up for air. Anyway, Aspen had a mischievous look in her eye, but I let it go. It was early as hell. However, when they"—he points to Aurora and me again—"walked out of the house, this is what she was blaring from her speakers."

"Aspen," Aurora warns.

"Sorry, Rory. This is just too good not to share."

Royce, Marshall, and Owen are already laughing. Layla and Sawyer are trying like hell not to if the way they're torturing their bottom lips, and the hand over their mouths is any indication.

"Hit it, maestro!" Conrad tells Aspen. Her thumb taps the screen of her phone, and the song, the same one as this morning, begins to play.

Dad cracks up, slapping his hand on the table, and Mom grins, rolling her eyes.

"Sleep with one eye open," Aurora tells her sister.

"Come on, Aurora, you have to admit that it was excellent timing."

"Here?" she says through gritted teeth.

"Babe, it's fine. We're both consenting adults."

"All right, you've embarrassed the poor girl enough. Put that thing away and eat. I didn't slave over this meal to have it go to waste," Mom says.

Aspen is quick to turn off the music and slide her phone into her back pocket. She, Conrad, and Marshall whisper to themselves while my older two brothers, their wife, fiancée, and my parents all try to have a civilized conversation. As the conversation begins to flow, Aurora relaxes beside me.

"I'm sorry if you're embarrassed, but I'm not. I don't care who knows that we're together or that I'm in love with you," I whisper in her ear, kissing her temple.

"Your parents," she whispers back. There is no heat in her voice.

"They love you almost as much as I do. We've done nothing wrong."

"You're not ashamed?"

"Never. Not with anything that involves you."

Her eyes water with tears. My mom must see it too because she pulls her into a baking question, and just like that, all is forgotten. Aurora handled it well, and I'm sure with time she's finally going to realize that I'm not him. I'm the man who loves her and will stop at nothing for her to see that.

CHAPTER
Aurora
TWENTY

"I LIKE THEM all," Layla says. She's perched on the couch with a small plate of six different flavors of wedding cake resting on her belly.

"Thank you. You picked out a small three-tier cake. I can do a flavor for each layer, so you need to narrow down to at least three," I tell her, laughing.

"Ugh. The pregnant woman should not be in charge of picking," she grumbles good-naturedly.

"Well, it is *your* wedding," I remind her.

"Hush it." She chuckles.

"When will Owen be home?" I ask. "Maybe we should have waited for him?"

"Good idea." She picks up her phone, taps the screen, and places it to her ear. "Hey, babe. When are you guys going to be back?" she asks. "Okay, yeah, no, I'm fine. Don't worry," she assures him. "Aurora is here with me. We're cake tasting, and I need help." She pauses. "Yes, I need help. I love them all." Another pause. "No, we can't have them all. I'll see you in a few," she says, ending the call.

"Let me guess, get them all."

"Yep. He's not going to be any help either," Layla sighs.

"How are you feeling?" I ask from my place on the loveseat.

"Amazing. I still find myself not believing that this is my life." She looks up at me with a sad smile. "How much do you know about my past?"

"Not much. Just that you didn't have it easy, and that something happened here, in this house. Grant said it was your story to tell."

She nods. "The Riggins family, they're something special, Aurora. They've never blinked an eye when it comes to bringing me into their family. They've all accepted me, and that is why it's hard for me." She pats the couch next to her. "Grab those tissues and come sit. Owen will be here in an hour, and in the meantime, I have a story to tell you."

Doing as she asks, I stand and take the cake samples, setting them on the table in front of us. I have a small cake of each flavor covered in the kitchen. I can cut her more later. Grabbing the box of tissues, I place it between us as I settle on the couch facing her. "I'm all ears," I say, reaching over and placing my hand on top of hers.

"My life growing up was nothing like this," she starts, and I settle in, letting her talk.

She tells me about her mom and her mother's boyfriends. By the time she gets to the attack, we're both crying, our hands full of wadded-up tissues. "You're so strong," I tell her.

She nods. "Yeah, but Owen made me that way. Sure, I fought to get out of there and never looked back, but it's the way he loves me. He pulled me from my darkness. I went from having two people, complete strangers when I met them looking out for me, to a family of rowdy brothers-in-law, and two parents who I couldn't love more if they were my own, loving me." She pauses to blow her nose. "I never had this kind of life growing up. I never got to experience holidays together or Sunday dinners. I remember thinking about how much I was going to miss it when Owen decided I wasn't the one for him."

"No." I shake my head vigorously.

"That was before I finally got it through my thick skull that he loves me. I had low self-esteem, and to be honest, it was too good to be true. From poverty to this." She waves her hand around the house. "I can still remember the first time I stepped foot in this house. I saw a life with Owen, our kids"—she rubs her belly—"running up and down the halls. I refused to let that vile woman who gave birth to me take that dream from me. She'd already stolen so much. Owen insisted we remodel to make it look different, and I agreed. He needed it more than I did. When you grow up the way I did, it's not the place but the people. And I love this house. Even with the renovations." She smiles.

"It's beautiful."

"Thank you. In a few weeks, this little guy, he's going to complete that dream."

I nod. She's been through so much, but here she is standing tall, grabbing onto the life she's always dreamed of, not letting her fear hold her back. "My life was good. My parents loved us, and we never wanted for anything. I was always shy, and Aspen, well, she was always the outgoing one." I pause, collecting my thoughts. "I was always the chubby one, my mom and grandma both loved to bake, and I spent more time with them than I did dating. I loved it, still do."

"Okay, let me stop you there. Please tell me you don't think you're chubby?"

I shrug. "I'm never going to be model thin."

"Aurora, you're fucking gorgeous. You have curves. Me, I'm this stick. I'd kill for your curves. Get that shit out of your head right now. Hell, I'm hoping after little man here is born, I'll get to keep some of the pregnancy curves." She chuckles.

I hear her words, and it's nothing that my family and Grant

haven't told me. I'm tired of letting the scars from my past control my future. I need to figure out a way to be secure in my own skin. I think back to when Grant and I first met, and I realize I've come a long way. I still have work to do, but I'm getting there. "Thank you for saying that," I finally reply as there's a knock at the door.

"Come in!" Layla calls out.

"Hey, hey," Sawyer says, walking into the room.

"Royce said there was cake tasting, and it involved Aurora and her mad skills, so here I am. What can I do?" she asks, taking a seat on the loveseat.

"I can't decide, but—" Layla glances at me, and I nod. "I was just telling Aurora about my past, and she was getting ready to tell me hers."

"I can go," Sawyer offers, but I can tell she doesn't want to.

"No. It's fine. You can stay." I catch her up to my story that's just starting.

"I can't imagine Grant is on board with you feeling this way," Sawyer comments.

"No." I shake my head. "Not even a little bit. That's what's so hard about it. My ex, he was my first, and initially I thought he loved me." I go on to tell her about my relationship with Elijah and the way he would tear me down, only to make me feel as though he was doing it for me, that he loved me, and was just looking out for me. I believed it all. Every sordid word, I let it settle into my soul.

"You're beautiful," Sawyer says, wiping at a tear.

Layla nods, pulling out a few tissues and tossing the box to her.

I ignore her and keep going. "Grant, he's every woman's dream, and he wants me. After believing you're less than for so long, it's hard to flip that switch and believe that a man like him, successful, smart, funny, sexy"—my face flames—"would want me."

"He loves you. We all see it," Layla chimes in. "That's something you'll learn about the Riggins brothers. When they love, it's with their whole hearts. Grant's not playing games with you, Aurora. He's not built that way."

"Exactly. Lena and Stanley have been married for years, and the boys all want that. They grew up watching their dad cherish their mother. He taught them how to love, and he did a damn good job," Sawyer declares.

"I love him," I say, wiping at my tears. "So much, and it wasn't supposed to happen. I told myself that I'd never let a man have my heart, not after what I went through, but with Grant, there wasn't really a choice. He swooped in, and I fell hard."

"That's a good thing. You can't let your ex win, Aurora," Layla says gently. "Don't let him steal your happiness. He wasn't there for you when you needed him, and he stole those years from you. Don't let him have any more control. Trust in yourself and your heart. I promise you Grant is one of the good ones."

"I second that," Sawyer agrees. "It's scary, I get that, but nothing in life worth having is easy. Just let go, have fun, love, and be loved."

"You sound like a greeting card," Layla teases, and the three of us crack up laughing. That's how Grant, Owen, Royce, Marshall, and Conrad find us a few minutes later. Eyes puffy and red from tears and laughter filling the room.

Royce, Owen, and Grant make a beeline for us while Conrad and Marshall stand stock still in the doorway. "Um, whose ass do we need to kick?" Marshall asks.

"No one's," Layla tells him. He studies her to make sure she's telling him the truth. "We're just some girls sharing stories and talking about life."

"The baby?" Conrad asks.

"We're all fine," Sawyer assures him.

"Aurora?" Conrad asks.

"All good." I smile, wiping my cheeks. At this point, I'm not sure if the laughter is from the pain of my past or the happiness of my present. "I have cake," I tell him. "This one—" I point to Layla "can't decide. She's going to need your help."

"I'm in," Conrad and Marshall say together as they step further into the room, taking the two remaining chairs.

"You good, babe?" Grant asks.

I turn to face him, placing my hands on his cheeks. "I'm better than good." Leaning in, I kiss him softly. "I missed you."

"You feeling okay?" he asks.

"I'm fine. Now, I need to serve up some cake." I kiss him once more before standing and making my way toward the kitchen to slice up some cake.

"Hey." He comes up behind me, caging me in. "What happened out there?"

"Therapy," I tell him, glancing over my shoulder.

"You kissed me. First. In front of the entire room."

"I did."

"I liked it," he says, moving my hair and nipping at my neck.

"Enough of that. She'll never get the cake cut and served," Sawyer says. "Go, let us take care of this."

"Love you, Rory," Grant whispers before pulling away and walking back toward the living room.

"I love you too." I don't lower my voice. He stops and turns to look over his shoulder, a smile pulling at his lips.

"I don't know what happened here today, but keep that shit up." He points at Sawyer and back to me with a wink, and then he's gone.

"Told you," Sawyer says, bumping her hip into mine.

"I'm still scared, but talking to the two of you helped me. He was already working me out of my shell. I think it was hearing Layla's story. She lived through so much, and she's not willing to let it keep her from living her life. It's not keeping her from loving and being loved. What she went through, it makes my ex look like a little old lady."

"Welcome to the family, Aurora." She smiles.

"Not yet," I tell her.

"Oh, it's going to happen. Mark my words. These guys don't toss out I love yous unless it's something they feel deep. That's fine. I'll get to say I told you so."

"I hope you do," I admit. "Now, we've got to serve up this cake." We get to work making up eight plates of all six samples and carrying them into the living room before passing them out. "Now, each flavor is a different color. I need you to taste each of them and tell me which colors are your favorite." That's all the encouragement they need. Everyone dives in, including Layla and me for the second time.

Over the next hour, we debate on the best flavor, and we're still not any closer to deciding. "This is all your fault." Owen points at me. "If you weren't so damn good at your job." He smiles, shaking his head.

"How about this? I change the cake from three small tiers to four, and then I surround it with cupcakes of the remaining two flavors?" I suggest.

"That's a lot of work for you," Layla says, chewing on her bottom lip. I can tell she likes this answer to our little dilemma, but she's worried about me.

"Pft." I wave off her concern. "This is what I do. Besides, I have the best assistant ever. We can do this, no problem."

"Are you sure, sis?" Owen asks.

I open my mouth to reply but shut it, fighting back my emotions. I nod instead. "Yes," I say, finding my words. "I promise it's nothing."

Owen stands and comes to me, bending. He hugs me tight. "Thank you, Rory."

I try, I really do, but a stray tear slides over my cheek. "You're welcome."

"Thank the lord," Marshall says, sitting back in his seat. "That was seriously stressful. I don't need that kind of negativity in my life," he says, making us all laugh.

I give him a watery smile, and he winks at me. Today has been full of tough talks and not so tough decisions, and somehow, I feel lighter. The weight of worry is no longer weighing on my shoulders. Instead, there is hope in my heart for what the future can hold. Layla and Sawyer gave me hope. They didn't tell me anything Grant hasn't, but I'll be the first to admit trusting men isn't something that comes easy for me, but I do trust him. Now, I need to trust in him, that this is what he wants. That *I'm* what he wants, and we can move forward. Who knows, maybe one day we'll all be sitting around our living room trying to decide on our wedding cake flavors.

A girl can dream.

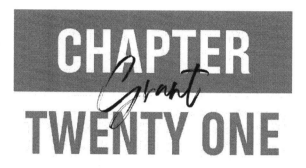

CHAPTER
Grant
TWENTY ONE

THIS IS THE second wedding I've been to in less than a year. As I sit here in Owen's living room, watching as he vows to love Layla for the rest of their lives, I feel it—the magic that Dad and my two oldest brothers keep preaching about. It's this moment watching two people who love one another so deeply that nothing else seems to matter or even exist. If I'm being honest, I saw it at Royce and Sawyer's wedding too. I was just too dumb to see it for what it is.

Leaning over, I press my lips to Aurora's temple. She's sitting as close to me as I can get her without her being in my lap. Our fingers are entwined resting on her thighs, and I know without a doubt that she's my magic. I wasn't looking for my forever, but it found me all the same, and the universe was looking out for me when they brought Aurora into my life. She's everything I never knew I wanted.

She glances over and mouths, "Are you okay?"

I nod, mouthing back that I love her. I do so completely that I don't even know who I was before she came into my life. As I watch my brother place his hand over his unborn child and lean in to kiss his wife for the first time, I know that is what I want. The wife, the kids, and Aurora. I want it all with her, and the crux of it all is that I'm not going to tell her. Not yet.

I don't know what happened last weekend when the girls were here all alone, but whatever we walked in on, it changed my girl. She's more open and affectionate, and even though the worry is still there lingering in the back of her mind, it doesn't stop her from pushing forward.

Today is Saturday, which means she's off tomorrow. That also means that I get her with me tonight, in my bed. I get to hold her all night long and wake up next to her in the morning. I tried like hell to get her to stay with me over the past two weeks, but she insists that it's just easier, and she gets to sleep a little longer staying above the bakery. I let it go, but we're going to have to do something about that. About her hours. The bakery is doing well. Aurora claims business is better each month, and I love that for her. Maybe I can drop a hint that she needs to maybe hire someone. I need more time with her. I need her next to me at night. I could stay there, but then Aspen is around, and I love her little sister, but I'm sure she doesn't want to hear her sister calling out my name in the middle of the night.

"Grant." I jerk out of my thoughts to find Aurora watching me. "You okay?"

I look around and see that we're the only two left still sitting. "Yeah, baby. I'm good. Just thinking."

"Everything okay?"

"Yes." I stand, pulling her with me. "I was just thinking about how I get you all to myself tonight and how I need to find a way to convince you to do it more than one night a week."

Her eyes soften. "I'll see what I can do. You can stay with me, you know."

"Aspen doesn't want to hear that."

"No, but you can hold me," she counters. Her face is still

flushed, but she's speaking without hesitation. She's telling me what she wants, and that's a huge leap in the right direction.

"Done."

She throws her head back in laughter. "Come on. We need to congratulate the happy couple."

Hand in hand, we make our way to Owen and Layla, passing out hugs and congratulations. We devote the next few hours to spending time with our family. Marshall and Conrad take turns spinning Aspen around the dance floor while the rest of us have our own women, not that Aspen seems to mind. She's lapping up the attention my brothers are throwing at her. I know because I keep checking on her. She's my girl's little sister, and I don't want her to feel left out or unwelcome.

"We're going to start putting everything back," Royce says as he and Sawyer step up next to where I'm spinning Aurora around the makeshift dance floor.

"I'll help." I kiss Aurora on the forehead and release my hold on her.

"What can I do?" she asks Sawyer.

"I think we should start in the kitchen."

"I don't know why she didn't let us hire this done," Owen grumbles as Royce and I join him and our younger two brothers to take down the decorations and put the furniture back.

"Stop bitching. She's yours now," Royce tells him, and that's all it takes to shut him up. It doesn't take us long to take down the decorations, setting the vases of flowers throughout the room, once we have the furniture moved back into place.

"Looks like home," Layla says as she waddles toward us.

"I thought you were putting your feet up?" Owen asks her.

"I was in the kitchen, but then I decided to help. The girls kicked me out."

"Good. Sit." Owen guides her to the couch.

"Nice to have it all back in order. Silly man changing it around so early." She smiles up at him.

"Any excuse to keep you from changing your mind, Mrs. Riggins."

"You're stuck with me."

"Fucking finally," Owen says, and the rest of us roar with laughter, including his new wife.

"I'm going to go check and see what else needs to be done so we can get out of your hair."

"You don't have to rush off," Layla announces.

"It's your wedding night," Royce counters.

"And we all know this one is eager to get you alone." Marshall wags his eyebrows, bending to give Layla a hug.

"Welcome to the family, sis," Conrad says, swooping in for a hug as well.

"You're good for him," I say, taking my turn to hug my new sister-in-law. There are tears in her eyes, but she nods, offering me a watery smile. I don't stick around to get yelled at by Owen for making her cry yet again today. Instead, I hightail it to the kitchen, looking for my girl.

"Thanks for the lift," Aspen says, reaching for the door handle.

I find her eyes in the rearview mirror. "Call us if you need us, and make sure you lock the door."

"Yes, Dad," she teases. "I'll be fine. You just take care of this one." She reaches up and squeezes Aurora's shoulder.

"She's in good hands."

"Oh, I'm sure she is." Her cackling laughter follows her all the way out of the SUV.

"Ignore her," Aurora says from her spot in the passenger seat.

"I don't know. Keeping you in my hands sounds like a pretty damn good plan to me."

"That's not what she meant," she counters.

"That's exactly what she meant, and you know I'm a man of my word, baby." Glancing up at their apartment, I see the lights come on, and Aspen comes to the window, giving me a thumbs-up, which is all I needed to see, and I'm pulling back out onto the road.

"I walked right into that one, didn't I?" she asks, resting her head back against the seat.

"You did."

"Thank you for looking out for her."

"She's family."

"You really feel that, don't you? That she and I are your family."

"Yes." There is no hesitation in my answer.

"I love you, Grant. Thank you for showing me what the love of a good man is supposed to feel like."

"Loving you is easy."

She reaches over and runs her fingers through my hair, which is where they stay the remainder of the drive to my place. We're quiet as we enter my condo. My hand rests on the small of her back.

"I'm going to take a shower. Is that okay?"

"Of course. You want some company?"

"Hmm." She moves to stand directly in front of me. "I could use some help washing my back."

"I'm your man," I say. My words hold more than one meaning and the softening of her eyes tells me that she understands that as well. "Come on, gorgeous. Let's get you out of the dress." I lead her to my bedroom and proceed to strip myself naked while she stands there watching me. "What are you waiting for?" I ask her.

"Your full attention."

"You have it," I tell her. "Always."

"Sit." She points to the bed.

This is new for her to command and ask for what she wants, and I'm the man who's going to give it to her. I take a seat on the bed. "Now what?" I ask her.

"Now, you watch."

"That I can do." I lean back, bracing my hands on either side of me on the bed. My cock is already hard just at the mention of her getting naked. I've got it bad.

"I'm going to need some help." She walks to where I sit and turns, giving me her back. "Can you unzip me?"

My answer is to take the delicate zipper of her dress between my thumb and index finger and pull the zipper all the way down. It ends just above her ass, and I swallow back the groan that wants to be set free when I see just a peek of her ass.

She steps away and turns to face me. She's just out of reach, which I'm sure is by design. She knows me well enough to know that if she's within reaching distance, I need to be touching her. It's not something that I can control. Hell, I don't want to. I give her my full attention as the little lavender dress she wore to the wedding slides over her shoulders and pools at the floor around her ankles. Underneath is a matching lace bra and panty set, the same color as her dress.

"I might have splurged a little," she says.

"I'll pay for it," I say, drinking in the sight of her.

"That's the reason you're sitting there, and I'm over here. I like these." She slides her hands into the band of the tiny piece of fabric she's calling panties and slides them over her thighs. "I didn't want you to rip them."

"You know me well, baby."

"Can you help me again?" she asks. Each step she takes that brings her back to me is accentuated from the sway of her hips, and I'm close to losing control. I'll buy her a thousand new sets as long as I get her naked now. She turns, giving me her back, and I waste no time unclasping her bra, only this time I don't let her go. No, I move in close, pressing my front to her back and slide my hands under the cups of her bra, and palm her breasts.

"That's cheating," she pants, resting her head back against my shoulder.

"I think I can convince you to forgive me," I say, pressing my lips to her neck as I pull the fabric from her skin and drop it to the floor. My hands go back to her breasts, cupping them, pulling on her hardened nipples.

"Maybe, I will. On one condition." She's breathless, and I want to beat on my chest. I did that to her.

"Name it." I'd give her anything.

"Make love to me."

Keeping one hand on her breast, the other travels down to her pussy, where I slide my fingers through her folds. "Is that what you want? For me to make love to you?"

"Yes."

"Tell me how you want it."

"I—Just you inside me."

"That's a given, sweetheart, but I need you to tell me how you want me inside you. It's just me, and you can tell me anything." I nip at her ear. "Tell me what you want, Rory."

"I want to feel desired. I don't want to worry about doing something wrong, and I want to feel." Her words are whispered and haunted with the ghosts of her past.

"You're in control," I tell her. Sliding from my spot behind her, I reach into the bedside table and pull out an unopened box of condoms and rip open the package. Reaching in, I tear one off and hand it to her. "This is your show, babe. I'm just along for the ride." With that, I climb onto the bed, resting my head on the pillows, placing my hands behind my head. "I'm yours, Aurora. There is nothing that you could do or ask for that I would deny you. Take what you want, baby."

I crave her hands against my skin. I want to feel her body aligned with mine, and I want to feel the warmth of her pussy as I sink deep inside her. I've been waiting for this moment—for the time when she and I become one—and I'd love nothing more than to hover over her and take what we both want.

However, she needs this.

My girl needs to be able to see my desire for her. She needs to know that there isn't a single fucking thing she could do that would make me not want her. I need her to take the control here, so that maybe, just maybe she can carry some of that over into her everyday life.

I need her to see that she's beautiful, and strong, and so damn sexy. My needs, they'll be met as long as she's here with me.

Right now, this is all about her.

CHAPTER
Aurora
TWENTY TWO

MY HEART SWELLS with love for this man. He's giving me the control that was taken away from me. He's giving me the chance for the first time in my life to explore a man's body. He's lying on the bed, hands behind his head, and his hard length is resting against his rock-hard abs. My mouth waters at the sight of him. "I don't know where to start," I confess.

"Anywhere. Everywhere. I need your help. Do you want the lamp off or leave it on?" he asks.

"On." My eyes widen at my quick reply, making him chuckle.

"On it is. The rest is up to you. Do what feels right. There is no right or wrong answer. There is no script for this. Just feel, Aurora. Feel my love for you, and take what you need from me. Trust me, baby. This is not a hardship for me. Unless you count the fact that I'm keeping my hands to myself a hardship, that's going to be torture, but I'm not worried. I know I'll get my turn," he says, his heated gaze gliding over my naked body.

My entire body is trembling, but this time it's not fear. It's anticipation. It's excitement. Climbing onto the bed, I lie down next to him and let my hands begin to roam. "When people look at you, they see the gorgeous blue eyes and the sexy hair, the body made for sculpting, but do you know what they miss?" I ask him.

"What's that, baby?"

"Your heart. I don't know how it fits inside your chest. You have given me so much. My confidence, my voice, your body…" My voice trails off as I continue to run my hands over him.

"And my heart. You have my heart and my kisses. Those all belong to you too."

"Those butterflies have moved to my chest," I tell him. "My heart feels like it's fluttering."

"Good. That means you feel my love. Now show me yours."

"Can I—" I start, but he's already shaking his head.

"No. Don't ask me, Aurora. Take it. What's mine is yours. Take what you need, baby. I'm right here with you, and I promise you anything you decide to do is okay with me. Well, unless you plan on leaving me here and you going home. I'm not good with that plan."

"I'm not leaving you." My words have a double meaning. I don't think I could ever walk away from this man.

Never.

Taking a deep breath, I move down the bed until my face is eye level with his length. Tentatively, I reach out and grip him, stroking slowly from root to tip. My mouth waters and I know what I want to do. I move to settle between his thighs and place him in my mouth. My tongue swirls the head of his cock, and he moans. The sound gives me the strength to keep going, so that's exactly what I do. I take him deeper each time, my tongue caressing him, and I know from the ache between my thighs and the moans coming from deep within his throat that I'm torturing both of us. It's time to move on, to conquer this void that only Grant can fill.

Climbing to my knees, I reach for the condom, and with shaking hands, I tear open the package and slide it over his length. "Did I do it right?" I ask, looking up at him.

His eyes are hooded, and his breathing is labored. "Y-Yeah, baby. You did good."

"You okay?"

"No. Not even a little bit. My sexy as fuck girlfriend just put on a show, and it's killing me that I can't touch you, but we both need this. I need you to know that you have the control here, and it's good for me to have to wait. Helps me work on my control."

"Your control?"

"Yeah, trying not to come with my cock in your mouth, that sexy ass of yours in the air, and your fucking gorgeous tits brushing against my thighs. So, yeah, I'm working on my control too."

"I'm sorry?" I pose it as a question.

"Don't be sorry, baby. I enjoyed every hot fucking second of it." He smiles, and those butterflies in my chest flutter their beat.

With cautious movements, I move to straddle him, gripping his cock and aligning him with my entrance. I fight the urge to close my eyes and hide from the intimacy of the moment. I stay strong, keeping my eyes locked on his. Instead of hiding, I'm memorizing this moment. I know it's one I'll never forget as long as I live. No matter where our future takes us, this will be a night I will forever remember.

"Oh," I say as I start to lower myself onto him.

"Almost there, beautiful," he says huskily.

I nod and settle fully onto him. "Wow," I breathe.

"Babe, that's damn good for my ego," he says through gritted teeth. "You feel so fucking good. Hot. Wet. Tight." He lifts his hips just a little, and he slides even deeper.

My breath stutters in my chest. "I need you to touch me now. I need your hands on my skin. I need you in this moment with me."

"I'm right here, Rory. I've been here the entire time, cataloging every detail, committing it to my memory."

"Touch me. Please, Grant." I watch closely as he removes his hands from behind his head and places them on my thighs.

"I don't know where to start."

"Take what you need," I say, tossing his earlier words of encouragement back at him.

He sits up and wraps his arms around me. "I need your smiles," he says, pushing my hair out of my eyes. "And these lips, I need them too," he says, leaning in and kissing me softly. "I need the feel of your naked body pressed against mine." He kisses me again. "I need your pussy milking my cock." Another tender kiss. "I need your heart, Rory."

"You have all of me."

"I love you," he says, pressing his lips to mine. His hands roam over my body until they land on my ass cheeks, and he begins to guide me to move back and forth, creating a delicious friction between our bodies. It's a euphoric feeling I've never in my life experienced.

"Nothing has ever felt like this," I say, breaking our kiss and tilting my head back, enjoying the feel of the fire coursing through my veins. "I'm close."

"Thank fuck. I don't know how much longer I can hold off." With that, he slides his hand between our bodies and uses his thumb to massage my clit. With the rhythm of our bodies, it takes seconds for the fire to turn to pure ecstasy as I explode around him, screaming out his name. He grunts his approval and yells out for me as he spills over inside me.

I bury my face in his neck as we both hold onto each other with an iron grip. I feel the first tear slide across my cheek, followed by another and another. I don't stop them from coating my cheeks, instead letting them fall unchecked.

"Hey," he says when he feels my tears. He pulls back enough to cradle my face in the palm of his hands. "Talk to me."

"These are happy tears," I say, offering him a watery smile. "I'm sorry that I'm crying, but tonight, you—it's been magical."

"The magic," he whispers.

I nod. "I've never felt this connected to someone else. I've never felt this deep, intense love that I have for you, and I've never had an orgasm like that. Ever. All firsts, and overwhelmingly so. I just… I love you, Grant Riggins."

"My girl," he whispers before his lips connect with mine.

He kisses me slow and deep. His tongue duels with mine as we meet one another stroke for stroke, much like our lovemaking. The butterflies take flight in my belly and in my chest as he heals a piece of me that I never thought could be repaired. It's not until we're both gasping for air, does he break the kiss.

"How about that shower?" he asks.

"Definitely." With slow movements, I lift up on my knees and climb off him. I miss our connection instantly, but Grant doesn't give me time to dwell on it. He's climbing off the bed and lifting me into his arms, carrying me into the bathroom.

"This time, we're taking that bath. Together," he says, kissing my bare shoulder.

I watch as he takes care of the condom, and starts the water, lays out a few towels for us for after. Once he deems the water warm enough, he holds out his hand and motions for me to step in. I stand, waiting for him to settle into the tub before I take my spot between his legs, resting back against his strong chest.

"We should end every day like this," he says, wrapping his arms around me.

"Well, for me, that would be at around seven each night." I laugh. "Three in the morning comes early."

"The bakery's doing well. Maybe you should look into hiring some help. Someone who can give you and Aspen a break. Maybe two someones?"

"I've thought about it. To be honest, I was just holding off to make sure that sales are going to stay steady like they have been. I still can't believe the success we've had."

"You know you kick ass at what you do, right?"

"I mean, yeah, I like my creations, but I wasn't sure that other people would like them too. At least not this much. The success has been more than I could have ever dreamed of."

"Come on now, you know better than that."

"Okay, so I admit that I'm good in the kitchen. The bakery's success is still surpassing my wildest dreams. I never imagined there would be a write-up about me in the paper," I state, referring to the article that ran last week. I think Lena had something to do with it when she announced publicly in the grocery store, from what Layla told me, that I was the one making the wedding cake.

"You're badass, baby."

"Well, this badass is exhausted," I say, standing and grabbing a towel and wrapping it around my hair.

"That's it? That's all the time I get?"

"We have forever," I say without thinking.

"Damn right, we do." His words have my pulse pounding in my ears, and my heart bursting with love for him. He stands and grabs another towel, enfolding it around my shoulders before grabbing the other for himself and releasing the drain on the tub. We quickly dry off, and I use the new hairdryer that Grant bought for me to dry my hair, and climb into bed. He wraps his strong arms around me, and it's no time at all before sleep claims us both.

CHAPTER
Grant
TWENTY THREE

THE OFFICE IS eerily quiet for a Monday afternoon. Royce and Owen are offsite at a meeting with the bank. We're looking to open a new site in Pennsylvania, and this is the first step. Marshall is at a marketing seminar, and Conrad just left for the day. There is an IT issue at the Nashville location, and he's going to offer his assistance. He doesn't need to, but it's nice to get out of the office every now and then.

It's just Layla and me holding down the fort. Sawyer is meeting Sam for pedicures. They tried to get Layla to go, but she's not feeling well. My nephew is making these last few weeks hard on her, which is why I've walked past her desk about fifty times since everyone left. I told Owen I would keep an eye on her. He's not exactly happy that she's insisting on working until the baby arrives, but in my opinion, it's better that she's here where someone is close if she needs us than home by herself.

Due to my Layla walk-bys, I've gotten shit done this afternoon. Instead of trying to focus, I grab my phone and text Aurora.

Me: How was your day?

Aurora: Great. We sold out of muffins twice!

I can picture the smile lighting up her face.

Me: That's great, babe. I'm proud of you.

Aurora: Thank you. I might have saved you one.

Me: You do love me.

Aurora: More than anything.

I never thought I'd see the day when a text message would make me all sappy and shit, but over the past few months, that's exactly what happens. Aurora Steele has turned my world upside down.

Aurora: How's Layla?

Me: Annoyed. LOL. I've been checking on her every five minutes.

Aurora: She'll tell you if she needs you.

Me: I know, but I would never forgive myself if she needed me, and I wasn't there.

Aurora: You're a good man, Grant Riggins.

Me: So I've been told.

I follow it up with a winking face emoji and an arms shrugging emoji.

Aurora: So modest. Get back to work, slacker.

Me: See you tonight.

Her reply is a thumbs-up, making me smile. She knows I'll keep texting her because no matter how much time I get with her, it's never enough. It will never be enough.

Tossing my phone on my desk, I try to get back to work, but

my concentration is complete shit. It's just one of those days, I guess. Standing from my chair, I stretch before grabbing my phone and sliding it back in my pocket. It's been almost an hour since I checked on Layla, so it's time for that. I know that I'm annoying her, but she'll get over it. I can't focus on work, so checking on her at least makes me feel productive.

I'm almost to the door when my desk phone rings. Walking back to my desk, I reach over the front of my desk and grab the handset. "Grant Riggins," I say, trying to lean over the desk and see who's calling.

"Grant?" Layla asks.

"Hey, I was just coming to see you."

"Okay. Well, I'll see you in a minute." I hear laughter in her voice, but it's not an "I'm happy you read my mind" laughter. It's more of an "I'm nervous about something" laughter.

Hanging up the phone, I make my way toward the reception desk where she is. "Hey," I say, leaning against the counter. "What's up?"

"Well, I was hoping I could ask you for a favor."

"Anything." I mean that. I would do anything for either of my sisters-in-law. I love them both and will continue to state that Sawyer and Layla are the best things to ever happen to Owen and Royce.

"Don't freak out."

"Layla, you can't tell a man not to freak out and not tell him what he's not freaking out about." I run my eyes over her, where she sits in her chair, and she looks perfectly fine.

"I need you to take me to the hospital."

"What? What's going on?" My feet are moving, and I end up behind the desk, bending down beside her chair so that we're eye to eye. "Are you hurt?"

"No. But my water broke."

My water broke. "Fuck. Okay. Um, yeah, let's get you to the hospital. I love you and my nephew, but I don't want to deliver him." I take a deep breath. "Are you okay? What do you need?"

"I'm fine. I don't need anything but a ride and for someone to call my husband. We have time. I've been timing my contractions all morning. They're still fifteen minutes apart."

"All morning? Layla!" I scold her.

"Oh, hush. I'm fine. You and I both know that if Owen was aware he would have made both of us stay home, and there is no point in that."

"You're awful calm for this to be your first rodeo," I tell her, holding out my hand and helping her stand.

"That's because I know everything is going to be fine. I've lived through the worst, and this is far from that. This is special, and I'm too excited to be worried. I get to meet my son. A piece of me and a piece of Owen." Her smile is wide and sincere.

"You're one of a kind, Layla Riggins."

"I love that. I don't think I'll ever get tired of hearing it."

"Well, Mrs. Riggins, let's get you in the car and call your husband. He's going to flip his shit, so I'd like to tell him you're safe and on your way to the hospital before I call him."

"Thank you, Grant. I'm glad it's you."

"What?" I ask, leading her to the elevator.

"I'm glad it was you who's here. Marshall watches me like a hawk after all that went down, and Conrad, I have a feeling he wouldn't be this calm, and Royce either. You're just the right amount of worried and calm for this kind of situation."

"Well," I say with a laugh. "I'm glad I'm here too." With cautious steps, I guide her to my SUV.

"Wait, I can't sit on your seats."

"You can, and you will. It's leather. It will clean. We're not waiting a minute longer to get your ass in this car," I tell her, my hands on my hips.

"Ugh. I should have called Sawyer." She smirks.

"In the car, Riggins." I smirk right back at her. I win, of course, and I help her into the car. "Now, I'm going to call Owen from my phone and not yours, so he doesn't lose his shit in the middle of their meeting. I'm going to ask him to step out for a quick second, but you, my dear sister, are going to be the one to tell him. He'll go off on me, not from anger, but fear. He will be the exact opposite with you, so you get the pleasure."

"Deal." She smiles, placing her hand over her baby bump.

Double-checking that she's buckled in and comfortable, I pull my phone from my front pocket and place it in the cupholder. Pulling out of the lot, I hit the button on my steering wheel. "Call Owen," I direct my Bluetooth. The phone rings through the car speakers, and after the third ring, he picks up.

"What's up?"

"Hey, can you step out for a minute?"

"Hold on." He doesn't hesitate and tells Royce he's stepping out. "Done," he tells me.

I turn to Layla and give her a look. "You're up," I tell her.

"What?" Owen asks.

"Hey, babe."

"Layla?" Owen asks. "What's going on?"

"My water broke. And before you freak out, I'm okay. Grant and I are on the way to the hospital."

"Fuck," he curses under his breath. "How are you? Are you in pain? Damnit. I knew I should have missed this meeting this morning when you were having contractions."

"What? How did you know that?"

"You're my wife," he tells her. Like that's the only explanation he needs. "I'm on my way. Grant!" he barks.

"Yeah?"

"You have my world in that SUV of yours."

"I've got them, brother. Drive safe."

"Layla, I love you. I love you so fucking much. I'm on my way," he tells her.

"Okay. I'll see you soon."

"Bye, baby." The call ends.

"That went better than I expected," I tell Layla. She's quiet, so I glance over and see her gripping the door handle, her face constricted in pain.

"Yeah," she says, releasing her hold on the door. "Sorry, contraction." She grins.

"You are the only woman in the world happy to be in pain due to labor."

"No. I'm not. And I'm not happy about the pain. I'm happy that I finally get to meet my son. I'm happy that my life is something I only ever imagined it could be. I'm just... happy, Grant. I'm so happy."

I'm man enough to admit that she's got me a little choked up. Instead of replying, I reach over and give her hand a gentle squeeze. I clear my throat before speaking again. "We should call everyone else."

"I'll call Sawyer and have her do it for us."

"I'm going to call Aurora," I say as I pull up to a Stop sign. I grab my phone and dial her number, moving the call from Bluetooth to my phone. The light turns green as she answers. I take Owen's words to heart and make sure it's clear in all directions before pulling through the light.

"Grant?" Aurora's voice greets me.

"Hey, babe. I have a slight change of plans."

"Okay."

"I'm on my way to the hospital."

"Oh, my—What's wrong? What happened?"

"Layla's water broke."

"I'm on my way."

"Drive safe," I tell her.

"See you soon. Take care of her."

"Always." I put my cell back in the cupholder. "Aurora's coming."

"Good. She can keep you calm," she teases. "Sawyer is on her way too. She's going to call your parents, and Marshall and Conrad."

Before I can comment, my phone rings. Owen's name pops up on the dash, so I reach out and hit Accept. "Hey," I answer.

"How is she?"

"I'm fine," Layla answers him.

"How far apart are they?"

"About fifteen minutes or so."

"I'm sorry I'm not there," Owen says, and he sounds tortured. Then again, I can imagine that he's worried about not being here for her.

"You have nothing to apologize for. We re—" she starts but grabs the door handle and grips her mouth shut.

"Lay? Baby, what's happening?" Owen asks, panicked.

"Contraction," I tell him.

"How long?"

"About ten minutes since the last one. I just pulled up to the Emergency Room. I'll text you and let you know what room we're in."

"Fuck. Okay. Thanks, man. Layla, I'm on my way. I'll be there in twenty minutes."

"Take your time. Drive safe. You're not going to miss it."

"I love you."

"I love you too."

"All right, bro. We gotta go."

"Take care of her, Grant. Both of them."

"I've got this," I tell him. I end the call and turn to Layla. "You stay here. I'm going to go grab a wheelchair."

"Definitely glad it was you." She grins. "I'll be right here."

"Grant." I look up to find Aurora and Aspen walking toward me with large bags in their hands. "How is she?"

"Good. Owen is in there with her. He and Royce just got here." I stand and give her a kiss. "What's in the bags?" I ask, then turn to Aspen. "Hey." I pull her into a hug.

"We brought food."

"By food, she means baked goods. But we can go back out for dinner later. This should hold everyone over for now," Aspen says, placing her bag on the small table.

"You didn't have to do that," I tell her.

"I wanted to. I usually donate it all at the end of the day anyway, so I figured I might as well bring it here for everyone to enjoy."

"By everyone, she means the staff too."

"You never donate that much," I say, pulling her into my lap.

"I might have grabbed a few extras."

"Babe, that's profit."

"Yeah, but this is a big deal. I can whip up the things we brought in no time."

"You work too much already."

"Well, it's a good thing my boyfriend talked me into hiring some help. I have interviews set up for next week."

"Really?" I can't hold back my smile. "That's more time with you."

"It's going to take some time to get someone hired and trained, but yeah, that's the goal."

"And you—" I look over at Aspen, who's sitting across from us, "you need to get out more."

"Meh." She waves her hand in the air. "Dating is overrated."

"Isn't that the truth," Aurora mutters.

"Hey!" I tickle her side.

"Sorry, not you, but you know what I mean," she rushes to say.

"I know. Lucky for you, you don't have to deal with that anymore."

"Lucky me," she says, kissing me lightly.

"The cavalry has arrived," Conrad says, taking a seat next to Aspen. My parents and Marshall are right behind him.

"What did we miss?" Mom asks, as Sawyer and Sam appear in the doorway.

I quickly fill them in on what I know, and everyone settles in for what is sure to be a long night. I'm holding Aurora in my arms, watching as my two younger brothers flirt with her sister. I hate to break it to them, but she's not interested. At least, I don't think she is.

"Are you excited?" Aurora asks, her voice is low just for me.

"I am. I can't imagine what Owen is feeling right now."

"You want kids?"

"Yeah. You?"

She nods. "I never really thought it would happen for me. I convinced myself that it wouldn't."

"And now?"

"And now I've met this amazing guy who has turned my world upside down, and I'm hopeful."

"This will be us one day. You and I will be the ones adding a new little Riggins to the clan."

"Big dreams," she says, kissing my cheek.

It's more than big dreams. It's facts. It's plans for our future. She's come such a long way in the past few months, so I'm not going to press the issue. We're not there yet, but we will be. One day this will be us, and I for one can't wait.

CHAPTER
Aurora
TWENTY FOUR

I'M RUNNING ON fumes—fumes and very strong coffee. I stayed at the hospital until after nine, which was later than I should have. I just had a hard time leaving Grant there without me. He insisted on Aspen and I going home and getting some sleep. What he didn't know is that I had to come home and replace everything that I took to the hospital for today. I was fine with it. I wanted to help, and by the time I left, almost everything that I brought had been eaten. I was up until midnight, not because I needed to be, but because I went ahead and did some prep for today. I was back up at three, and to say my ass is dragging is an understatement.

"I'm so tired," Aspen says, plopping onto a stool behind the counter.

"You didn't have to stay up with me last night."

"I know, but I wanted to. Not to mention I couldn't sleep. Being on baby watch is exhausting."

"Yes, but he's such a cutie. I can't wait to see him." Layla delivered a healthy baby boy at four this morning. I was in the middle of pulling my first batch of apple fritters from the oven when the call came in. I could hear the happiness in Grant's voice when he told me the news. That baby boy is going to be so spoiled; it's not even funny.

"Did they decide on a name? We got busy, and I forgot to ask."

I nod. "Carter Owen Riggins." I can't hide my smile.

"Aw," Aspen coos. "Let me see the picture again." She holds her hand out for my phone. I pass it over, and she pulls up the message. "It's hard to look at him and not want that," she says, smiling down at my phone.

"Yeah," I agree.

"At least you have a man, which you need for this to happen." She hands my phone back to me.

"You don't need a man to have a baby, but that's the way I would prefer."

"Me too. But I'm too tired to say my own name, let alone think about dating."

"Go to bed. I'm going to lock up and run over to the hospital."

"Are you not dead on your feet?"

"I am, but I want to check on everyone."

"Are you going back later?"

"Probably." I shrug. "Grant mentioned going back to his place for a little while, then taking over dinner or something."

"I imagine that Lena has that covered."

I laugh. "I'm sure she does. Anyway, go to sleep. I'll keep you posted."

"You don't have to tell me twice. Be safe," she says, turning and heading through the kitchen to the back stairwell that leads to our apartment.

I finish wiping down the counters and grab my purse and phone. Realizing I forgot to bring the sign in from the sidewalk out front, I place my things on the counter and snatch the keys. Unlocking and pushing open the door, I grab the sign.

"Hello, Aurora." A voice I never wanted to hear again greets me.

I close my eyes, wishing and willing for me to be wrong before slowly turning to face him. "Elijah."

"I heard you had a nice little place downtown. I see you've continued to ignore my request to give up this hobby that's obviously not good for you," he says, skimming his eyes over my body.

"What are you doing here?" I spit out the question. The disgust at seeing him again is clear in my tone of voice. I grip the sign in front of me, using it as a barrier between us. I never thought I would see him again, and now that he's standing here in front of me, I hold my breath, waiting for all the self-loathing to return with a vengeance.

Nothing happens.

I'm a stronger person. I've changed. Images of Grant pop into my head. It's incredible what the love of a good man can do for you.

"Can I not come and visit my fiancée?"

"Are you fucking kidding me?" I hiss. "I am not your fiancée. You left me. On our wedding day," I add, just in case his delusional ass needed a reminder.

"Aurora," he tsks. "Did you really think that I would marry you?" He laughs maniacally.

I think he's lost his damn mind. "Leave." He's always been cruel, but this manic, harried man standing before me is something new. Something foreign that I want no part of. He is my past, and that's where I'd like for him to stay.

"This is a public sidewalk." He waves his arms around. "Besides, we need to talk."

"I have nothing to say to you." I'm not even mad at him. I'm just... indifferent, I guess. Sure, I hate the way he treated me, but I let it happen. I stood by and took the proverbial hits. I stayed. It's not all on him.

"You owe me," he seethes, taking a step closer.

"You're fucking crazy. I don't owe you a damn thing."

"You're wrong. I let you live with me for over a year."

"I paid my share of the bills, and I bought all the food that you claimed I was the only one who ate it!" I say, my voice raising an octave.

"You owe me," he says, spittle flying from his mouth. His eyes are dark, and he legit looks as if he's not slept in days.

"Leave." My voice is loud. Firm. Decisive.

"Ma'am, are you all right?" An older gentleman approaches us slowly.

"He was just leaving." I point to Elijah.

"We can do this the easy way or the hard way. I need cash, and I need it now."

"I owe you nothing. I haven't seen you in almost two years. You show up out of the blue demanding money after you left me on our wedding day. I don't think so. Get lost before I call the cops."

"You're going to regret this, you fat bitch!" he roars.

"Hey, that's enough of that. You best be moving on." The older man steps in.

"This isn't over." Elijah points at me before turning and stalking off.

"Are you okay?" the man asks.

"Yes." I stand taller, pushing my shoulders back. I am okay. I'm stronger without him. "Thank you," I tell him, offering him my hand to shake.

"We should call the police," he offers.

"Nah. He's all bark and no bite. He's a bully from my past."

"He's wrong, you know," he says, watching me closely. "You're not fat, and I don't know you, but I can tell from our brief interaction, and how you're handling yourself, you're not a bitch either. Don't let his hate darken your good."

Tears prick my eyes. "Thank you. I appreciate you stepping in. Come on in, and I'll give you some treats to take home."

"That's not necessary, but my wife, my Susie, she'd love this place," he says, peering in the windows. "I think I'll stop back by sometime when she's with me."

"Well, it's on the house…" I say, not knowing his name.

"George. Name's George. And you are?"

"Aurora. Aurora Steele."

"I'll be seeing you, Miss Aurora." With that, he leaves me standing in front of my bakery. I watch him walk away until I can no longer see him. Lifting the sign, I head back inside and lock the door. I'm quick to type in the code, just in case Elijah does have some bark in him after all.

Tiptoeing up the steps, I peek in on Aspen and see that she's sleeping soundly. I debate on waking her up to tell her, but I know she's exhausted. I'll just tell her when I get home. I change my clothes so I don't smell like a bakery and head out. As soon as I'm in my car, my cell phone rings. I smile when I see *Mom* flash across the screen.

"Hey," I answer, pulling out onto the street.

"How are things?"

"Good. Layla had the baby," I tell her.

"Oh, good. I hope everyone is well."

"Yes. Grant texted me a picture. He is the cutest little boy ever."

"I want to see when you have time."

"Absolutely. So—" I pause, debating on whether I should tell her but decide to just go for it. "I had a visitor just a few minutes ago. I was taking the sidewalk sign down before leaving for the hospital."

"Okay. Are you going to tell me who it was?"

"Elijah."

"Oh, dear," Mom says. "Aurora—" she starts, but I interrupt her.

"I told him to get lost. Mom, I felt nothing. Not even anger. Sure, I was mad that he was there, but it's all in the past. To be honest, I'm glad he showed up. It's the proof and closure I needed. He's no longer a person of significance in my life."

"Wow. That's not what I was expecting you to say. Then again, I shouldn't be surprised. Moving to Nashville has been good for you." I can hear the smile along with the approval in her voice. "What did he want?"

"Get this. He says that I owe him money."

"For what?" Mom asks in disbelief.

"Apparently because I lived with him for over a year. He's full of it, Mom. I paid for all the groceries and my half of the bills. He looked like he might have been strung out on something, or maybe had no sleep for a few days. Something was definitely off with him."

"You girls need to make sure you're locking your doors and using the alarm system."

"We are. We'll be fine. I can handle Elijah. He's a bully. He's not physically abusive."

"I don't know, Rory. If he is on something, he sounds desperate, and that changes a person."

"We'll be careful. Listen, I just pulled into the hospital. I'm going to go in and get my baby Carter fix. I'll call you later."

"Send me pictures. Love you."

"Love you too. Tell Dad hello," I say, ending the call.

"He's so tiny." I stare down at the perfect baby boy in my arms. Grant is kneeling next to me.

"Didn't feel tiny," Layla jokes.

I look up to see her tired smile. You can tell she's exhausted from a long labor, but she's a trooper, and her smile tells me that all the pain was worth it. Not that I would think anything less. I'm not a mother, but I can imagine it's the best feeling.

Carter stretches in my arms, and I pull back his blanket, giving his little arms and legs the space he needs to do his thing. "Feel better, buddy?" I ask once he's finished. I try to wrap him back up, like the little burrito that he is, but I'm going to need to lay him down.

"Dad's got this," Owen says. He walks around the bed and takes him from my arms. I stick my lip out in a pout, and he chuckles. "I'll give him right back. I've perfected the burrito," he tells me. His blue eyes are also shining with so much love and happiness. It's radiating off both of them.

"I need to watch this," Grant says, standing.

"Something you're not telling us, little brother?" Owen asks.

"Nope. Trust me. If this was my future, I'd be screaming it from the rooftops. I need to work on my burrito skills if I'm going to claim the favorite uncle title," he says.

Layla and I both burst out laughing, not because of the "favorite uncle" remark, but because Grant's gaze is focused. He's concentrating on watching Owen, who is also the model of concentration.

"How are you feeling, Momma?" I ask her.

"Good. Tired and sore, but happy."

I nod. "He's perfect," I say, glancing back at Carter, who is now the perfect little baby burrito. "Gimme." I hold my hands out for him, and Owen smiles. He kisses his son on top of his head and places him back in my arms.

"Looks like Aurora is going for favorite aunt," Owen jokes.

My heart swells at the thought of being a part of this family. Of being here to watch this little boy grow up. Watching his Mom and Dad be amazing parents, and his four uncles compete for his affection, which he will surely figure out as he gets older and takes full advantage of them. As he should.

"What's that smile for?" Grant asks.

"Nothing. Just picturing you and your brothers spoiling this little guy rotten to be the favorite uncle."

"Oh, it's going to happen," he agrees.

The four of us talk for a little while, and when Layla covers her yawn for the third time, I know it's time to let them get some rest, and just the thought of rest has exhaustion washing over me too. It's been a long couple of days, and I could use a nap. "You ready?" I ask Grant.

"Yeah." He takes Carter from my arms, whispers something I can't hear into his ear, kisses his head, and then hands him off to his dad. "We're going to head out. If you all need anything, you call us."

"We will. Mom and Dad are coming back later, so are Conrad and Marshall. Royce and Sawyer were here earlier."

"They'll be back." Grant chuckles. "Get used to it. This little guy is the most popular Riggins."

With a round of hugs, we're out the door. "Why don't you ride home with me? We'll come back later and get your car."

"Depends. Are you going to let me sleep? I'm running on about three hours."

"Yes. And now you no longer get the choice. I'm not letting you drive that exhausted."'

"You slept here," I remind him.

"Yes, but I went home and got a shower and about five or so hours of sleep before I came back."

"I need food too," I tell him. My eyes widen in surprise. I can't believe I just said that.

"I'll swing through a drive-through and get us something." When we reach his SUV, he pulls me into his chest and buries his face in my neck. "I fucking love you, Aurora."

"What brought this on?" I ask, even though I already know.

"You. You're opening up to me. You're trusting me, and, baby, I've got to tell you. I love it when you tell me what you want. From food to the bedroom, I love your confidence."

"That's all you."

"No, that's all you." Standing on my tiptoes, I press my lips to his. "It's your kisses, they're magic."

"I definitely believe in the magic," he says, stepping back to pull open the door for me.

I'm not certain that I believe in magic, but I do believe in him— in the man who has loved me back to life.

CHAPTER
Grant
TWENTY FIVE

I T'S SUNDAY MORNING. I'm lying in bed with my sexy as fuck girlfriend curled up against my side, and I can't help but think that life doesn't get any better than this. With each day that passes, Aurora and I grow closer. Not only do we grow closer, but she's opening up more each day. She's her own person, and she's fucking vibrant.

"Morning," she says, giving me a sleepy smile.

"Good morning." I kiss her temple.

"What are we doing today?"

"Owen texted me." I hold up my phone that's lying beside me in the bed. "He's trying to rally up the troops to get everyone out on the boat today."

"The boat? It's the beginning of May. Isn't the water still too cold?"

"Nah, we won't get in. Not on purpose." I chuckle. "I guess he wants to get him and Layla out of the house for a few hours. Mom and Dad are going to watch Carter. He's a month old today, and Layla has barely left the house. I think my brother's feeling a little neglected from his wife. What do you say?"

"Sure, I just need to shower, and I need to check my mail. I haven't been to the post office since Wednesday. And I bet your parents are going to be over the moon. As far as Owen being neglected, I doubt that, but I know he loves Layla fiercely and some mom-and-dad time is never a bad thing; in fact it's good for all parents to get a break."

"I agree with you. Owen and Layla know they will be close, and it will more than likely be a quick trip out on the lake. Just enough to get us all some fresh air. Now, how about you get your fine ass in the shower, I'll run to the post office for you, and when I get back, we can stop by my place so I can shower?"

"Sure. I wish Aspen were here. She'd love this."

"What time is she getting home?"

"I don't know. I'm sure Mom will keep her there as long as she can."

"Call her. She's more than welcome."

"Okay. She's going to be sad she missed it. She was leery about leaving for the wedding anyway. But like I told her, we can't let this place control our lives. I spend a lot of time with you, and she's just here hanging out on her own. She's made a few new friends, but I still worry about her."

"We should plan a night out. I'll put Conrad and Marshall on that. They'll be all over it."

"That sounds like something she would love." She laughs. "My keys are on the counter. The post office key is on there. Thank you, babe."

"I'm on it." I climb out of bed, and she rolls over on her belly.

"This bed feels cold and way too big without you in it."

"Mine's a king. How do you think I feel?" I ask her. Sliding into my jeans, I button them and quickly pull my shirt over my head. "Get moving, lazybones." I smack her on the ass and head for the small living room.

After slipping into my shoes and socks, I grab her keys and make my way down the steps. The post office is just two blocks over, so I decide to walk. It's a nice morning, warmer than normal for early May. It's going to be a great day to be out on the water. Maybe a little chilly with the wind, but I'm still looking forward to it. Not only do I love being out on the lake, and the first time of the season is always full of anticipation after a long winter, but this time Aurora is going to be there with me. That alone is a game-changer.

I'm headed back to the bakery with my arms full of mail. I need to remember to check this for her at least every other day. I know her hours are crazy and she's exhausted trying to do it all on her own. Well, with just her and Aspen. She's finally placed an ad in the paper that's supposed to go out today. Her previous interviews didn't show up. Hopefully, she gets some good candidates out of the ad so they can both get a break.

As I round the corner, I spy a man with his face pressed to the glass of the bakery. "Hey!" I call out to him as I quicken my steps. "Can I help you with something?" I ask him.

"Nah, just looking for my fiancée."

"Well, the bakery is closed today." Something about this guy is off. He's shady at best.

He nods, mumbling something under his breath. "You should probably get going," I tell him.

"Yeah," he says, turning to look back into the bakery windows. "She knows I'm around," he says cryptically.

I'm ready to tell him to move the fuck on when he turns and walks away. I watch him go until I can no longer see him. An uneasy feeling sits in my gut. I'm not getting a good vibe from this guy. I need to make sure Aurora and Aspen both know to keep an eye out, and I need to get someone in here to take a look at their security system. Hell, maybe they should move in with me for a while. My condo has three bedrooms, one is an office, but we only need two. Aurora can room with me.

Unlocking the door, I slip inside, ensuring that it's locked and the door is pulled tight. I take the stairs two at a time. "Aurora!" I call out for her.

She sticks her head out of her bedroom door. "What's wrong?"

"Nothing. There was just some creepy guy standing outside the bakery, and my first instinct is to make sure you're okay. Even though I knew you were." I take the final few steps down the hall and press my lips to hers. "I have your mail. I'm going to have to start checking this for you. Look at all of this." I hold up the stack of mail.

"That's unusual. We're on paperless billing for most of our accounts. We hardly ever have any mail. Just place it on the counter in the kitchen, and I'll look at it later."

Going back to the kitchen, I place the mail on the counter and grab a bottle of water out of the fridge, just as she comes out dressed and ready to go. "Ready?" she asks.

"Change of plans, we're just going to stay home." I let my eyes roam over her curves and fuck me, I want to take her back to bed.

"What? Why?"

"Because you look hot as fuck, and we have the place to ourselves."

"Actually, we don't. Aspen is on her way home. She's going to meet us at your parents' place in an hour."

"Fine." I pretend to be put out when I'm anything but. "I guess we better get moving. You want one?" I hold up my bottle of water.

"Yes." I reach into the fridge and grab her a bottle, following her to the front door. "I'm going to have a guy come out and check your security system. That guy freaked me out. I hate the two of you living here all alone."

"We're big girls, Grant. We can handle it," she says on our way to my SUV.

"I knew you would say that. That's why I didn't start with the two of you staying with me." I toss the suggestion out there. I open her door for her, lean in, and press a kiss to her lips before rounding the SUV and sliding behind the wheel.

"No. That's crazy. We're fine. Don't let some random stranger make you paranoid."

"When the love of my life has some lunatic snooping around her closed bakery looking for his fiancée, I have a right to be worried."

"Calm down, hulk," she teases. "You can have your guy come check out the system, but I know it's good. I had it installed new when I leased the building."

"How long is your lease?"

"A year. I wanted six months, but I couldn't get them to agree to the shorter terms. Luckily, it's worked out, and here I am six months later and still going strong."

"Because you kick ass."

"Oh, go on," she jokes.

"Is Sunday dinner still on for tonight?" she asks.

"Yes."

"What time do we have to meet everyone at the lake?"

"Not until two."

"Aspen is going to be there at noon. Do you care if I have her come to your place to hang out? And can we stop at the store."

"Yes, she's always welcome, and yes we can stop at the store. Wait, what do we need from the store?"

"I want to make something to take to dinner. We could always go back to the bakery."

"No. I like the idea of you baking in my kitchen. Preferably, naked, but I'm thinking Aspen wouldn't like that too much."

"She'd cheer us on." She laughs, digging in her purse for her phone.

I love that she's so carefree these days. She doesn't clam up when I talk about intimacy or tell her that she's beautiful. I'm damn proud of how strong she is and how quickly she let the past fall behind her—where it needs to stay.

"Hey, a slight change of plans. We're not meeting until two at the lake, so you should just come to Grant's and hang out." She pauses. "Okay. See you soon and drive safe."

"She coming?"

"Yep. She's making good time, so she should be there in about thirty minutes."

"Sounds like Aspen has a lead foot."

"The open road with no traffic and the radio blaring, it's easy to do."

"Here we are," I say, pulling into the grocery store. "I need to pick up a few things anyway." Together we make our way into the store. I grab a cart and begin to navigate each aisle while we both toss things into the cart. It's very domestic, and I don't hate it.

"Stop." Aurora swats at my hand as I try to sneak another one of her magic bars.

"I can't help it. They're so good," I say, popping one into my mouth. "And it's magic." I wink at her, licking my lips.

She shakes her head, a smile playing on her lips. "I'll give you magic."

"You two do remember that I'm sitting right here?" Aspen asks, a smile wide on her face. "I might need therapy after watching the two of you and let's not get me started on the fact that you two are couple goals times one million. My expectations are high." She points at me. "Thanks for that. Now I'm going to die a lonely old cat lady."

"Who's getting a cat?" Conrad asks, walking into the kitchen.

"Con, we've talked about this. You have to start knocking."

"I saw Aspen's car in the drive. I knew you two love birds weren't getting your freak on with her here, or who knows—" He shrugs. "You three might be into that kind of thing."

"Nope. No. Just no," Aspen says vehemently.

"So, no girl-on-girl-on-guy. Are you into two...?" He raises two fingers in the air with one hand and points to his crotch with the other.

"S-Stop!" Aspen sputters with laughter. "We are not discussing my sex life or the lack thereof."

"Aw, sweetness, you need me to help you out with that?"

"Have you been tested?" she fires back.

"Yep. And, I've had all my shots." Conrad smirks.

"How do you handle this? All this Riggins testosterone all the time?" she asks her sister.

"They know she's mine," I answer for her.

"Oh, Aurora knows that if she wants a real man, that I can show her around," Conrad says confidently.

"Out." I point to the door. "You're no longer welcome here. Don't be slinging your game at my girl." I'm kidding, and we all know it. Mostly. I know he's my brother and would never make a move, but the thought of any man other than me touching Aurora still has my hackles raised.

"There!" Conrad points back at me, grinning triumphantly. "You admit I've got game." He nods. "I'm telling you, Aspen, I can help you out with the dry spell." He winks at her.

"We should leave them. Give them some alone time." I slide up behind Aurora and wrap my arms around her waist. "We should definitely use our time wisely," I say, kissing her neck.

"That—" Aspen points to us. "How am I supposed to have realistic expectations of a man when this is what I'm witness to?"

Conrad places his hand over his chest. "Aspen, beautiful, you wound me. Am I not man enough for you?" he asks.

I watch with amusement as she takes her time looking him over from head to toe. "Meh," she replies.

Aurora and I both crack up laughing, and Conrad just shakes his head. He's a Riggins. He knows he has the looks and the bank account. He grew up in the same house as me, watching our father love our mother with every ounce of his soul. My guess is his game is definitely on point.

CHAPTER
TWENTY SIX
Aurora

"**T**HAT WAS SO much fun," Aspen says, plopping down on the couch in our apartment. "When can we do it again?" she asks Grant.

"Whenever you want. If I can't take you out, I'm sure Conrad or Marshall will."

"I can't believe that you grew up doing that every summer. I'm jealous," she says with a wistful smile.

"It was pretty badass," Grant agrees with her. He takes a seat in the chair and pats his lap for me to sit.

"I need to go through all that mail," I say, grabbing the stack and moving to sit on the floor between his legs.

"Take the chair." He starts to stand, but I stop him.

"I'm fine. I'm going to pull the table close and sort through this madness." I place the stack on the table and grab the first envelope. "Anyone need an extended warranty on their car?" I ask, skimming the paper, seeing that it's most definitely junk mail, and tossing it to the side. Reaching for the next one, I repeat the same process. I'm about seven or eight items in when I tear open an envelope that has me sitting up straighter. "What the hell?" I ask out loud.

"What is it?" Aspen turns her head to look at me from where she's still lying on the couch.

"This says that our loan payment bounced. How is that possible? The checking account is with the same bank the loan is through." My eyes skim over the statement again.

"There must be some kind of mix-up," Aspen says.

"I'm sure if you call them in the morning, you'll get it all figured out," Grant offers.

"I just don't understand how that happens." I say, setting the letter to the side and reaching for another. My mind is still on how our loan payment to the bank that my checking account is with would bounce. "Maybe they put my deposit in Aspen's account or something?" I muse. Shaking out of my thoughts, I finish opening the electric bill.

Past Due.

"I paid this. I know I did." Moving the table back, I climb to my feet and grab my purse. I take a seat next to Aspen and dig out my checkbook. "See." I hold it up for them to see even though I'm sure they can't make it out. "I paid that two weeks ago. What the hell is going on?" I ask. I can feel my panic start to rise. Why would two bills not go through? "They're saying we're a month behind. I paid this bill." I look over at Grant. He looks concerned, and that look on his face is just another reason why I love him.

"I'm sure it's a simple mix-up. Maybe they did put your money in Aspen's account. Your names both start with A. It must have been an oversight."

"Here, let me pull up my account." Aspen sits up, and her fingers fly across the screen of her phone. I can tell from the look on her face, our assumption is wrong. "It's not in my account. The check you paid me bounced." She holds her phone up for me to see.

"What?" I whisper.

"Yeah, I mean, I have money in there, so I'm not overdrawn or anything, but it says it bounced. They deducted the full amount plus a fee from my account."

"Aurora, you have online banking too, right?" Grant asks.

I nod, already digging my phone out of my purse. I quickly log in and what I see has bile rising in my throat. "I-It's negative," I choke out. "Thousands of dollars in the negative."

"What?" Grant and my sister ask at the same time.

"Rory, that's not possible. You are meticulous with your bank account and finances. What the fuck is going on?" Aspen asks.

Grant stands and pulls me to my feet. It's not until he wraps his arms around me do I realize that I'm trembling. I had enough money in that account for almost a year's worth of expenses. The bakery has done really well, and I've been saving. Now it's all just gone.

Gone.

How could this have happened?

"Baby, I need you to breathe," Grant says soothing, running his hand up and down my back. Doing as he asks, I focus on taking in a deep breath and slowly exhaling. "Again," he says, his voice calm and soothing. I repeat the process several times until I feel myself start to calm down.

"I don't know what's going on. How could this happen?" I look up at Grant as the first tear slides across my cheek.

Gently, he wipes it away with his thumb. "Where do you bank?'

"Nashville Horizon."

"Okay. This is what's going to happen. You're going to sit with Aspen while I make some calls. Can you do that for me?"

"Yeah." Moving out of his arms, I take a seat next to Aspen, and she pulls me into a hug.

"Babe, I'm going to need your account information."

"My checkbook is there, and I'll give you whatever else you need."

He bends and presses his lips to my forehead. "I love you. I'm going to get to the bottom of this." He grabs my checkbook and stalks off toward the kitchen with his phone already at his ear.

"I can't believe this. Just when I think all is going right in the world, life knocks you back on your ass."

"It's okay. Grant is going to find out what happened. Have faith."

"Should someone not have called me? Are thousands of dollars missing from someone's account, not a huge red fucking flag? Come on. Something isn't right here. I just don't know what it is."

Grant comes back into the room, his phone still pressed to his ear. "Thanks, Owen," he says before ending the call.

"So, Riggins Enterprises has a relationship with Nashville Horizon. Owen is the chief financial officer, so he works with them more than the rest of us. He's going to make some calls and get back to me."

"It's Sunday night," I remind him.

"I know, but Riggins runs a hell of a lot of money through that bank. He'll answer for Owen. We might not have answers tonight, but there will be a fire under their ass. Especially since Owen is going to make sure he knows that they're fucking with his brother's fiancée."

I cough at the word fiancée. "W-What?"

"I had to give him leverage for why he was calling. If they think we're going to pull our accounts, they'll get to the bottom of this. I promise you that."

"I don't get it. I'm just a small business."

"Yes, but you're engaged to a millionaire." He smirks.

"Millionaire?" I know that my mouth is hanging open right now, but I'm shocked.

"Just one of the many things I love about you, Aurora. You don't give a shit about my money."

"No. I would never—" I start, and he leans down, pressing his lips to mine.

"I know that, baby. That's why I said it. Besides, the look on your face is a dead giveaway."

"Is kissing always the answer to getting her to shut up? No wonder nothing has worked for me over the years," Aspen jokes, trying to lighten the mood.

"I don't know, babe? What do you think? Are my kisses distracting?"

"Very," I admit, with not a single ounce of shame.

"You've ruined romance for me, Riggins," Aspen whines. "You're not a normal man, are you? Are you some kind of alien from outer space?" she teases.

"I'm a man who loves your sister, and it's nothing more and nothing less than that."

"See what I mean? Men don't talk like that."

"I know six that do," he counters.

"Anyone with the last name of Riggins doesn't count. You're all aliens." She sputters with laughter. "You, my dear sister, are engaged to an alien who's going to give you adorable little alien babies."

"He's not an alien, and we're not engaged." There is a pulling in my chest. It's a yearning, and it hits me that I want to be engaged again. I'm no longer afraid to think about the future, and I know without a shadow of a doubt that if I'm ever lucky enough for Grant to propose to me, that he will not leave me at the church, in my dress with tears, and in embarrassment, alongside a blanket of regret.

He's one of the good ones.

"You know, I have two single brothers." He raises his eyebrows at Aspen.

"You're like a brother to me." She wrinkles up her nose.

"But they're not."

"Guilty by association." She shakes her head, as if dating one of his brothers is the craziest idea she's ever heard in her entire life.

"What's that saying about the lady protesting too much?" Grant teases as his phone rings.

He taps at the screen, holding his phone out in front of him. "What did you find out?" he asks.

"Not a lot," Owen replies on loudspeaker. "Martin Hamilton, the CEO of that branch, doesn't really know his ass from a hole in the ground when it comes to the inner workings of the operations. However, what he does know is that Riggins Enterprises runs millions of dollars through his bank. Once I told him Aurora was your fiancée, he changed his tune. We need to be at the bank in the morning at eight to sit down and see what we can find out. I can guarantee you he's not going to get much sleep tonight as he starts to look into this."

"Thank you, Owen."

"You're family." He says it so simple as if it's written in stone. Or, in my case, a marriage certificate.

"Thanks, man," Grant tells him. "I owe you one."

"Nah, he's a prick. I don't mind going head to head with him. You want me to meet you all there, or are we meeting somewhere else first?"

"You're going? You don't have to do that. You have your job and Layla and Carter."

"I have nothing pressing at the office that can't wait, and my wife and son are going to be at home, safe. I'm going to be there, Aurora. I've dealt with this guy on behalf of Riggins. He knows I have the power to pull our accounts. Something he knows I won't hesitate to do."

"I don't know how to thank you for this. I'm sorry that you're being dragged into my drama. Both of you."

"We love you," both Riggins men reply at the same time, and tears build in my eyes.

"We'll meet you outside the bank at eight in the morning," Grant tells him.

"See you then," Owen replies, and the line goes dead.

Before I have a chance to ask him what he's doing, his phone is ringing, and Lena's voice comes through the line.

"I knew you were my favorite, Grant Riggins. Calling your mom out of the blue." She laughs.

"You know it," Grant replies. "Listen, Mom. I have a favor." He goes on to explain what's going on and how he and I with Owen are meeting at the bank in the morning. "I was hoping you could come to the bakery and help Aspen while we're gone. That's their busy time, and it's a lot for one person."

I didn't even think about that. Shit. I start to tell her we'll just close for the day when her reply comes quick. "Of course, I will. Oh, I'm so excited. What time should I be there?"

"We have to leave there about a quarter till eight."

"What time does it open?"

"Six."

"What time do they get in?" she asks, sounding exasperated.

"Three."

"Perfect. I'll be there when you ladies start your day. I'm excited to see the inner workings. Was that all?" she asks.

I'm shocked by her easy acceptance and willingness to help out. Then as soon as the thought filters through my mind, I know that's wrong. Lena Riggins is a selfless and amazing woman who raise five incredible sons. She's just being who she is. Helping out someone in need. Tomorrow, I'm that someone. I need anyone and everyone in my corner, and I'm blessed to know that the majority of them carry the last name Riggins.

"No. Thank you, Mom. We owe you."

"Great, then I need to get off here and tell your father and get in bed. I'm so excited."

"Thank you, Lena," I finally speak up.

"You're welcome, sweet girl. Is Aspen there?"

"I'm here," she answers.

"Be patient with me." Lena laughs. "I've only ever ran my kitchen."

"It's going to be fine. We appreciate you helping us out in a jam. Besides, if you can handle those five rowdy boys of yours, this will be a walk in the park."

"I love the park," Lena replies, and I can hear the smile in her voice. "No problem at all. I'll see you all bright and early. Love you." The line goes dead, and Grant chuckles.

"She's excited. I should have arranged for her to come and hang out with you two a long time ago." He grins before his face sobers. "Now hopefully, you can sleep better tonight. Aspen and Mom will take care of Warm Delights. You, me, and Owen, we'll get to the bottom of this tomorrow."

Grant and I say goodnight to Aspen and disappear into my room. I doubt I'll get much sleep, but I do know that having Grant in my corner has eased my fears. He's a man of his word, and I know I can count on him. It's freeing, and any love that I thought I had for him tripled tonight. He thought of my sister and me, and he made sure we would both be taken care of.

Grant Riggins is definitely my magic.

CHAPTER
Grant
TWENTY SEVEN

WE WERE BOTH wide awake when the alarm went off. Neither of us dozed more than a few hours the entire night. I don't know who's fucking with her, but I can guarantee that they're going to regret it. All night long, my mind raced with how this could have happened. I didn't mention this to Aurora, but this isn't a clerical mistake. Not with over fifty grand. Something is going on, and I hope like hell we can get to the bottom of it today.

"Thank you, Lena, for being here. I don't know what we would have done without you," Aurora tells my mother.

"Are you kidding? This is the most fun I've had in ages. I love being in the kitchen. You two go on and do what you need to do. Aspen and I've got this covered." Mom walks around the counter and pulls us both into a hug.

"I don't know how long we'll be," I tell them.

"Go," they both say, waving their hands in the air.

"See? We're already finishing each other's sentences," Aspen points out, grinning at Mom. "We'll be fine. Everything is ready to go, and the first morning rush has passed. Go. Do what you need to do. We're good here."

"You want to walk or drive?" I ask Aurora once we're outside in front of the bakery.

"It's just a couple of blocks. Do we have time to walk?"

"Doesn't matter. I can promise you that he's going to be waiting for us as long as it takes."

"Yeah, but Owen too."

"We have time. Let's go." Hand in hand, we begin walking toward the direction of the bank.

"It doesn't matter how many times I turn this over in my head, I can't seem to find a solution that makes sense."

"There has to be a paper trail of some sort. They're going to be able to tell us where your money went. The bigger issue is how did it get there without your consent."

"Maybe I was hacked?"

"I thought about that, but I think we would see charges appear. We're only seeing a negative balance. There is nothing on the dashboard of your online banking that indicates the money was there. Thankfully we have your bank statement from two weeks ago proving your balance, along with your deposit slips since then."

"I guess being organized actually paid off for once."

"We'll figure it out, babe." We're quiet the remainder of the walk, both of us lost in our thoughts.

"You ready for this?" Owen asks as we approach him outside of the bank's main entrance.

I give Aurora's hand a gentle squeeze. "I think a more fitting question. Is he ready for this?" By he, I mean Martin Hamilton, the CEO of Nashville Horizon bank. All I can say is he better have a damn good explanation as to how this happened.

"Thank you both for being here." Aurora looks at Owen, and then up at me.

Owen nods, and I pull her into my side. "Let's see what he has to say," Owen says, tugging open the door and motioning for us to walk in ahead of him. Once inside, we step back and let Owen take the lead. He and I talked earlier this morning and thought that would be best. At least to start.

"Welcome to National Horizon. What can I help you with today?" a young woman sitting at a welcome desk asks.

"Owen Riggins for Martin Hamilton." Owen's tone is clipped and leaves zero room for anyone to think he's not a man of authority or that his distaste for Martin Hamilton isn't present.

"Oh, of course, sir. He's expecting you." She stands and motions for Owen to follow her. "Um, if you just want to have a seat." She motions toward Aurora and me.

"They're with me," Owen says.

"O-Okay, right this way." She turns as fast as she can, placing her back toward us, and leads us to a locked door. She has to try three times to put in the code for us to enter. I have to bite down on my bottom lip and look to the right to avoid laughing. I don't have to see the twitch of Owen's lips to know he's doing the same thing. With the beard and those penetrating eyes of his, my older brother can be an intimidating fucker. The most intimidating out of all of us.

Finally, the lock releases, and we follow her down a long hallway. She stops in front of an elevator and pushes the up arrow. Silence surrounds us as the doors slide open, and the four of us step inside.

I watch as she presses the button for the sixth floor—Aurora's hand trembles in mine. We damn well better get some answers. I hate that this has happened to her, and I won't stop until I get to the bottom of it. The elevator doors slide open, and we file out, following along behind the young woman who stops at another reception desk. "Mr. Riggins for Mr. Hamilton," she says, her voice shaking.

Nashville Horizon is one of the largest banks in the city and employs some of the best financial investment bankers around. That's why Riggins banks here, but we're prepared to change that.

Owen talked to Royce, Conrad, Marshall, and Dad last night after he talked to me. They're all prepared to pull our business if necessary. The text came in around midnight. That tells me my family has a plan, and that plan includes having Aurora's back. Not that I expected anything different.

The woman behind the desk pushes her glasses up her nose and lets her eyes linger over the three of us. They stop on Aurora, and her eyes widen. I'm about to ask her what the fuck her deal is when Martin himself appears from a doorway just across the hall.

"Owen," he greets.

"Mr. Riggins," Owen counters. He's got his game face on.

"Right. Mr. Riggins, Mr. Riggins." He nods to me. "Ms. Steele, I presume?"

"This is my fiancée," I tell him. I release her hand and move mine to the small of her back.

"Come on in," Martin says, refusing to make further eye contact. "Lucy, hold my calls," the bastard says like he's something special. Little does he know we'll have his fucking job if this isn't cleared up.

"Yes, sir," Lucy says, her voice shaking.

I'm not sure what this chick's issue is, but it's not my problem either. It's time to get some answers.

"Martin," Owen says, deliberately using his first name. It's a kick in the nuts to him, knowing that Owen refuses to let him use his own. "What have you got for us?" Owen turns to Aurora and points to one of the guest chairs directly across from Martin's desk. She takes the hint and moves to sit. I stand behind her with my hands on her shoulders, with Owen standing next to me.

"Well, I'm afraid that I don't have the best news, Mr. Riggins," he says, his gaze locked on me.

"You're stalling." Owen crosses his arms over his chest.

"Well, it appears that Ms. Steele's fiancé has withdrawn the funds from their joint account." He smirks.

My blood boils.

Fiancé? I'm her fucking fiancé, or at least I'm going to be. I look down to find Aurora turns in her seat, peering up at me. There is confusion written all over her face. My gut tells me that this isn't her cheating on me or playing me for our money.

Looking up at Martin, I pin him with a deadly stare. "I need a name."

"Elijah Daniels." He smirks.

"What?" Aurora is out of her seat. "That man is not my fiancé. Not anymore. We were engaged, and he stood me up on our wedding day," she says before the first tears begin to fall. "How does he even have access to this account?"

"You opened the account together," he says, holding a folder out.

Owen grabs it and takes a look at what's inside. "These are copies. I want the originals. Now," he adds.

"No, we most certainly did not. I don't want anything to do with him. My sister and I opened that account when we moved to Nashville."

"Well, I-I—" Martin stumbles over his words.

"Let me tell you how this is going to go. You're going to leave this room and not come back until you have the originals in hand. If it was electronic, I need to see the date and time stamp of the signature. And before you tell me you don't have that information, don't waste your breath on the lie. I know you do." Owen tosses the folder in the chair and takes a step forward, placing his hand on the desk. Leaning over, his voice is lethal. "I want those documents. You have one hour to retrieve them, or Riggins pulls their money, and this bank will be hit with a lawsuit that will have the walls of this six-story building crumbling all around you." He stands to his full height. "We'll be here waiting."

"R-Right. I-I'll just go get those," Martin says, hurrying from the room.

"Grant," Aurora cries. "What's going on? How could Elijah have access to my account?"

I don't know what to say to her. My mind is still trying to catch up to my heart that tells me she's not in on this scam that's being played. That this isn't some ploy for her to extort money from me. I know her. I know she's not capable of something like this, but the years of women chasing me and my brothers for our money... Hell, Royce's ex-wife comes to mind, and my mind is a little slow to get on the same page as my heart. So, I keep my lips clamped shut because I'm not sure what to say or to think right now. I'm smart enough to know she didn't do it, but these conflicting feelings are racing through me. I just need a minute. Instead of my words, I place my hands back on her shoulders and give them a gentle squeeze.

"Rory." Owen sits in the seat next to her, placing the folder on Martin's desk. I watch as he reaches over and takes her hands in his. "I trust you. I need you to know that before we have this conversation. However, I need to ask these questions for the sake of absolute clarity. You with me?" he asks her.

"Y-Yes."

"Who is Elijah Daniels?"

She keeps her eyes on him as she begins to tell the story. "He was my fiancé." She goes on to tell him about the mental and verbal abuse he threw at her and how he pretty much ignored her when her gran died and then left her sitting at the church just minutes before they were supposed to be married.

"Bastard," Owen seethes, his eyes catching mine.

I can't speak for the anger coursing through my veins, hearing the story all over again. My arms ache to hold her, to take this all away. I remember the night she told me her past, and my mind finally catches up. She has nothing to do with this. I know that. I feel like a fucking tool for even considering it.

"When did you open your account here?" Owen asks.

"When we moved here. I had a small inheritance from my grandmother. I used most of it for the lease on the bakery, and the little I had left went into my account here. They gave me a loan for the renovations. That's how this mess started. I got a letter telling me that my payment failed."

"Is there anyone else on the account?"

She nods. "Aspen." Her tear-filled eyes find mine, and I break. After walking around her chair, I drop to my knees and cradle her face in the palm of my hands.

"We're going to figure this out. I promise," I say, leaning in and kissing her forehead.

"I'm sorry. When he showed up at the bakery, he wanted money. He said I owed him, and he looked... crazy. I just blew it off to him being him. He told me that he would get it one way or the other, but I didn't take his threat as serious. His words hurt me for so long, and seeing him... it was like my time with him didn't exist. You healed me, Grant, and I just wanted him to go away. I ignored him, and he left. I haven't heard from him since."

"He came to see you?" My voice is tight. I don't want to yell at her, but fuck me, she should have told me about this. She nods. "Why didn't you tell me?" My question seems to light something inside her. A fire I've never seen before. She sits up taller, squaring her shoulders, and although tears are still falling from her eyes, she locks her gaze on me, and I know that whatever she's about to say is going to tip my world on its axis.

CHAPTER
Aurora
TWENTY EIGHT

"**H**E STOLE MY life from me. He annihilated my spirit and broke my faith in men. He tore me down and left me when he knew I was the most vulnerable. I've told you the basics, but do you know what it's like for a man to tell you to not eat for at least a month, if not longer, in order to look good in your wedding dress?" I pause when Grant's hands drop from my face and his fists clench. "Every day he would ridicule what I was wearing, how bad I looked, and what I was eating. I gave up everything I loved for him. I stopped baking. I stopped eating the foods that I loved to create, and I ate what he told me to eat. It sounds petty when I say it out loud."

"Fuck," Owen mutters.

I have their full attention, and I make myself push forward. "I thought he loved me. He told me so, and I didn't know any other way. He was my first serious relationship. I knew that our love was different than my parents,' but I was okay with that because it was us against the world. I was young and dumb, and I have so many regrets."

"Rory," Grant grits out.

"He broke me. It took my sister and my parents constantly riding me to follow my dreams to bring me to Nashville. Their suggestion of a new start on life, to take the risk and open my own bakery, it finally took root, and I began to look at local listings, but nothing was available. It wasn't until I looked outside of Memphis that I started to get excited. A new start. Moving away from the memories of him and how I let him control me. I wanted that. When I saw the listing for Nashville, I jumped on it. I was prepared to come here alone, but my sister wanted no part of that. She hated her job and said it would be an adventure."

This time it's me who lays a palm against his cheek. "I felt this pull to this city that I couldn't explain. I love the shop location, and the apartment above sealed the deal. Then I met you." I pause, searching for the right words. "You were this handsome storm who rolled into my life without warning. You were unlike any man I'd ever met. Your confidence in what you wanted, both with me and out of life, was resolute. Trusting was hard for me, but you didn't let that stop you. You chipped away at my walls and my insecurities until they were both nothing but the dust in the wind of my past. With each day, you taught me what it's supposed to feel like to be respected. You taught me that true love is all-consuming. It's passion and acceptance. It's patience and perseverance. Most of all, you taught me that being me is okay. That I can speak my opinions and order whatever food sounds good to eat without feeling as though I'm doing something wrong. You taught me that curves are okay too." I give him a watery smile. "You showed me what true love means, how it feels, and what it can do to your heart and your soul if you accept it."

"I love you." He leans in and presses his lips to mine.

"I love you too," I tell him, but I'm not done. Dropping my hands from his face, I turn to look at Owen. He has a soft expression on his handsome face. One I've only seen when he's looking at his wife and son. "You and your family,"—I shake my head—"you've accepted me into Grant's life without question. You've supported my business and my love for your brother. You treat both my sister and me like we've always been family."

"You are family."

I nod. My lips tilting in a grin. "I love all of you like family. Owen, I can't tell you what it means to me that you're here with me today." I take a quick glance at Grant. "Both of you. And your mom, she's slaving away at the bakery, and I-I'm not sure how to show you all what that means to me. To have people who I love and trust in my corner. To know that it's not just me and Aspen in this big city alone." Grant stands, and so do I. Only it's not him that I go to. It's his brother. I wrap my arms around Owen in a hug. "Thank you for being here for me."

"Aw, sis." Owen's deep voice rumbles.

"Rory." I turn to look at Grant, and his arms are wide open. "I need you over here." I waste no time moving into his embrace. He holds me tight. No words are spoken, but we don't need them.

The door opens, and I try to pull out of Grant's arms, but he's not having it. Martin Hamilton takes a seat behind his desk, and there is sweat beading on his brow.

"Let's hear it," Owen says.

"Well, it looks as though Mr. Davis was added to the account. You signed off on the change two weeks ago," he says, turning his beady eyes toward me.

"I did no such thing. Show me," I demand. He nods and places a piece of paper on the desk, sliding it our way.

"That's not her signature," Grant says immediately. He reaches for a notebook and a pen without asking permission and hands it to me. "Babe, sign your name," he tells me.

Taking the pen and paper, I scrawl my name across the page. Grant hands it to Martin. "Not hers."

"Martin, it seems we have an issue," Owen tells him. "A case of forgery?"

"This was an addition made by my personal receptionist."

"Is that something that your personal receptionist often does?

Alters people's accounts?" Grant asks. He's barely maintaining his composure.

"She used to be a teller. She helps out from time to time."

"Let's bring her in, shall we?" Owen suggests.

Martin wipes his brow and presses the intercom button on his phone. "Lucy, could you join us, please?" He doesn't wait for her to reply. A few minutes later, his office door opens, and Lucy hesitantly steps in.

That same eerie feeling I got when she greeted us, the way she looked at me, prickles my awareness. "Yes, Mr. Hamilton?"

"Lucy, can you tell me if you recognize this woman?"

"I've never seen her before," she replies, and then her eyes widen.

Busted!

"Can you tell me why you approved a signature on an account without verifying identity?"

"I—" She opens and closes her mouth.

"We know it was you," Owen tells her. "It was your account. You just admitted to not knowing who she is. You've backed yourself into a corner."

"You stole from him!" she shouts, pointing her finger at me. "He loves me, and we want to get married, but we can't because you stole from him. He was just taking back what was his."

"Who?" I ask calmly.

"Elijah. My fiancé."

I can't help it. I laugh. Not just a low chuckle, but a full-out head-thrown-back, deep-from-your-gut laugh. No one says a word until I'm able to gain composure. "Oh, Lucy." I shake my head. "He's a con artist. A bully."

"No. You're wrong." She's quick to defend him, and suddenly my laughter is overshadowed by pain. Hers and mine.

"Let me guess. He loves you and wants you to be your best self. That's why he nags you about what you eat, what you wear, and how you wear your hair. He tells you that you're the most important person in his life, then tells you that you're a disgrace in your current state." Her eyes well with tears, and that's all I need to know. Elijah is never going to change. Men like him rarely do. "Lucy, I was you. I believed his lies and took his abuse. He tore me down to nothing and left me there. Just like he left me at the church on the day of our wedding." A sob breaks free from her chest, but the final piece of the hole he left in mine heals.

"No." She's shaking her head.

"Do you realize what you've done?" I ask her. "You've committed a crime. Fraud for him."

Panic crosses her features as her eyes dart to Martin, then to the door. Owen moves to stand in front of it, blocking her exit. "Martin," Grant speaks up. "You have a choice to make."

Martin nods and picks up his phone. "Can you send up security?" he asks whoever is on the other end.

"No. You can't do this. Please, no. Let me call Elijah. He'll tell you that she's lying."

"What did you do with the money, Lucy?" Martin asks her, pinching the bridge of his nose.

"We have an account here together. We're using it for our wedding. It's his money," she cries.

Martin rolls his eyes and turns to his computer. His fingers tap against the keyboard. Whatever he sees has him shaking his head. "This account?" he asks, turning his screen so that we can all see it too has a negative balance.

"What?" Lucy whispers. "That's not right. It can't be."

"You've been played," Grant tells her.

"And you're going to jail," Martin adds. "You do realize that the bank is responsible for this fiasco that you've created? The money you stole from Ms. Steele has to be returned."

"I-I don't have that kind of money," she says as there's a knock at the door.

"Security," a deep voice announces.

Owen steps back and allows them to enter. Not only is security entering the room, but the Nashville Police are right behind them. I called in a favor to a friend of mine, asked him and his partner to hang out in the lobby. I wasn't sure what we were getting into, but I knew that if we needed them, I wanted them close. Martin explains the situation, and Lucy is quickly read her rights and taken out in handcuffs. Part of me wants to stop them to tell them that she didn't know any better, but she did. She knew right from wrong. She knew she was forging my name on a document. No matter how many times Elijah tore me down, I never broke the law for him, and I never would have. My moral compass wouldn't allow it.

Lucy is crying uncontrollably as she's escorted out of the office. The room is silent until we can no longer hear her cries.

"Ms. Steele, I owe you an apology."

I nod. "How do we fix this, Mr. Hamilton?"

"Nashville Horizon has fraud protection coverage for *rare,*" he emphasizes the word, "occurrences as these. It does take some time to get it all processed and through the insurance carrier."

"What do I do until then? This is my livelihood. The livelihood of my business."

"I'm sorry." His shoulders slump. "I'll make some calls and see what I can do."

"You've got until tomorrow morning to notify us of the next steps," Owen informs him. "See to it that we hear from you." With that, he nods at Grant, who links his fingers through mine and leads us out of the office and to the elevators.

"Wow," I say once the doors slide closed.

"That's not at all what I was expecting," Owen tells me.

"I'm sorry to drag you both into this mess. Thank you for being here."

"Are you kidding? I live to make that man squirm. He's a pansy-ass who sits in his big office all day and does jack shit. He has no idea what was going on under his nose."

The elevator doors open, and with our heads held high, we make our way out of the building. The warm May sun beats down on us, and I take a deep breath, filling my lungs with fresh air. I don't know how this mess is going to turn out, but I have to have faith that everything will be all right.

"You going back to the office?" Owen asks.

"No. We're going to go back to the bakery and relieve Mom, and then we're... we're just going to *be*."

He nods. "Love you, brother. You too, Aurora. I'll let you know if I hear anything."

Grant steps forward and gives his brother one of those back-slapping man hugs men do. "Thanks, O. I appreciate everything you've done."

"Me too." I move forward as Grant steps back and I give Owen another hug. "Thank you for being here." I know I've told him already, but I feel as though it deserves to be repeated.

"You kids have fun. I'll call you later," he says, climbing into his car.

"You can go to the office," I tell Grant. "I'm sure you have a ton of work waiting for you."

"Nothing that can't wait. Today I just need to be close to you." He doesn't say why, but he doesn't need to. I could feel the tension rolling off him in waves as I told Owen my story. And let's be real, we don't ever need an excuse to spend time with the ones we love. Even if it means missing work for a day. We'll call it a mental health day.

When we make it back to Warm Delights, Aspen and Lena are laughing with a group of women at one of the tables. "Oh, we didn't expect you back so soon," Lena greets us.

"Grant and Owen, they were incredible. You should be proud," I tell her.

Lena nods. "I am. I'm proud of all of my boys. Did you get everything worked out?"

Grant and I tell them about Lucy and Elijah, and the epic mess at the bank. Despite the shitshow, it's still turned out okay. We were lucky to be able to figure out what happened so soon, and they can work on getting my money back in my account where it belongs.

"Oh my," Lena says. "I'm glad you found out who was behind it and can move forward."

"Me too," I agree. "How did it go?" I ask my sister. I'm over talking about Elijah and the way he keeps screwing with my life.

"Great. It was busy, but this one handled it like a champ." She hip checks Lena gently.

"I raised five boys. This was nothing," she jokes, and the ladies sitting around the table all laugh. "We've got this handled. You two shoo." She motions for us to go. "Take the day to just… be."

"No, I can't ask you—" I start, and she's already shaking her head.

"You didn't ask me. I volunteered. Besides, Aspen and I are making a new creation. You can't see it yet."

"Should we be worried?" Grant laughs.

"Nope. We've got this," Aspen assures him. "Go."

"Thank you both." I give them both a big hug, wave to the ladies at the table, and pull Grant back out to the street.

"That was easier than I thought it would be. I was sure you'd insist on staying."

"They were having fun and looked as though they had it all under control. Besides, there is something else that I need right now."

"What's that?" he asks, concerned.

"You." His eyes soften. "Emotionally and physically," I add. I can see when he picks up on what exactly it is that I need. Never again will I fear or shy away from asking for what I want or need. Not with this man, holding my hand as if it's his lifeline.

CHAPTER
Grant
TWENTY NINE

I T'S BEEN TWO weeks since Owen, Aurora, and I confronted Martin Hamilton. Two weeks since my girl has been stressed beyond measure, and two weeks of me offering to help her and her refusing. She's adamant that this is her mess, and she's not pulling me into it any further. I love her newfound confidence. I love that she tells me what she wants, but with this, not so much. I love her. It's a love so deep I know we're the real deal. It's going to be the two of us until the end. Until I take my last breath. I can afford to help her, yet she continues to refuse.

Tossing the pen I'm using across the room, I rub my hands over my face. "Fuck," I mutter.

"What did that pen do to you?" Royce asks, entering my office.

"Casualty of being near," I tell him, leaning back in my chair. "What's up?"

"Just wanted to check-in. You've been quiet these past few weeks."

"How do you help someone who refuses help?" I ask him.

"Aurora?"

"Yeah. She's struggling financially until this fucking shitshow is taken care of, and I hate it. Aspen and her parents are helping, but damnit, I can help her."

He nods. "Have you taken the time to look at this from her point of view?"

"The stubborn one?" I fire back.

He chuckles. "You've told her, I'm sure, that women have gone after us for years for our money. I'm sure she knows my story, my first wife. My guess is she's trying not to be one of them. Someone who uses you or our family for money."

"It's fucking different. I love her."

"I know you do, but she's still fragile. She's come a long way, but I'm sure in the back of her mind, there is still this lingering worry from what he put her through."

"What do I do? Her landlord sent her a letter letting her know he's selling the building. She can't purchase it because her down payment and assets are fucking locked because of that douche and his piece of ass, and now Aurora is paying for it. I know she's worried about losing the bakery. The location. If the building sells and they kick her out, she's fucked. She won't let me help. I've tried to convince her. I've tried to have Aspen talk to her. Hell, I even sent Mom into the trenches to talk to her. Nothing." I run my fingers through my hair.

Royce shrugs. "You're too close to this. You're not thinking objectively. You're feeding off your emotions and hers. Think about this from a business standpoint. How would you handle it then?"

"I'd fucking buy the building!" I blurt.

A slow grin tilts his lips. "So buy it."

"She won't let me."

"Do you really need her permission? The building is going to sell. That's a prime area in the heart of downtown. It might as well be you."

"Fuck me! Where were you two weeks ago?"

He laughs. "That's why I'm here for you. You need me on this, or any of us for that matter, let me know."

"She's going to be pissed," I tell him.

"Maybe. She's also going to be relieved. She's going to insist on paying you, and blah, blah, blah, but that's minor details you two can fight or fuck about later." He smirks. "But at least you know she has her home and her livelihood. Put you both out of your misery and just buy the fucking building."

"And that, ladies and gentlemen, is why he's the CEO," I say in a fake as hell announcer voice.

"Nah, just the oldest. Like I said. You're too close to this. You're thinking with your heart and not your head. Not that I can blame you. I'd be the same way if it were Sawyer."

"Thanks, brother." I stand, walking around my desk to hug him.

"Who died?" Marshall asks, snacking on a bag of pretzels that look as if they came from the vending machine in our breakroom.

"No one died. Royce just talked me off the ledge."

Marshall nods. "You good? Need anything?"

"Nah, I'm all good for now. I've got some calls to make."

"You know where to find us if you need us." Royce pats me on the back and walks out of my office. I hear him and Marshall talking about a new marketing campaign for the summer and smile. For as much shit as we give each other, I know that they're all there for me if I need them. And today, Royce came in strong.

I don't know why I didn't think of it from that angle. It's going to sell. It might as well be me. That eliminates my stress from worrying about her, and she'll know that her bakery can stay open. It's a win-win. Sure, she's going to be pissed at first, but I'm confident she'll get over it once she realizes this is the best-case scenario for both of us.

Pulling up the realtor site from the paper Aurora showed me, I find their number and call them while pulling up the listing. Ten minutes later, I've put in a cash offer. The agent assures me it's as much as a done deal and will call me back after promising to keep my identity from the current tenants — namely, my girlfriend.

Girlfriend.

That needs to change too. I've got some work to do, but first things first. Get through this sale, get her money back. No way will I get her to agree to marry with that hanging over her head. I'm just going to have to improvise. Grabbing my phone, I text my friend Tommy.

> **Me:** It's that time again.

> **Tommy:** Been a while.

> **Me:** Yeah. You got time? It will be quick.

> **Tommy:** The next three hours are open. I'll block them out for you.

> **Me:** I'm on my way.

Closing down my computer, I go in search of Royce and find Owen in his office. "Hey," I say, stepping into his office.

"You good?" Royce asks.

"Yeah. Put in a cash offer. It's as good as done."

"Good. Better?"

"Getting there." I smile. "I'm heading out for the day."

"What's up?" Owen says.

"I'm more than likely going to have to grovel when she finds out. I need to be prepared."

He laughs. "I hear ya. Let me know if I can help."

"Thanks." I direct that at both of them. "I'll catch up with you guys later."

Thirty minutes later, I'm walking into Tommy's shop. "Grant Riggins." He walks out from around the counter and offers me his hand. "What's up, my man?"

"Needed a little therapy," I tell him.

"You know what you want?"

"Yeah. I need a butterfly."

"A butterfly? You going soft on me, Riggins?"

"Maybe." I laugh. "I need my girl's name wove into the design."

He whistles. "That's some heavy shit, Riggins. You know this is forever, right?" he asks.

"I'm well aware."

"And if this doesn't work out."

"It's going to work out."

He nods. "Let me draw something up. Come on back." He turns toward his room and sits down at the small sketch table. "So, who is she?"

"My future wife."

He chuckles. "Does she know that?"

"Not yet." I grin.

"And the butterfly?"

"Fuck, man, can't you just do it and not ask questions?"

"Nope."

"She says I give her butterflies." I expect him to give me shit.

"I like it." He gets busy drawing, and I take the time to look at the new work he has showcased on his walls. "You are one talented fucker," I tell him.

"I know." He smirks. "Take a look at this." He motions me over. "I was thinking about putting her name down the center of the body."

"Perfect."

"Well, I need a name to see if it will fit."

"Aurora."

"That's hot." He nods his approval.

"She's mine."

"I'm just saying. The name's hot. Does she have a sister?"

"Yeah." I grin. "Aspen."

"That's hot too. I need to see these two," he says, his head bent over the sketch, working her name into the design.

Reaching for my phone, I scroll through my camera roll until I find a picture of the two of them that I took that day on the lake. "My girl's on the left. Her sister, Aspen, is on the right."

"Damn," he mutters. "I'd be inking her name on my body too." He laughs. "All right, check this out." He hands me the sketch. "I assume you wanted something small?"

"Yeah, I'm going to put it on my chest. Over my heart."

He nods. "It's a good size to cover up later if we need to." He grins. I know he's just giving me shit.

"Not happening, Tommy."

"Didn't Owen and Royce both tie the knot too?" he asks.

"Yeah, just Conrad and Marshall left."

"Y'all are dropping like flies."

I shrug. "The love of a good woman."

He nods. "Touché, my friend. Touché. All right, take a seat in the chair, and we'll get this going."

My phone rings. "I need to take this," I say, glancing at the screen.

"We've got plenty of time."

"This is Grant."

"Grant, hi, this is Kiersten from Markle and Associates Realty. The seller has accepted your offer. Can you stop by our office to sign the contract? All we need is a title search and appraisal, and an inspection if you choose to do so."

"I don't need an appraisal or inspection. The title search, yes. How fast can we make this happen?"

"I'll have it in a few days."

"When can we close?"

"With a cash offer, I can get someone on this and a week or two."

"Kiersten. This is a gift for my girlfriend. Can we do it any sooner?"

"I can put a rush on it, but it's another—" I stop her there.

"I don't care what it costs. Make it happen."

"Yes, sir. I'll see you in an hour or so."

"Yeah, make it two just in case."

"Sure thing, Mr. Riggins."

Ending the call, I take off my shirt and climb up on the chair, letting Tommy do his thing. In a matter of a few hours, I've managed to find a solution to a short-term problem and give my girl a gift I hope she understands. I'm not going anywhere. I want her now and always.

"You fall asleep on me?" Tommy asks.

I open my eyes. "No."

"You're all set. Wanna see?" He hands me a mirror, knowing damn well I'm going to say yes.

I take in the swirls of ink, in the intricate design of the wings, and right there down the center is her name—inked over my heart. I always said I'd never do this. I'd never ink a woman's name on my body. But that's the me before her. Now I know what it's like to have her love, to have her in my arms, in my bed, and in my life. This was one of the easiest decisions I've ever made.

CHAPTER
Aurora
THIRTY

"**T**HIS HAS BEEN the longest week in history," I tell my sister as she goes to lock the front door.

"I think you said that last week too." She laughs.

"I've barely seen Grant this week."

"He and his brothers run an empire. You know how much work it takes just for this place. I can't imagine the weight on their shoulders."

"Yeah, I just... feel off when I don't get to see him."

"Aw, young love," she teases.

"He calms me. Our connection is unlike anything I've ever felt. I can't explain it, but when he's close, when I'm with him, I know everything is going to be okay. With all of this mess, the money missing, and now the building being sold, my stress level is through the roof. He makes that better."

"I'm happy for you. Even through this shitstorm, you're holding strong, and that man loves you. You know that, right?"

"Yeah." I smile. "I love him too," I say, just as his face appears outside the bakery front door. He peers and waves.

"I'll get it," she says, walking to unlock the door and let him in. "You're just in time. We just closed up."

"Good day?" he asks.

"Busy as always."

"That's a good thing."

"Yeah, if we could hire help," I add. Every interview we've had have been duds. They either don't show, or show up smelling like cigarette smoke and alcohol. I placed adds online and am hoping to set up more interviews. I can only hope that we find someone soon.

"Hey, baby." He leans down and kisses me. "This is all going to be over soon, and you can hire help, and then I get more of you." He turns to Aspen. "And you can get out more."

She gasps, placing her hand over her heart. "Are you insinuating that I have no life?" She laughs.

"No. But you gotta admit you spend a lot of time just hanging out."

"I went shopping with Sam and Aria this week."

He nods. "Good. I'm glad you're getting out."

"What are your plans for the rest of the day?" he asks me.

"Nothing much. We were able to get Monday's prep done, and we're all cleaned up."

"Good. I was hoping to talk to both of you." He holds out his hand and guides me to a table, Aspen following along behind us.

"You're kind of freaking me out right now," I admit. I glance at my sister, who is also wearing a worried expression.

"It's not bad, but I'm not sure you'll see it that way at first. That's why she's here." He points at Aspen. "I might need backup, and she can keep you from attacking me." He winks at us.

"Spill it, Riggins," I say, crossing my arms over my chest.

"Earlier this week, Monday, in fact, I was talking to Royce, and it hit me that there was something that I needed to do."

"Okay?" I say cautiously.

He reaches out and takes my hands in his. "I love you, Aurora. Deep in here." He places his hand gently over his heart. "I want a life with you. I want to see this place succeed. I want you and Aspen both to have everything you've ever dreamed of. Not only that, but I want to be here to watch it happen. You're my family." He glances at my sister. "You're my little sister, and you... well, one day, I hope that you'll be my wife."

I gasp, and Aspen sniggers. "See why I needed you?" he asks her. She holds up her hand and offers him a high-five that he returns.

"I have something for you, but I need you to hear me out. Can you do that?"

I nod. I don't know where this conversation is going, but the butterflies that only he causes are going about a thousand miles a minute as he reaches into his back pocket and produces an envelope.

"What's that?" I can't help but ask.

"Open it." He hands it to me and sits back in his chair.

I can feel his eyes on me as I pull the document out of the envelope and begin to read. I read the first paragraph a million times, sure that it's the tears in my eyes that have me reading this wrong.

"W-What did you do?" I ask him.

"It's your baby. I bought the building. You don't have to worry about being kicked out, or finding a new place, or even paying rent. I know that money is tight until this shit that Elijah caused is worked out, but I had to do something. You wouldn't let me help you, and I need to. It's yours," he says again.

"You can't buy me a building."

"I can. I did. It's all legal and in your name. I just need you to sign this paper."

"I can't do that."

"Then, I'll have Aspen do it." He looks over at my sister with a look of pleading. He wants her to agree to this.

"Grant, this is crazy."

"No, it's not. What's crazy is that you're refusing to let me help you. Let me ask you this. If it were me in your situation, and you were in mine, if you had the means to help me, what would you do?"

My shoulders sag. "I don't want to be your burden." I know as soon as I say the words that they're wrong. I know Grant would never think of me that way. I guess old habits die hard. Will I ever be rid of the negativity that Elijah made me believe? Made me feel?

"Baby, look at me."

I keep my eyes downcast in my lap as hot tears burn my eyes. I hear him rustling around, but I refuse to look up. I hate that he's seeing me cry. Again. I'm tired of feeling weak. That's not who I am anymore, but my tears say otherwise.

"Oh my God," my sister breathes.

My head jerks up, and I see Grant with his T-shirt off, sitting on the table. My eyes go to his chest, and that's when I see it. "Grant." I reach out to touch him but quickly pull my hand away. "What did you do?"

"I wanted a piece of you with me always. You're always telling me that I give you butterflies, and you do the same for me. You're my butterfly, my magic." He moves in close, grabbing my hands again. "I love you. I want to build a life with you, a family. Please don't be mad at me for doing this. I can afford to buy this building twenty times over, and I would if that's what I needed to do to help you."

"You got a tattoo. Of a butterfly."

"I did, but it's more than just a butterfly, Aurora. It's you."

My eyes zero in on his new tattoo, and that's when I see it. My name. "That's me," I say, losing my battle with the tears that have been threatening to fall.

"That's you, baby. Now." He taps the papers on the table. "Please sign these."

"I—" I start to protest and then think better of it. I can't keep fighting the good in my life because of the evil. Fighting the man I love, the man who is sitting here with my name permanently marked on his chest, who is offering to take my fears away. I won't let Elijah take from me like that ever again. Swallowing back my protest, I try again. "Thank you for what you did. I accept this amazing gift that you have given me. So many of my fears have been diminished by this, and I don't know how to thank you. However, I don't want to sign those papers. Please keep the building in your name."

"No. I know you're going to fight me on rent, and damn it, Aurora, I'm not doing that. You are not paying me a fucking dime."

"Okay," I agree. "I won't fight you on it. But please keep it. If something happens."

"I'll sign it over to you. But, baby, nothing is going to happen. You and me, we're forever."

Forever. My heart stutters in my chest, and hope blooms. I want Grant to be my forever. I want everything life throws at us, because I know with Grant by my side, we can tackle anything. "I'll buy it from you. Once this money situation is figured out, I'll buy it from you. The bank is telling me another two weeks."

A slow, sexy grin lights up his face. "Deal. I get to name the price."

"Grant Riggins, you can't say something crazy like a dollar," I warn him.

"Oh, no. I've got a price in mind."

"Let's hear it," I say, glancing over at my sister, who I see is also crying. She smiles, wiping her tears, and shrugs.

"I want all your kisses. From today, and for our lifetime, I get all of your kisses."

"You'll get those anyway."

"That's the deal. Take it or leave it."

"And if I don't take it?"

"I put the place in Aspen's name."

"She won't sign it." I glance over at my sister, who is grinning. "Tell him you won't sign it."

"No. I'm sorry, dear sister, but I can't do that. He's just given you the grand gesture of all grand gestures. I'll sign the papers and then find a way to give it to you."

"Traitor."

She laughs.

"Do we have a deal?"

Everything I've ever wanted and never thought I'd have is sitting here in front of me. Grant is my lifeline and he's asking me to reach out and grab it.

Hot tears threaten to fall, but I push them back, square my shoulders, and look the man I love in the eye, sealing our fate with the promise of our future. "Yeah," I say, relenting. "We have a deal."

He leans in and presses his lips to mine. His hand slides behind my neck as he holds me close. I get lost in his kiss. In the love that we have. I will forever be grateful for the day that Grant Riggins walked into my bakery. Kiss by kiss, he's stolen my heart, and I never want to know what a day in my future looks like without him in it.

When we finally pull out of the kiss, I notice Aspen has disappeared. "I need you," I tell him. I don't know where my sister is, but I don't care if she heard me.

"Tell me when and where."

"Can we go to your place?" I don't want Aspen to have to listen to us, and the way I'm feeling right now, so overcome with the need for this man, I know I won't be able to be quiet.

"Let's go."

I grab my purse from behind the counter and send Aspen a text letting her know we're going to Grant's, and telling her that I love her. I don't know if I would have gone through with this adventure had it not been for Aspen coming along, and it's been the best thing to ever happen to me. *He* is the best thing to ever happen to me.

The drive to his place is full of sexual tension. At least for me. He keeps glancing over at me with those blue eyes of his, and the look he gives me... it's carnal. Not only that, his thumb is tracing lazy circles on my palm, and his touch, it's igniting a fire deep inside me. I'm more turned on than I have ever been in my entire life. However, Grant doesn't seem fazed. He pulls his SUV into the garage, and with leisurely steps, he makes his way to the passenger door. His hand lands on the small of my back, and the heat from his touch is searing, even through my clothes.

"Would you like something to drink?" he asks.

"No."

"Are you hungry?"

"Yes."

He turns to look at me for the first time since we've walked in. "What sounds good?"

"You."

My single word confession has him dropping all pretenses as he stalks toward me. "You have me, baby."

"You naked." I amend my earlier request.

"I'm barely holding on right now, Aurora. I'm trying to be a gentleman and not take you here on the counter."

"I'd like that. Please and thank you," I say sweetly. He laughs, a deep rumbling sound from his chest. He takes a step back, just out of my reach. "You're going the wrong way," I tell him.

"Naked." He points at me. "I need you naked."

"What about you?"

He rips his T-shirt over his head, and with speed I wasn't sure anyone was capable of, he's stripping out of his jeans and kicks them to the side. He stands there, arms held out beside him, his body on display. "I'm all yours, Rory. Now tell me, baby, what are you going to do with me?"

Following his lead, I start pulling off clothes, letting them fall into a pile on his kitchen floor. When I'm fully naked, I hold my arms out just as he did and toss his words back at him. "I'm all yours, Grant. Now tell me, baby, what are you going to do with me?"

He lunges for me, and I squeal with both surprise and laughter as he tosses me over his shoulder and carries me to the island. The granite is cold on my bare skin, but I barely have time to notice before he's fusing his mouth to mine. His kisses steal the breath from my lungs. He pulls back, his chest heaving, and rests his forehead against mine. "I don't have a condom down here."

I let the words hang between us as I consider what it means. What it is he's asking. "I'm clean. I've been tested every six months since... him. I didn't trust him, so..." I shrug.

"There's been no one but you for over a year, and I'm clean. I promise you. I would never do anything to put you in danger."

I run my hand over the butterfly tattoo on his chest. "I don't want anything between us. I'm on the pill. We're protected."

"The pill isn't always 100 percent."

I nod. "I know."

"You're willing to take that chance with me?"

"I do owe you a lifetime of kisses."

"Damn right you do." He kiss me hard. Reaching between us, he grips his cock and aligns himself at my entrance. "This is going to be fast, beautiful. Just the thought of sliding inside you bare, with your pussy gripping my cock, has me ready to blow."

"Good. Because you've been driving me crazy with need since we got in your car."

He smiles. "Hold onto me."

I do as he says, sliding my hand behind his neck. He pushes in deep, causing me to hold on tighter, burying my face in his neck.

"You okay?"

"Never better. Take what you need, Grant. I'm not fragile. I'm not going to break. I need this just as bad as you do."

He nods and pulls out, slamming back in. His hands grip my thighs, keeping me in place as he brings us both to the edge of pleasure. "So… good," he says, his voice tight. "We're never going back," he says, pumping into me. "Never going to be anything between us ever again."

"Yes," I say. I'm agreeing with him, but also telling him that I want more. I *need* more. Over and over again, he pumps into me at a rapid pace, and even though I don't want it to end, I can feel my body start to tingle, and I know I'm falling. My moans, as my orgasm races through me, would give a porn star a run for her money.

"Fuck!" Grant yells as his body stills, and he empties himself inside me. "You're trying to kill me."

I smile into his neck. "I love you."

"I love you too. Let's get you cleaned up and in bed, where I can worship you as you deserve."

He gets no complaint from me as he lifts me into his arms and carries me upstairs. "I say we lock ourselves inside until tomorrow night."

"Done." He kisses my temple.

Grant makes good on his promise. We shower, and he worships my body. As I drift off to sleep sometime in the early morning hours, fully sated, I can't help but wonder if I can talk him into this every weekend.

EPILOGUE
Grant

THIS WILL BE the first year since the lake was built on our parents' property that we don't spend the Fourth of July on the water. That was the plan until Aurora broke the news that she and Aspen were meeting her parents in Gatlinburg for a weekend getaway. Her parents went to North Carolina to the beach for the week and are driving home. They want to see their daughters, and I can't spend that much time away from her. So I rallied the troops. My parents own a cabin in the Smokey Mountains. It's huge, with ten bedrooms and twelve bathrooms. I invited her parents to stay with us: us meaning me, my four brothers, my sisters-in-law, my nephew, and Mom and Dad. We take six rooms, Aspen takes another, her parents take another, and I still don't know if Aurora will be lying next to me each night. I'll respect her wishes about whatever she decides to do, but I want her with me. Always.

"You ready for this?" Dad asks, helping me unload the back of my SUV.

"Yes."

"Confident as always." He laughs.

"I love her."

"I know you do."

"It's time." I don't have to elaborate for him to know what I'm talking about.

A slow smile crosses his face. "You finally ready to admit the love of a good woman is magic?"

"Yep."

He clamps a hand on my shoulder. "Never forget it. Treat her and your love like the special gift that it is."

"What's going on over here? Is this some kind of meeting of the minds?" Conrad asks.

"Nah, Dad and I were just talking about magic."

"Ugh," Conrad sighs dramatically. "He got to you too. Dad, you're turning my brothers into love-sick fools." He points at our father. "You keep yourself and that voodoo love stuff away from Marsh and me. We're sowing our wild oats."

"The magic finds you, son. It's not something I can curse you with. Besides, it's not a curse." He glances over at my mom. "It's a blessing."

Owen and Layla pull up in their loaded-down SUV. I make a beeline for the back door and lift Carter and his baby seat out. "Hey, buddy," I say to my smiling nephew.

"Hand him over," Conrad says, trying to reach for the baby seat.

"Nope. Get your own."

"Not when I have this little man to spoil."

A car coming up the driveway catches my attention. My entire family is already here, including Aurora and Aspen. With Owen and Layla the last to arrive, I know this is her parents. I pull my phone out of my pocket to call Aurora and let her know they're here, but the slamming of the screen door and the pounding of feet across the deck and down the steps tells me that she already knows. I watch with a smile as the sisters greet their parents. It's been way too long since they've seen them. I wonder what it would take to get them to move to Nashville. Carter coos as Conrad steals him away from me.

Grandkids.

That's what it will take. We'll be there soon enough. If this weekend goes like I'm hoping it will, we're definitely going to be on the right track. I take my time walking over to where the four of them are standing in the driveway. Aurora grins and loops her arm through mine. "Mom, Dad, this is Grant. Grant, this is our mom, Sheila, and our dad, Hank."

I offer her mom my hand first. "It's a pleasure to meet you. Thanks for letting us crash your trip."

"Come here." Sheila bypasses my offered hand and pulls me into a hug. "It's so nice to finally meet you in person."

When she finally releases me, I offer Hank my hand. "Sir."

"Nice to meet you," he says, taking my hand.

"This place is beautiful," Sheila comments.

"Oh, Mom, you have no idea," Aspen tells her.

"Each bedroom has a bathroom, and you all can pick from any that are not already claimed," Aurora tells them. "Aspen, Grant, and I chose the third floor, Conrad too, I think."

"Any room will be fine. We're just glad to see our daughters in the flesh," Hank says, pulling both girls back into his arms for a hug.

"Need help with bags?" Marshall asks, joining us.

"Marshall, these are our parents, Hank and Sheila," Aspen introduces them. "Mom, Dad, this is Grant's youngest brother, Marshall." The three of them exchange handshakes. "I put your bags in your room," he tells Aspen.

"Thank you." She smiles up at him, and I make a mental note to ask Aurora or even Marsh himself if there is something going on there.

"Dad stole the baby," Conrad says, stepping up and placing his arm around Aspen's shoulders.

"Serves you right. You stole him from me." I glare at him, making him laugh.

"You had to meet your girl's parents," he counters.

"Mom, Dad, this is Conrad, another one of Grant's brothers," Aurora introduces us. "Con, these are my parents, Sheila and Hank. The baby he's talking about is Owen and Layla's. He's one of Grant's older brothers, and their son is three months old and the cutest tiny human you've ever seen," Aurora gushes.

I don't tell her that the title should be saved for our kids. I'm not sure her parents would appreciate that.

"Like your kids aren't going to be adorable," Aspen fires off.

"Um, yeah, he's going to be a Riggins," Marshall comments.

"Is there something you're not telling us?" Sheila asks Aurora with a coy smile.

"No. Trust me, that's not something I would be able to hide in this family." She gives her sister a pointed look.

"Ooh, you're in trouble," Marshall teases Aspen.

"Come on in. I'll introduce you to my parents and the rest of the family."

"We'll grab the bags," Conrad tells them.

"Thank you." Hank shakes his hand, and then the four of us head inside. More introductions are made, and Mom pulls the girls away to the kitchen, leaving me standing alone with dad and Hank.

"You want to see the property?" I ask him.

"Sure."

"Dad, you want to come with us?"

"Nah. I'm going to find my grandson. Hank, make yourself at home. Your daughters are family to us. That means you are as well." They share another handshake before Dad walks away.

"Let me grab us a couple of waters." I move into the kitchen and find Aurora sitting at the island with the rest of the women. "Hey, babe. I'm going to walk your dad around the property." I lean in and kiss her temple. "We'll be back soon."

"Okay," she replies, her voice low. "Be safe."

"Always." I wave to the women in my life and turn to find Hank in the doorway watching me. "All set," I say, holding up two bottles of water, and lead him out the back door of the cabin.

"It's a beautiful place," Hank says, breaking the silence between us.

"Yeah. We love it here. Although, back home, Mom and Dad have a lake, and it's where me and my brothers spent most of our time growing up."

"You and Aurora seem to be close."

I nod. "I love her." There is no point in holding back.

"She's changed since the move to Nashville. Aspen says we have you to thank for that."

"No, sir. I never want you to thank me for loving her. It's as easy as breathing for me."

"I guess I don't need to ask you your intentions." He chuckles.

"Actually, I was hoping to talk to you about that." I stop and pull the ring I bought weeks ago out of my pocket and hand him the box. "She's my everything. I'll love and cherish her for the rest of my life."

"You have my full support. You brought the happiness back into my baby girl's eyes. That tells me all I need to know about the man that you are."

"Thank you," I tell him, my voice cracking. "You've just given me the greatest gift. I—knowing that we have your blessing, that means the world to both of us."

"Take care of her," he says, handing me back the ring box.

"Always," I assure him, accepting the box. "You didn't look at it."

"Nope. I want to see it for the first time on her finger. I want to see the light and the sparkle in her eye that should have been there the first time. When do you plan on doing it?"

"This weekend at some point. I'm not sure exactly. I wanted to ask for your blessing, and the rest I have faith will just fall into place. Everything with her always does."

EPILOGUE
Aurora

TODAY HAS BEEN the best day. The. Best. I'm thrilled to have finally formally introduced Grant to my parents and have our families meet. When Grant and my dad got back from their walk, we had dinner ready. Me, Mom, Aspen, Lena, Sawyer, and Layla grilled steak and chicken and made a ton of sides. We do have an army we're feeding. The sun is setting over the horizon as we all watch my dad and Stanley start a fire.

The past few weeks have been insane, but life is finally starting to settle. My money was returned to my account, and Elijah and his sidekick were both charged with fraud and extortion. They're both serving two-year sentences in county jail. I'd love to say that I feel bad about it, but I don't. They knew they were breaking the law. It was their choice to do so.

I was finally able to hire two full-time employees, and they are working out fantastically. Aspen and I have not had three full days off since we moved here, so that's another reason to celebrate on this little weekend getaway.

"Jase and Sam are coming up tomorrow. They're bringing Aria too," Royce says, looking at his phone, and pulling me out of my thoughts.

"Oh, good." Lena claps her hands. "Another baby to love on. You know—" she starts, but Sawyer interrupts her.

"We're pregnant."

I look over to find my brother grinning like a fool. He's looking at his wife with so much love in his eyes. "Babe, I thought you wanted to wait?"

"I couldn't do it." She laughs. "We're all here together, and I had to tell them."

Royce has eyes for no one but her as he walks to where she's sitting, holding Carter, and drops to his knees. "I love you."

"Finally!" Stanley laughs. "I'm tired of fighting your momma for Carter. She's a baby hog, that one." He points at Lena accusingly. However, the smile on his face and that look in his eyes, the same one that Royce is giving Sawyer, is unmistakable.

We all take our turns passing out hugs and handshakes of congratulations, and just like that, the best day got even better. I don't think that anything could top this. I'm surrounded by the people I love. Our bellies and our hearts are full. What more could you ask for?

Dad pulls out his guitar, and to my surprise, Stanley does the same. We spend the next hour requesting songs, singing along, and just being together.

"I'm going to get a drink from the cooler. You need anything?" Grant asks me.

"No, thanks."

He stands and bends to kiss my lips before making his way to the other side of the fire where the cooler is sitting. I watch him as he stops and chats with our fathers for a few minutes. The three of them are wearing matching smiles. My heart is full, and the butterflies are in full swing.

Speaking of butterflies, I have a surprise for Grant later tonight. With the help of his brothers, I found out who did his tattoo and got the same exact one, swapping his name for mine. It's on my hip, and it hurt like hell. It's been hard to not wince when he touches me, and thankfully we've both been busy this week so that we could take off for this trip. What that means is that no naked time, so hiding it has been easy.

Grant comes back and places his bottle of water on the ground by my chair, and holds his hand out for me. "Let's take a walk."

Placing my hand in his, we stroll toward the edge of the mountain. The final remnants of the setting sun are disappearing beyond the horizon. "It's beautiful here," I say as Grant wraps his arms around me from behind.

"You're beautiful." He kisses the top of my head. "Can you see it? Us spending holidays here. Our kids running and playing with their cousins?"

"I can see it," I say, turning in his arms. "I have a surprise for you later."

"Yeah? Does that mean you're sleeping in my room tonight?"

"That's where all of my things are."

He nods. "Good. I wasn't looking forward to not having you next to me."

"You know in your arms is my favorite place to be."

"I'm glad you think that," he says, pressing a kiss to my lips. Pulling back, he raises his hand in the air, and before I can ask him what he was doing, the song that our fathers were playing changes.

"This is it," he says.

"Yeah, I love this song." Scotty McCreery definitely has a hit on his hands with this one.

He takes a step back and drops to one knee. "No, Rory. This is it. This is our moment." He reaches into his pocket and pulls out a ring box. I watch as his hands tremble, opening the box and pulling the ring from inside.

My hand covers my mouth, and tears are already welling in my eyes. "Grant," I breathe.

"This is our moment. The one where we decide to spend the rest of our lives loving one another. The one where the dreams of our kids growing up vacationing here with their cousins comes true. My dream of one day calling you my wife and making you an official member of my crazy family." He pauses, wiping at his eyes. That's when I realize he's emotional too. "Aurora Steele, will you make my dreams come true? Will to me the incredible honor of being my wife? Will you marry me?"

"Yes."

No hesitation.

No second thoughts.

No fear.

"Yes, I'll marry you." I offer him my hand, and he slides the ring that feels way too heavy and is sparkling from the light of the moon and the fire onto my finger.

Behind us, our families cheer and clap, and all I can do is hang onto him. I jump, and he catches me as I lock my legs around his waist. He's always going to catch me, and I know that deep in my soul. My tears are falling, and my smile can't be contained as I feel the first set of arms wrap around us. Before I know it, they're all there, hugging us together, because neither of us are willing to let go.

Not now. Not ever.

"Are you happy?" he asks once it's just us again.

"Butterflies," I tell him. "Kiss by Kiss, you brought me back to life."

"I own all your kisses," he counters, pressing his lips to mine.

Thank you for taking the time to read Kiss by Kiss. Are you ready for more of the Riggins brothers? Grant's story is next in Touch by Touch.

Never miss a new release:
http://bit.ly/2UW5Xzm

More about Kaylee's books:
http://bit.ly/2S6clWe

Facebook:
http://bit.ly/2C5DgdF

Instagram:
http://bit.ly/2reBkrV

Reader Group:
http://bit.ly/2o0yWDx

Goodreads:
http://bit.ly/2HodJvx

BookBub:
http://bit.ly/2KulVvH

Website:
www.kayleeryan.com

OTHER WORKS *by* KAYLEE RYAN

With You Series:
Anywhere With You | More With You | Everything With You

Soul Serenade Series:
Emphatic | Assured | Definite | Insistent

Southern Heart Series:
*Southern Pleasure | Southern Desire | Southern Attraction |
Southern Devotion*

Unexpected Arrivals Series:
*Unexpected Reality | Unexpected Fight
Unexpected Fall | Unexpected Bond | Unexpected Odds*

Standalone Titles:
*Tempting Tatum | Unwrapping Tatum | Levitate
Just Say When | I Just Want You
Reminding Avery | Hey, Whiskey | When Sparks Collide
Pull You Through | Beyond the Bases
Remedy | The Difference
Trust the Push*

OTHER WORKS *by* **KAYLEE RYAN**

Entangled Hearts Duet
Agony | Bliss

Co-written with Lacey Black:
It's Not Over | Just Getting Started | Can't Fight It

Cocky Hero Club:
Lucky Bastard

Riggins Brothers Series:
Play by Play | Layer by Layer
Piece by Piece | Kiss by Kiss

ACKNOWLEDGEMENTS

To my family:

I love you. I could not do this without your love and support. Thank you for everything.

Wander Aguiar:

It's always a pleasure working with you. You and Andrey always go above and beyond to help me find the perfect image. Thank you for your talent behind the lens and bringing Conrad's story to life.

Tyler Collins:

Thank you for doing what you do. You brought Conrad to life. Best of luck to you in all of your future endeavors.

Tami Integrity Formatting:

Thank you for making the paperbacks beautiful. You're amazing and I cannot thank you enough for all that you do.

Lori Jackson:

You nailed it. You were patient with me, and worked your photoshop magic. Thank you for another amazing cover. It has been my pleasure working with you.

Lacey Black:

My dear friend. Thank you for always being there with life, and work. I value our friendship, and our working relationship more than you will ever know. I can't wait to see what our co-writing journey takes us.

My beta team:

Jamie, Stacy, Lauren, Erica, and Franci I would be lost without you. You read my words as much as I do, and I can't tell you what your input and all the time you give means to me. Countless messages and bouncing idea, you ladies keep me sane with the characters are being anything but. Thank you from the bottom of my heart for taking this wild ride with me.

Give Me Books:

With every release, your team works diligently to get my book in the hands of bloggers. I cannot tell you how thankful I am for your services.

Tempting Illustrations:

Thank you for everything. I would be lost without you.

Julie Deaton:

Thank you for giving this book a set of fresh final eyes.

Becky Johnson:

I could not do this without you. Thank you for pushing me, and making me work for it.

Marisa Corvisiero:

Thank you for all that you do. I know I'm not the easiest client. I'm blessed to have you on this journey with me.

Kimberly Ann:

Thank you for organizing and tracking the ARC team. I couldn't do it without you.

Brittany Holland:

Thank you for your assistance with the blurb. You saved me!

Bloggers:

Thank you, doesn't seem like enough. You don't get paid to do what you do. It's from the kindness of your heart and your love of reading that fuels you. Without you, without your pages, your voice, your reviews, spreading the word it would be so much harder if not impossible to get my words in reader's hands. I can't tell you how much your never-ending support means to me. Thank you for being you, thank you for all that you do.

To my Kick Ass Crew:

The name of the group speaks for itself. You ladies truly do KICK ASS! I'm honored to have you on this journey with me. Thank you for reading, sharing, commenting, suggesting, the teasers, the messages all of it. Thank you from the bottom of my heart for all that you do. Your support is everything!

With Love,

Kaylee Ryan
AUTHOR

Made in the USA
Middletown, DE
30 March 2023

27721360R00146